A CIGAR CITY THRILLER
BLUEBIRD

CHRIS KNEER

A CIGAR CITY THRILLER

BLUEBIRD

CHRIS KNEER

This is a work of fiction. Unless otherwise indicated, all the names, characters, businesses, places, events, and incidents in this book are either the product of the author's imagination or used in a fictitious manner. Any resemblance to actual persons, living or dead, or actual events is purely coincidental.

Bluebird
Published by Spartan Entertainment
Tampa Bay, Florida, USA.

Copyright ©2024, CHRIS KNEER. All rights reserved.

KNEER, CHRIS, Author
BLUEBIRD
CHRIS KNEER

Library of Congress Control Number: 2024919614

ISBN: 979-8-9913666-0-1 (hardcover)
ISBN: 979-8-9913666-1-8 (paperback)
ISBN: 979-8-9913666-2-5 (digital)

FICTION / Thrillers / General
FICTION / Thrillers / Crime
FICTION / Thrillers / Suspense

Publishing Management, Editorial, and Art Direction: Pique Publishing, Inc.

For quantity purchases or additional information,
email Chris@ChrisKneerAuthor.com.

All rights reserved by CHRIS KNEER
This book is printed in the United States of America.

To my wife Jodi and my son Andrew.
Without your inspiration and motivation,
this book would not have been possible.

CHAPTER 1

Jerusalem, Israel
2013

"I am just a bank security officer," I say to a collection of hard men in a small, dark room somewhere in Jerusalem. I was plucked off the street an hour earlier and placed in a black SUV before being roughly ushered into this room.

No one speaks for a very long time. A pungent smell hangs in the air—the result of too many men with too much testosterone in a tight space. Sweat drips down my back and forehead despite a chill in the air. Their intense stares are boring into me, and I feel dizzy. I search for a sympathetic face but can't find one.

I am seated at the end of a rectangular, metal table, farthest from the door that leads to freedom. There is no way I can make it through all the men if I decide to make a run for it. Even if I want to try, I doubt my shaking legs will carry me far. A man with a thick, black beard and shortly trimmed salt-and-pepper hair is seated to my left. He finally speaks.

"How long have you been working for the Bank of Israel?" he says with a heavy accent. He seems like a man who asks questions to which he already knows the answers.

"I have been with the bank for almost two months. What is this about?"

The man seated to my right has a shaved head and a beard. He wears a skintight T-shirt that highlights massive biceps and two sleeves of tattoos. He has a notepad and grips the pen like a claw as he writes. Around his shoulders are two straps that hang down and hold two black handguns. If he is positioned to intimidate, it works.

"What is your full name?"

"Jason Miles, no middle name. Did I do something wrong? I don't know about this country, but in America, you can't just take someone off the street and drag them to some god-awful room," I say, doing my best to sound confident as my leg bounces under the table.

I can't believe this is happening. Alone and paralyzed with fear, I have trouble thinking clearly. I don't know if I am being arrested or maybe something even worse. I don't have much back home and thought a job in a foreign country might offer a fresh start. Clearly, I made a mistake.

A woman with jet-black hair walks through the door. She is feminine, but her black tank top shows off her arms, which are a little too muscular. She nods to the behemoth on my right, and he gives up his chair without a word.

Her hair is pulled back into a ponytail, which showcases a perfect face. Her eyes are the color of coffee beans and shaped in a way that makes me think she is a mix of nationalities. Her accent is not nearly as strong as the man's to my left.

"Jason, everything is fine. You are free to go at any time you like. You are not being held against your will," she says.

If this is good cop, bad cop, I am going with the good cop.

I will myself to stand. "Great, then I am going home."

The man to my left stands and shoves me down as he growls, "Sit down."

The magnitude of the situation sets in. I am imprisoned in this room without any chance of escape. I won't be able to talk my way out of the mounting danger. I am having trouble breathing and feel a pain in my chest. When the heat starts to spread from my chest to my neck and then my face, I know I am on the cusp of one of the attacks I've been having since I was thirteen.

Close your eyes and take deep breaths. It used to help.

"Can someone tell me what this is all about?" I ask.

The woman sits and scoots a little closer. She places her hand on my arm. "My name is Lia. We'd like to know how an American started working at Israel's largest bank as a security officer."

Her voice is gentle, but her eyes are intense. I ignore everyone else and speak directly to her. "Have you ever heard of Oak Williams?"

Her brilliant smile is warm and disarming. I notice a small gap between her front teeth. A small imperfection that makes her more interesting. "Of course, the famous actor."

"That's right," I say. "Oak is my best friend, and he was promoting his latest movie, *Blind Rage*, in Israel. He asked me if I wanted to come with him, and I'd never been here, so I said yes. We had an amazing time, and I fell in love with the country and applied as a security analyst at BOI."

The man to my left interrupts before I fully finish my sentence. "Why would Israel's largest bank hire you, an American who knows nothing about this country, for security?"

"You should ask them," I say trying to keep my leg still. "I assume it was due to my resume. This is what I did back in the States."

He stands up, sliding his chair back, and pokes his finger into my chest. His face is just inches from mine. "I think you are lying, and I think you are a spy."

CHAPTER 2

I hold up my hands. "This is insane."

The man pulls me out of my chair and pushes me up against the wall. The chair topples over with a loud bang. He is so close, I feel his warm breath. The tightness in my chest grows more painful, and I can feel tears welling up in my eyes. I am more scared than ever, but I need to figure out why these people think I am a spy and convince them I'm not. I look to Lia for help, but her eyes don't offer safety.

"I want to know who you are working for," the man screams as the veins in his neck bulge. "Is it the CIA? Are you a spook? We have people in your government. You might as well tell me. I will find out."

"I don't know what would make you think I'm a spy. I told you. I am a security officer at a bank. That's it. We can get Oak on the phone, and he can vouch for me."

The man on my left sits back down. "Call him," he says.

I notice he is squeezing some sort of ball in his hand. The muscles in his massive forearms move up and down. His veins look like snakes pulsating under his skin to some kind of music. One tattoo stands out from the others: a powerful lion roaring with sharp teeth.

"Someone took my phone," I state.

The bald man with the tree-trunk arms removes it from his pocket and tosses it to me.

I put in the security code and open to my favorites. I try to hide the fact that my hands are shaking. In the first spot is a picture of me and Oak standing on the world-famous seventh hole at Pebble Beach. I press the picture to dial.

"Put it on speaker," he grumbles.

I do as he asks, and we all hear "You know what to do." It is the voicemail message I have listened to a thousand times. Oak never picks up his phone and usually has no idea where it is.

"Hey, Oak, it's Jay-Bird. I need you to call me back ASAP. It's important."

Lia smiles at me, and for a moment, I relax. "Why did you call yourself Jay-Bird?"

I return the smile. "It is just a silly nickname. Oak has called me that since we were little kids."

"Is that his nickname—Oak?"

I shake my head. "No, his parents named him that. He weighed fifteen pounds at birth, so I think they knew the name would fit."

The man to my left stands up again. "Everybody out but me and Lia."

On cue, each member of their team shuffles out of the drab room. It instantly feels twice as large. Lia leaves for a moment and returns with a bottle of water for me. My throat is dry, and I drink greedily.

"Jason," says the man, "we are going to thoroughly check you out. If you are lying to me and you are anything except a banker, you and I are going to have a much different conversation. Do you understand me?"

I gather all the courage I can muster, take a deep breath, and say, "I have told you the truth, so help me God. My name is Jason Miles, and I am an American working at the Bank of Israel. There is nothing else to tell. I am not and have never been a spy."

I run my hands through my dark hair. The sweat pushes it up even higher in the front than it usually stands. I rub my palms on my jeans.

Without a word, they exit the room. I hear the click of the lock, reminding me that I am basically a caged animal. All alone, I blow out a deep breath. I don't appear to be under arrest, and I am still alive. I say a quick prayer and ask my parents to look out for me. They taught me from an early age to always do the right thing and everything would work out. I'm not sure that will happen today.

I try to think of anything I have done wrong, but my life in Israel has been uneventful. I go to work and, in my free time, try to make a couple of friends along with experiencing a new culture. I have a lot of baggage from back home that I need to unpack or bury, and a new country seemed like a great idea.

I want to know more about the woman named Lia. How does she fit in with this group of alpha males? Is she kind or just playing a part? She seems to be full of contradictions.

****

In a long hallway with a view of the interrogation room, an elderly man stands leaning on a cane. He has deep lines on his face and reading glasses hanging around his neck. A wisp of white hair sits on top of his head. He is clean-shaven except for a spot on his cheek he missed this morning.

"What do you think?" asks Lia. "Can he handle the role?"

The man cocks his head and squints his eyes. "Maybe. He is not a spy. He is not calm enough. He is too scared. A spy is always cool and collected—until you get rougher than Avner did in there."

Avner Cohen looks away from the man, feeling admonished. A light slap from a demanding father figure. "I was just testing him a little. No need to get rough at this stage. He's a visitor to this country and an American."

"You are getting soft, my boy. Lia, you need to lead the recruitment. I saw how he looked at you. Maybe set a honey trap," he suggests with a quiet laugh that turns into a cough.

"I'm not sleeping with him. Go find yourself a Russian if you want a honeypot," responds Lia.

The old man pulls out a handkerchief and coughs some more. "Find out what motivates him. Is it money, ideology, corruption, or ego? Dig into his background. Find out about his past. Look at his parents, girlfriends, and vices. Find something we can use to manipulate him into helping us. Everyone has a weakness, you just need to find it," the old man says as he lights a cigarette. The smoke hangs in the air, giving off a foul smell.

"You know those things are going to kill you," Lia tells him as she covers her mouth and nose.

"We live in the most dangerous country in the world. Most of our neighbors would like to see us blown to smithereens. The last thing I worry about are these things," he replies taking a long drag. "Keep in mind, this young man might not survive this mission. Make sure you can live with that. I know I can."

****

"We talked it over, and you are free to go for now. But we're keeping your passport so you can't run away. Don't tell anyone about meeting us. We'll give you a ride home, but take a long look at me and ask yourself if I look like someone you want as an enemy," the snake-vein guy states.

As we walk out of what has been my cell, Lia grabs my arm. "Jay, everything is going to be fine. Trust me."

They lead me to an idling SUV. Everything is blacked out, including the windows and rims. The bald guy with the tattoos opens the passenger door and barks at me to get in. The interior is black leather, and the car smells like chewing tobacco. He drives me two blocks from my corporate apartment and nods for me to get out.

I turn to face him. "I want to know what the hell that was all about. Who are you people, and what do you want with me?"

He exits the car and opens my door. "Get the fuck out of here before we change our minds. If you want to know who we are, we're either your best friends or your worst nightmare."

As I enter the building, the chest pains lessen, and I stop sweating, although my shirt is still damp from the interrogation. I am happy to be back around others and safe from that gang of thugs. I sit down on one of the brown couches in the lobby and breathe deeply for several minutes.

I feel like I should report the incident to someone, but who can I trust? I am in a foreign country, and now I don't even have my passport. And that lead ruffian also made it clear I was not to tell anyone.

I swipe my work ID card to open the elevator. I press the third-floor button and ride up in silence with a guy wearing earbuds. My card also opens the door to my room. The apartment is one bedroom, one bath and comes fully furnished with what looks like IKEA furniture. Bright colors and pictures of famous Israeli cities cover the walls.

The room is fine for now, and the price is right, since it is free if I am employed by the bank. But I want a lot more from life. Successful people wear nice clothes and live in fancy homes. I will get there someday. For now, I just need to put in the time and be a good employee.

When I moved in, I set up a small bar next to the kitchen. There is a bottle of bourbon, a half-filled Grey Goose Vodka, and a nearly empty bottle of ouzo is in front. I take pride in my Greek heritage and enjoy the national drink from time to time. I pour myself a shot to calm my trembling hands. The warm licorice flavor burns as it travels down my throat. I immediately have another.

I feel some pain in my upper lip from hitting the car doorframe when I was shoved into the SUV. It is swelling and only partially hidden by my dark beard, which is already way past a five o'clock shadow. A bag of frozen peas helps bring the lump down.

It is Saturday, and I worked a half day at the bank. Employees simply call it BOI. I was hired as an Assistant Bank Security Officer after several interviews and a reference from Oak that they thought was cool. Our team spends days dealing with perceived threats to the bank, which can include employee theft, computer viruses, or physical threats like bank robberies. I am grateful for the job and hope to advance up the ladder quickly. My dad always said the only way up the ladder is one rung at a time.

I try calling Oak again and get the same voicemail message. Having no luck, I attempt to process all that has happened.

Who is that group of hard men who swept me off the street and why did they accuse me of being a spy? Who is that woman who called herself Lia? Can I trust her?

I don't know the answer to any of these questions, and more alcohol isn't calming my anxiety any longer. I don't know who they are, but they know me, and I have a feeling I will be seeing them again.

CHAPTER 3

It has been two weeks since I was dragged off the street by those men and the beautiful lady. I constantly feel like I am being watched during the day, and my nights are haunted by dreams of abduction and lack of resistance. I wake in a pool of sweat with my heart pounding. I want to forget about the incident and resume normal life.

My corporate apartment is only six blocks from BOI headquarters. I wake up early, stretch for fifteen minutes, and shower. Men are required to wear a suit and tie every day, so I pick one from the three neckties I have and meticulously knot it, making sure the dimple is near the top. I don't have the nicest clothes, but they are well taken care of, and I try to look professional. Dress to impress.

I don't have a car, so I walk the streets of Jerusalem in a pack with others. Most are already texting or talking on their phones. I listen to music to get my day going. First Rush's "Working Man" and then several songs by Jay-Z.

Jerusalem feels like a big city, but while it is the largest in Israel, you can walk it in three hours or get about anywhere in a fifteen-minute drive. The Bank of Israel headquarters is located near the Downtown Triangle, a commercial and entertainment district. The area has plenty of traffic and smells of all kinds, some good and some awful.

Students and men wearing kippahs walk the narrow, curving streets intermingled with those rushing to work. Most of the buildings are made of Jerusalem stone, which is a pale limestone that has been used since ancient times. Young men can be seen making deliveries on bikes, and families roll up the doors to their stores, where they sell everything from souvenirs to newspapers to fresh produce. At night the streets are filled with musicians, artists, and entertainers.

I sit outside the Cafe Kadosh drinking Turkish coffee and eating a pastry. A couple of my co-workers—an expat from Australia and another from Ireland—join me, and we plan a night out after work. Quite a few foreigners are working at the bank, and we've become friends. On the weekends, we take turns planning adventures to new places. I consider telling them about the abduction but remember the hulking man's stern warning.

After properly caffeinating ourselves, we trek off to the office. They exit a couple of floors before me, and I wish them a great day. My team is on the ninth floor, and every morning we start with a meeting, accompanied by more coffee. My boss David leads off, and then we each update everyone on the miscellaneous projects we are working on.

I try to focus on work, but my mind inevitably drifts back to that small room. I picture Lia's dark eyes and wonder again how she has ended up with that group. They never told me who they were, but they felt like cops, military, or something more sinister. I try to pack the memory away, but that part of my brain is getting full.

Maybe they picked up the wrong guy and have now moved on to real threats.

When I leave the office, anxiety wraps around me like a boa constrictor. Every burly man with a beard and tattoos seems to be looking at me out of the corner of his eye or over the top of a magazine. People seem to be sitting a little too close and listening to my conversations. I try to ignore the paranoia, but it won't let go.

The only place I feel truly safe is at work. My department is a tight-knit group bonded over our shared sense that we are protecting the bank from all kinds of risks. We are constantly chasing fraud suspects, securing branches, and observing large transfers of cash in and out. We need to have access to a lot of sensitive information.

I spent my teenage years feeling abandoned and scared. The idea of protecting the bank and its customers fills a hole that has been empty for a long time. It makes me feel brave, like I am making a difference.

I leave work at six-thirty in the evening with plans to meet some friends for a drink and listen to a local band. I put in my earbuds and press play on the Eagles' "Hotel California" to get me in the mood. I am aware of two people very close, one on each side. They came out of nowhere. I remove an earbud.

A hand grabs my shoulder. "Hello, Jason," says the man I remember as "bad cop." A black baseball hat with a flat brim is pulled low on his head, nearly to his eyes. His beard is even bushier than I remember. I smell a little too much cologne. We are nearly the same height, a smidge under six feet, but he is much thicker.

On the other side is Lia. She slips her arm in mine and asks, "Can we buy you a drink?"

CHAPTER 4

I can't help but tremble a little as they lead me through the front doors of the Waldorf Astoria hotel. The lobby has a gorgeous tan-and-white marble floor and an expensive-looking chandelier. The staff are dressed impeccably and smile at us as we walk by.

This is the moment I've feared for the past couple of weeks. I wanted to believe that the first encounter had just been a mistake, but somewhere deep down, I knew they would be back. I think about screaming for help but instead just keep walking with them.

Instead of turning at the bar, we take the elevator to the fourteenth floor and then back down. We walk through a door and ignore a sign that reads "Staff Only." The laundry room is packed with machinery and soiled linen in rolling baskets. It smells strongly of detergent. We exit through another door and are out in an alley.

"Where are we going?" I ask. I feel my heart beating faster. I stop walking. "I am not going anywhere until you tell me what's going on."

The man grabs my elbow. "Come on, we don't have time for this. We don't know who is watching."

We cross the street into another alley and walk midway down. Lia knocks four times on a dirty metal door. It is opened by a handsome-looking man in his sixties. His face is tan and set against thick salt-and-pepper hair.

"Welcome to the Lion's Den," he says as we walk through the door. He hugs the man and Lia then bolts the door shut.

The room is a knockoff of Bar Hemingway in Paris. The carpet is green with a diamond print, and the walls are paneled in light wood with pictures of the famous writer placed throughout. Instead of the bull skull mounted on the wall, like they have in Paris, there is a lion's head.

Lia nods to a table set up front with three green leather chairs. Our host walks behind the shiny wood bar and mixes four drinks that have champagne, cognac, and lemon juice. He serves them to us and takes his drink to another table to read the newspaper.

"What is this place?" I ask, as I inspect my drink. I have no idea whether it is spiked or possibly even poisoned.

"We can't really be doing business out in the open," the man says. "So our friend created this little place."

I look around and take a deep breath. "I want to know why the hell I'm here. Why do you keep taking me against my will, and who would be watching?"

The man removes his jacket and hangs it on the back of his seat. On his hip is a black handgun. I assume a Glock or something similar. He takes a long drink and licks his lips.

"The drink is wonderful," he says.

The man at the other table gives us a little bow.

"You already know that this is Lia, and my name is Avner. We are agents of Shin Bet, the equivalent to your FBI."

"I thought that was Mossad." I give them a quizzical look.

Lia laughs. "Everyone thinks of Mossad because they are in the movies and books, but we protect Israel from internal threats. Mossad is like your CIA, dealing with the external. We often work together as well. Israel is a small country with lots of enemies. We must communicate to keep it safe."

I take a sip from my drink, despite my concerns. I need the booze to calm me down. I can feel the chills and a headache coming on. The last thing I need is another attack.

I'm happy to see Lia again. I don't know what power she has over me, but she is more beautiful than I remember. I steal glances at her every chance I can get. She notices and gives me a playful smile. I am brought back to reality when the brute who calls himself Avner snaps his fingers.

"We need to have a chat," he says. "And I need you to focus."

"What do we need to talk about? What could I possibly have to do with internal threats to Israel? I told you the first time. I am a banker from America, not Tom Cruise in *Mission Impossible*."

Avner takes a long drink and closes his eyes. "Nectar of the gods."

Lia slides my passport across the table. "Jason, we checked you out thoroughly, and we know you are who you say you are. We need you to help us with a problem."

"What could I possibly do for you?"

Lia smiles and seems to think about her next words. "What we tell you needs to stay between us. You cannot discuss this with your friends, your family, and especially not anyone at work."

"Discuss what?" I ask.

Avner finishes his drink and pushes the glass aside. "Do you know your apartment is full of listening devices and that the Bank of Israel is having you followed?"

It was my turn to finish my drink. "Why would my employer have a mid-level security officer followed?"

Two fresh drinks appear on the table. Lia has not touched hers. I notice the ice cubes have the imprint of a lion's paw on them.

"You are in security, with access to sensitive information," Lia replies softly. Her accent is a little thicker. "They need to know they can trust you."

"Is that the reason for all the silliness to get here? Up and down the elevator and through the woods to grandmother's house we go."

Avner grabs a napkin and starts working it over in his hands. His forearms rise and fall. He shreds it strip by strip and then balls it up.

"We want you to work for us, Jason," he says.

Are these people crazy?

"Is this a joke? Work for you doing what?"

"We need someone inside the Bank of Israel. Someone with your skills to get information," remarks Lia.

"What kind of information?"

Avner walks over to the bartender and whispers something in his ear. The man nods and then winks at me.

Avner sums up the situation. "We believe there is corruption in the bank and large amounts of cash being laundered. We believe the cancer is throughout and spreading."

I consider this. The Bank of Israel is huge, and the amount of money moving through it is massive. During my time there, I have mentioned strange transactions and accounts with murky ownership to my supervisors, but they always tell me to pay it no mind and that they'll investigate it.

"Don't you have a government organization that handles things like this?" I ask.

Lia touches my arm lightly. "Jay, this is complicated. It is a lot of money and even people in our government might be involved. We'll train you and you'll become part of our team. We'll be your handlers."

I look her in the eyes, pleased by the shortened nickname she is using to address me. "How do I even know you are who you say you are? How do I know you aren't really from the bank to test me? What if I say no?"

Avner stands over me, the strength of his accent increasing as he says, "I guess you would disappear from Israel."

CHAPTER 5

As I sip ouzo on ice at a lakefront bar several miles from my corporate apartment, I think this could be my chance. I am by myself and don't care if I am being watched. I order hummus and delicious deep-fried falafel. A cool breeze blows off the water, and a huge orange moon hangs in the air.

Lia and Avner are offering me a chance to make a difference and do the right thing. I've lived much of my life suppressing thoughts telling me I had failed those I love when it mattered most. These guys are offering me the chance to be a hero or at least start that journey. Avner also made it clear that I must leave Israel if I say no. I wonder what my parents would want me to do.

There is nothing more terrifying in the world to a child than being alone. Nothing fucks them up like being scared. Add guilt to the equation, and it gets messy.

My parents were the most important people in the world to me when I was young. Unlike most kids, I preferred to spend time with them at home as opposed to running around with my friends. Our house was modest but filled with laughter and happiness.

Doug Miles, my father, was my guy. Some kids worship athletes or musicians, but I worshipped my dad. Almost every day we'd play catch or tennis, or shoot baskets in the driveway. He was a busy financial planner but always prioritized time for me. I think back to family vacations in Michigan, Arizona, and Texas. My dad and I would get up early and have breakfast at the motel's restaurant or somewhere close by. Nothing fancy, just pancakes, bacon, and cereal. I would drink milk as he savored cups of coffee.

He made me feel safe and important. I could tell he liked being around me. He would ask me questions about my life and listen to my answers. Dad didn't preach but offered advice that I realized years later was dead-on.

Mom called me his shadow or Mini-Doug I followed him everywhere and wanted to be just like him. When I was little, I cried when he went to work, until I finally realized he'd be back at night.

I was also close to Mom. We'd spend hours in the kitchen cooking or curled up together reading on the couch. She loved to listen to music, and we'd sing along with Hall & Oates or Journey at the top of our lungs until Dad would yell to keep it down. We'd look at each other and sing louder. I could tell her anything, and she didn't judge; she just loved me.

It was a great childhood until one awful night when I was thirteen and everything changed. That night, fear replaced safety and dug deep beneath my surface, like a mole burrowing further and further into my psyche.

Mom and Dad were going to a fundraiser for my school with their friends and dropped me off with my grandparents. I remember the night like it was yesterday and often revisited it in my nightmares. I begged my parents to take me with them, but they laughed and told me it was for adults—a casino night so the school could upgrade technology. My anxiety was off the charts. I sensed something was wrong.

Pops and Mimi only lived a few miles away, so I spent a lot of time with them. They were in their seventies and Pops had asthma, so we spent most of our time playing board games or watching television. They lived in a big house that my grandfather had painstakingly refurbished when he was younger. To me, it smelled musty combined with pipe smoke and butterscotch.

My parents dropped me off at six and promised to be home in a few hours. I was mad at them, so I refused to give them hugs when they left, but they smiled and told me they loved me. Mimi ordered pizza, and we all played Monopoly. After they let me win, we watched baseball until Mimi went to sleep. They were big Cubs fans and never missed a game.

Pops drank his favorite cocktail—a whiskey sour—which inevitably put him to sleep in his leather recliner by the seventh inning. I sat by the window looking for my parents. They never came back.

Late that night, Mimi woke Pops, and they told me to go into the spare room to get some sleep. I listened to them call around to friends and finally the police. There had been an accident, and my parents had been killed by a teenager who had stolen a car. He'd been going thirty miles over the speed limit. I heard Mimi wail, and Pops told her to keep quiet for my sake.

The next day, they sat me down and told me that my parents were gone. I would move in with them immediately. That was the first time I had a panic attack. I couldn't breathe, and my eyesight became fuzzy. They laid me down, and Mimi put a cool washcloth on my head. It passed in time, but I was in a state of shock and unable to cry. I should have been with my folks and maybe I could have done something. Maybe I would have seen the other car or convinced them to take another route for ice cream. It had been my fault, and that burden attached to me like a barnacle. I hadn't even told them I loved them before they'd left.

The funeral was a blur. Everyone hugged me, with tears and pity in their eyes. I wanted to tell them it was my fault. It was my stupid school after all, but I just said thank you. I was ashamed and alone.

My grandparents were dealing with their own grief and had little time for me. I tried to stay busy with sports and friends, but sadness hung over the house like a rain cloud. Pops drank more, and Mimi spent a lot of time in her room.

Thank God for my best friend, Oak. He spent the night every weekend, and we were inseparable. His home life was even worse, so our dysfunction felt normal to him. My grandparents were just happy they rarely had to deal with me since he was around. I heard them telling a friend that raising another child was not how they'd planned to spend their retirement.

I wanted to leave and make amends for letting my parents die. A counselor at school told me it was not my fault, but I knew it was. I became reckless with too much drinking and partying. Anything to help me dull the pain. I knew there was something more for me in the world. I vowed to take care of myself, be brave, and protect those around me. Someday, I'd be a hero.

As I drain my drink and order another, I think this is my chance. I will take Avner and Lia up on their offer and become part of their team—part of their family. It feels good to make the decision, but something deep inside me wonders if I will fail them too.

CHAPTER 6

I walk into Hemingway's in the alley with a swagger. I've spent the last six months as a contract foreign agent for Shin Bet. I fill my days spying on the Bank of Israel and my nights training with the team. I am confident, physically strong, and becoming fearless. Avner interrupted our usual training schedule and called me here tonight. I'm not sure why.

There is no doubt in my mind I am consistently being followed. Early on, the team taught me situational awareness. Most people walk through their lives in a daze thinking about their problems or staring at their phones. I keep a mental notebook of people who look familiar and what cars are parked around my building. Testing myself daily, I change my routes and gait. I also double back to see if I can catch members of the surveillance team.

During my training sessions, Avner or Lia hide along the route in disguise looking for a tail. When they notice someone, they take pictures and send them through facial recognition software. As the year goes on, there are more hits. I am on the bank's radar. It makes me nervous, but it also makes me feel alive.

When I exit corporate housing this evening, I wear a blue baseball cap and a hoodie, and I carry a red backpack. Moving at a slow pace, I notice a sedan with a man inside who appears to purposely ignore my glance. I enter a local restaurant and order a drink. In the bathroom, I switch the blue cap for a white one and remove the hoodie. I have a duffel bag stuffed in the backpack that I now carry at my side.

I slip out the back and nearly run into a man coming my way. I notice a small earpiece and a lump under his jacket. There is a farmer's market around the corner that opens at six, and I move that way. I blend into the crowd before dropping my duffel bag and baseball cap in the trash. I put on a pair of sunglasses and pick up my pace. I move from the fruit stands to a family selling honey. I slip behind a lady selling jewelry and turn toward the street. Fifteen minutes later, one of Avner's men calls my cell to let me know I am clean.

During my walks, I spend a lot of time thinking about the last year. I have learned to be an effective asset, but I treasure the relationships most. Late into the night, Avner and Lia teach me the skills of being a spy. We discuss how to pass along sensitive information, and then I test what I learned the next day. Their lessons on how to survive interrogations freak me out, but I don't think that will ever happen.

Avner calls me Luke, and he is Yoda. My feelings have become stronger for Lia as I spend more time with her. We talk late into the night about our rough childhoods, her time in the military, and how she ended up becoming an agent for Shin Bet. I share everything she wants to know about me, even the things I've only told Oak.

Three nights a week, I train in Krav Maga—an Israeli martial art derived from a combination of aikido, judo, karate, boxing, and wrestling. I've become proficient in aggressive self-defense. I don't care if I am being followed to the gym, but I still like to test my surveillance detection techniques.

My path around Jerusalem can last an hour or more on the nights I meet the team. I refuse to let them down by being followed. This isn't a game; it can be life or death for us all. Earlier this week, we worked with weapons. Armed forces around the world use the Beretta 22LR pistol, and we spend hours at the range shooting targets in a specially designed course. We also fire submachine guns but agree I will never need such a powerful weapon.

Watching Lia shoot her sniper rifle is a real treat. She learned to shoot in the military and is proficient up to a thousand meters. She places her DAN .338 bolt-action rifle on its sling to keep the arm still, takes a breath, and fires. A true combination of beauty and violence. A continued study in contradictions.

I don't know if her attention is real or part of the recruitment, and I don't care. I'll do anything to spend more time with her. I want to believe she is genuine, but there can be a coldness about her that races in like a fast-moving storm.

"She's complicated," Avner tells me. "Focus on your training to stay alive, not your teenage crush."

After a year as a spy, I am getting more daring at work. Lately, someone always seems to be looking over my shoulder or following me throughout the building. The bank is corrupt at many levels, and I can't trust anyone. We know money is coming in and out, but determining its final location is difficult. It bounces all over the world, in and out of limited liability companies and partnerships.

When I arrive tonight, Avner and Lia are already at our table, but there are no drinks. They are both jumpy, like they've had too much caffeine. Avner tells me to sit down.

"What's wrong?" I ask.

"Jason, we are getting a lot of chatter from our sources close to the bank. They know there is a leak, and you are high on their list. We are going to pull you," Avner states matter-of-factly. "You have done a great job, but it is getting too dangerous."

I run my hands through my hair as I lean back in the chair. I can't lose my chance to be a hero. "Avner, I have been careful and followed my training. We are almost there. How dangerous can it be? These are bankers, not mobsters."

"You have no idea what these people are capable of. Israel is not America, and danger comes in many forms," he says.

I shake my head. "I am trained for this. I am one of you now. We are family."

Lia pounds her fist on the table. "No, you've only been doing this for a year. It's too dangerous, and it's time for you to go home. We are not going to have your blood on our hands. We'll find another way to get what we need."

It takes me a moment to recover from the coldness in her tone. I refuse to believe I am just a pawn for them. I stand and say, "I disagree. I signed up for this, and it has been the best year of my life. I finally feel alive, and I am doing something good."

Avner is quiet for a long moment. He scratches his thick beard and closes his eyes, dark rings circling them. His shoulders slump. "Two more weeks, but there are conditions."

"Avner, no." Lia leans across the table and points her finger at him. "This is not a fucking game. We are not playing make-believe. You know the horrible things people do. We see it all the time."

I interrupt her. "I'll do anything."

"First, we're going to implant a tracer under your skin," Avner resumes. "We'll be able to track you and hear everything you say. We'll always know where you are, and there is no way anyone can find it. It is the newest technology, so sometimes we lose the connection, but we'll reconnect if we do."

"Done."

"Second, we need to agree on a doomsday word. You say it and we are coming in with extreme violence. Say the word and drop to the ground. You only use it under extreme duress."

It takes a moment for his words to sink in.

Am I letting my ego override common sense? Do I think I am an Israeli agent, and am I willing to die for this?

"What is the word?"

"Bluebird," says Lia with moistness in her eyes.

"Why bluebird?" I ask.

"Bluebirds symbolize angels in disguise, and blue is also the color of your eyes."

CHAPTER 7

Entering the bank event at the hotel, I feel the pressure of Avner's two-week deadline. I need to network and make new bank contacts who I can mine for information. Only two days have passed since his warning, but things are growing more tense at work. I try to be extra careful and avoid prying eyes. My boss David is around more often, but he is a bit of a micromanager anyway.

The usually boring bank event offers a lukewarm chicken or vegan dinner, small talk with customers and co-workers, and the biggest plus: an open bar. I check my hit list of ten people I want to visit with and mingle until I find each one.

From the beginning of the night, something is wrong. Everyone is cold to my approach, and I feel like a pariah. I check my breath and body to make sure I don't smell.

After the speeches, I drink with David and watch our CEO, Uri Friedman, make his way around the room. He walks with his chin up and is quick with a handshake. His thick silver hair is parted on the left side, and I notice his stylish suit. A decade into the job, he looks younger than his fifty-eight years.

I admire how he floats from group to group. He offers what seems like a genuine smile to everyone, but I notice that it fades as soon as he moves on. He is visible from anywhere in the room and bends down to get closer to eye level. Skilled at working a room, Uri plays the part of a large bank CEO perfectly.

After half an hour, he approaches our group. David shakes his hand and introduces me. "Mr. Friedman, I would like you to meet Jason. He is on my security team."

Uri smiles, showing off perfectly capped teeth. His cologne smells like leather and spice. His presence makes me feel small, and I stand straighter. He offers his hand. "It is nice to meet you, Jason. David tells me good things about you. How do you like the Bank of Israel? And call me Uri."

I match his tight grip and reply, "I like the bank, and the country is amazing. I appreciate the opportunity."

"I'm glad. Why don't you and David join us at the after-party? You can get to know a few of the execs. I like to keep my eye on up-and-coming talent."

Something is not right. The CEO must know about the money laundering at BOI, even though I can't prove it. This invitation feels like a trap, but how can I say no?

"That would be great," I respond.

"Excellent," he says, smiling and moving on to the next group.

I excuse myself and slide into the bathroom. I hide in the last stall and call Avner on the secure phone. "Something is wrong here," I whisper into the receiver. "Everyone is acting strange, and I just got invited to an after-party for no reason. I'm out of here."

"Trust your gut and get out. Take the phone apart and toss it in the trash. Lia and I are on a stakeout, but we'll have someone monitor the tracer," he says before hanging up.

I feel sweat dripping down my lower back, and my heart thumps in my chest. My feet feel numb, causing me to stumble as I walk out of the stall. I nearly run into David who is standing just a few feet away. Had he heard what I was saying?

"Hey, man. Are you ready for the party?" he asks. "Follow me to your destiny."

I go to wash my hands at the sink.

"I'm not feeling great, David. I think I'm going to head home."

His face contorts in anger for just a microsecond and then he regains his composure. "Just come for a little bit. Uri invited you, and he will be offended if you don't attend."

Making a run for it seems like the only way out, but if I do, I will be burned at BOI forever. The project will be over, and I will fail the team. Letting Lia and Avner down is not an option. If the project is over, then I will likely be alone again.

"Lead the way," I say.

I follow him out of the bathroom and through several private conference rooms before entering a small space used for storage.

"I think we took a wrong turn," I comment as I turn around.

That's when the lights go out.

CHAPTER 8

A splash of cold water pulls me from an unconscious haze. It takes me a moment to realize I am in my underwear tied to a chair with a tarp underneath me. My wrists are taped to the arms of the chair, and the heavy industrial tape is cutting off feeling. My vision is blurry, and it is difficult to make out faces.

My tongue feels heavy, and my throat is dry. I must have been drugged. I try to say something, but it comes out as a mumble. I panic and start to thrash around in the seat, but it just makes the tape cut deeper into my wrists. I am in big trouble.

"Look who's up," says David. "Did you enjoy your nap, sleeping beauty?"

I look around the room the best I can. I take deep breaths and think about Avner's words. *Assess the situation, and look for opportunities to escape.*

My arms and legs are useless, and I am surrounded by Uri, David, and a couple of security types with shaved heads and scowls. We are in a cold, gray industrial building. The smell of chemicals fills the air.

In the corner is a short man with a bow tie and apron. He has small round glasses and leans casually against the wall. He holds a small metal baton in one hand and an unlit cigarette in the other. My predicament is dire. Even worse, I am alone. I keep looking around waiting to be saved, but it doesn't happen.

Why isn't the tracer working?

Uri steps forward, still wearing the beautiful suit, but his tie and smile are gone. His hair is ruffled, and his face is a light shade of red. "Young man, you are in a terrible situation. We need to get the answers to some questions. To help facilitate those answers, I am going to introduce you to my associate, Dr. Levi. I would suggest you do as he says and answer everything truthfully. If not, you are going to have a bad night."

He uses his hands to smooth down his hair. "As CEO, I must leave, as I cannot condone any of this ugliness. Good luck, Jason. You are going to need it," he says as he nods to Dr. Levi and walks out the door.

The man with the bow tie moves in front of me. His apron reads "Black Sheep of the Family." In a different situation, I might have laughed. With goggles on top of his bald head, he looks like someone's kooky dad or grandfather.

"This is going to take as short or long as you like. I don't care either way. I am paid by the job, not the hour. So you know, the cavalry is not coming. We checked you thoroughly for wires, and the boys were careful transporting you to this location. Everyone breaks sooner or later. It just depends on how much pain you're willing to endure."

"I think there has been a mistake. I am a banker from America."

He slaps me hard in the face. "While that may be true, that is not the whole story. Are you a religious man, Jason Miles?"

This man is insane. The slap pulls me from my haze. There is something about his squeaky voice that makes the hairs on my arms stand up. I consider the question and answer honestly. "I guess so."

He smiles and lights his cigarette. "If you have ever read the Bible, you know about the lion and the lamb. In this case, I am the lion. I can be your savior or your destroyer. You are the lamb that fully depends on me."

"Not to interrupt you, Dr. Levi, but I am not sure that is the meaning in the Bible."

He considers my comment and presses his cigarette into my thigh. I scream out. "Fuck."

"You might be right, Jason. I'm Jewish; we don't believe in Jesus anyway."

"Can we end the theology lesson and move this along," says David.

Dr. Levi turns his head slowly toward my former boss and smiles. "Would you like to join him, David? We have another chair for you. Do I have to remind you who I work for? I am simply being lent out by my people to Uri as a favor."

David holds his hands up and walks to the back of the room, mumbling to himself.

"Now, where were we? That's right. Do you believe in God, Jason Miles?"

"Yes," I say. The burn on my leg is only the size of a dime, but it is deep and bright red. I feel tears welling up in my eyes and will them to go away.

"Good. You might want to start praying to him. Let's begin. Now, who do you work for?"

I taste blood in my mouth and shiver from a combination of the cold and fear. "The Bank of Israel. Would you be kind enough to give me my clothes? It is freezing in here."

Despite being petrified, I need to show strength and build rapport with my captor. Lia taught me over and over during my training to establish a relationship. It might be the only way to buy time until they find me. I wonder again why the tracker isn't working. I check the room once more for exits, but my odds of escape are slim—or none.

"Strike one," he says, relighting his cigarette. "Why are you taking Krav Maga every other night and sneaking all over town? We've watched you attempt to avoid surveillance. For a rookie, you are pretty good. They taught you well."

"I have always wanted to learn martial arts, and I thought this was a perfect time. Would you like to untie me and see what I have learned?"

He laughs out loud. "I don't think so, Jason, but I appreciate a good sense of humor. We might be friends if it wasn't for your regrettable situation. Now, were you US military before being recruited by Shin Bet?"

My voice trembles a bit, but I try to sound confident. "I don't know what Shin Bet is."

I try and pull my wrists from the tape, but it is tight. I do my best to pull my ankles apart, but my legs are tied just as tightly.

"Strike two," says Dr. Levi, as he inhales deeply and blows out several smoke rings. "David, be a dear and unwrap my tools."

CHAPTER 9

David hands Dr. Levi his medical bag, and the doctor removes a syringe. "I am going to give you a shot that will help you stay alert and feel everything intensely," he says, grabbing my arm and pushing down on the plunger to inject some unidentified substance.

A jolt of electricity shoots through my veins, and I sit ramrod straight in the chair. Any residual fuzziness is replaced by intense clarity. My only chance is for Lia and Avner to find me. I must survive whatever is coming. I'm scared but steel myself for unknown horrors. I think of my parents and ask them to help me be strong.

"Jason, if you tell me everything, I will let you walk away. You can go back to America and live a normal life."

This was Interrogation 101. Give the prisoner some hope and all secrets will spill out.

He's lying. He will kill me once he has what he wants. I need to think of something.

Dr. Levi walks to the back of the room and picks up a piece of black iron at the end of a rod, along with a handheld blowtorch. The cigarette is hanging from the corner of his mouth. I watch him heat the branding iron for several minutes until it glows red. I am squirming in my seat.

"How long have you worked for Shin Bet?"

I close my eyes. "I am a banker from…"

Before I finish speaking, I feel the iron press into my right forearm. I let out a roar of agony. My body thrashes on the seat, and my hands try to rip off the chair arms. The smell of my burning flesh is sickening. The red gash is blistering in seconds.

"I am going to ask one more time, and if you don't tell me the truth, your face is next. If you are honest, I will extinguish this tool and pour some cool water on your new beauty mark."

Fighting through the pain, the answer escapes. "I have worked with Shin Bet for just over a year."

He claps and pours cold water from a bottle onto the burn. He places the branding iron in a bucket. "Thank you, Jason. Now, why did they recruit you to join them?"

"I guess they thought an American would go unnoticed."

"Who recruited you to Shin Bet?"

I'm not giving up my friends. "I don't know their real names. They call themselves Jack and Jill."

Dr. Levi ignores my answer. Walking back to his medical bag, he pulls out a pair of needle-nose pliers with a red handle. I cringe knowing something bad is coming. He slides the sharp nose under the pinky nail on my left hand, locks the tool in place, and applies a little pressure upwards.

"Please don't," I say.

"The real names."

When I don't answer, he rips the nail from my finger. My body spasms, but no sound escapes my mouth. Instead, I vomit from the pain.

I hear what sounds like a distant voice say, "We're just getting started."

****

I'm done. Avner told me that everyone gives in sooner or later. Tell them enough to give your team time to find you. If you can't escape, you must stay alive. Make yourself valuable.

Over the past hour, I've been punched several times as Dr. Levi screams questions at me. He shows me his instruments of torture like a proud child holding up trophies. When he pulls out the hammer, I give up.

David has been sitting off to the side looking at this phone like a bored parent at a soccer game.

"No more," I say with tears running down my cheeks. "I will tell you anything you want to know."

The corners of Dr. Levi's mouth turn down. "I know Americans are soft, but this is embarrassing. We are used to Israelis and Middle Easterners. I didn't even get to show you my dismemberment tools. David, please start recording."

David comes closer and holds up his iPhone. "Smile for the camera, dumbass."

I vow to snap David's neck if I ever get the chance, but that doesn't look probable. The transmitter didn't work. Dr. Levi is right; the cavalry is not coming. I keep hoping and praying that Lia is watching through her sniper rifle scope, but I'm losing faith. I wonder what went wrong.

"Let's start again," says Dr. Levi. "What is your full name?"

"Jason Miles. No middle name."

"Are you US military?"

"No."

"Who recruited you?"

"Shin Bet agents."

"Where are the documents you stole from the bank?"

"I transmit them every day or deliver them by hand."

"What do you know about *The One*?"

This is a new question. "I have never heard of anything called *The*

One," I say truthfully.

"Okay, maybe we'll come back to that."

This goes on for another hour until he asks everything several times and in different ways. The only things I do not tell him are Avner's and Lia's names. I vow to take those secrets to my grave if necessary.

I shake uncontrollably, sensing the end is near. No one is coming, and I am going to die in this disgusting room with these disgusting people. All alone and a failure. I thought I would be braver, but I am scared and sad that my life is ending so young. I am not a hero. I picture Lia and settle on her face as my last memory.

"You have earned yourself some mercy, Jason," says Dr. Levi, lighting another cigarette. "Do you prefer a needle, swift cut across your artery, or gunshot?" he asks, as if he is taking my order at a deli.

"I would prefer to walk out that door and go back to America as you promised," I answer. "This can be between just us, and I won't tell anyone."

"Fuck you," yells David. "Time to slice and dice this fool."

Dr. Levi tilts his head to the side and looks me in the eye. "Unfortunately, that is not my decision to make. I've been paid to do a job that includes your extermination."

As he moves toward me, I have one last memory pop into my head.

I can't believe I forgot about the doomsday word. Worst case, I drop to the ground and nothing happens. Best case, someone is listening. This could be a game-changer.

"I have one last request," I say.

"Make it quick," David responds. "I want to tuck my kids in and read them a story."

I take a deep breath. "I would like to see a bluebird."

As I say it, I tip my chair as hard as I can to the right. Dr. Levi's head explodes, and the room is full of agents in body armor. The two hired goons are down before they can pull their weapons, and David is hog-tied on the ground with a black bag over his head.

Avner rushes to my side. "Jason, are you okay?"

I look up and say, "What took you so long? And where is Lia?"

CHAPTER 10

Tampa, Florida
Present Day

The valet stand is backed up, so we patiently wait, listening to an old Alanis Morissette song about life being ironic. I check my steel Rolex Submariner for the third time. We are late for the charity event sponsored by Safe Harbor Bank, and I am annoyed.

This is my chance to spend some quality time with the bank's executives, especially our CEO. I have been at the bank for five years and have moved up the ladder slowly but surely. I am starting to be invited into the "boys' club," and I don't want to blow it. I am also hoping that my wife will start to enjoy our acceptance into a new world. Most of the time, I need to drag her to these events, and I need her to be engaged to make this work.

When it is finally our turn, I pull my blue Tesla Model S up to the waiting attendant. He opens the passenger door and then comes around to give me the claim ticket. He sneaks a peek at my date and winks at me. "Aren't you the king of the world?"

I smile, smooth down my suit, and button the top button. If he only knew what I have been through and how nervous I am, he would know I am just an actor trying to play the role of a confident up-and-coming C-suite employee. Subconsciously, I begin to rub my missing left pinky nail, and my wife takes my hand.

We walk through Armature Works past rows of mini restaurants. There are affluent families everywhere, dressed casually, with their kids running around close by. The smell of BBQ and Mediterranean food fills the air.

We move past the crowds toward the ballroom. The lights are low, and there is a huge sign that reads "Night of Dreams Sponsored by Safe Harbor Bank." A hostess directs us to table number one in the front of the room while a waitress hands us champagne.

Approaching the table, we see Terrance Browning, Safe Harbor's CEO, moving our way. Terrance is the son of a wealthy family in Connecticut. He went to work as a Wall Street trader and made his first million at twenty-five years old. He then led a group of investors during the Great Recession that started in 2007 and purchased a failing community bank. They recapitalized and set on a course to take over the market. Sixteen years later, Safe Harbor Bank is the largest privately held bank in the country. The internet claims Terrance's net worth is over one hundred million, and his annual salary has grown to five million a year plus stock options.

Terrance is an inch taller than me, but there are rumors of lifts in his Gucci slip-ons. His receding hair is very short; he has a sharp nose and a thin, but not frail, frame. At first glance, he is attractive, but upon closer inspection, he seems less so. Every day, he wears his trademark tan slacks, a pink shirt, and a blue blazer. The only thing that changes is the color and pattern of his pocket square.

"Look at this beautiful couple. You two look like movie stars," he says with his arms outstretched. He gives me a weak handshake. Everyone knows that Terrance is a germaphobe, and a handshake is a real effort.

"Lia, you look gorgeous. Black is your color." He gives her air kisses on both cheeks.

Lia does look beautiful. The ten years since we left Israel have done nothing to diminish her appearance. Her long black hair hangs down around her bare shoulders. I bought her the black dress earlier in the week, and she reluctantly agreed to wear it to the event. She said it was too short and tight. I disagree as does every man who steals a look at her.

I make the rounds, saying hello to several co-workers and community movers and shakers. Lia follows closely. I know she hates these events, but it is part of the job. I was recently promoted to head of security for the bank, and this is a rare opportunity to hobnob with the execs.

"Can you at least get me a real drink?" Lia asks as she drains her champagne.

I take her hand, and we move through the throngs of people. Most of the men are dressed in suits, but some have on tuxedos. The women are dressed in party dresses of all different colors and styles. Earth, Wind & Fire's "September" plays a little too loud.

I order two Kentucky Mules, our favorite drink. It is a wonderful concoction of bourbon, ginger beer, mint, and lime juice. The drink immediately makes Lia more comfortable, and I see her start to smile and giggle at my dumb jokes while we look at items available for auction. I tell her how lucky I am to be with her, and she blushes and turns away. She hates being complimented, but I am feeling the bourbon and have so much gratitude for my new life.

Walking back to the table, my path is suddenly blocked by Eric Gruber, Safe Harbor's Executive Vice President in charge of the Executive Banking Division. He is holding a glass of whiskey and invades my private space. I can smell the booze seeping out of his pores.

"I want to know why your team is sniffing around my division," he gripes with a slight slur.

"Hey, Eric. I'm not sure what you're talking about. Have you met my wife Lia?" I try to change the subject.

He ignores me. "We have our own compliance, so stay out of my business. Got it."

Eric is a bank executive, and I don't need to get into a clash with him. I am sure it is the booze talking, and we will work things out on Monday.

"Who's that asshole?" inquires Lia.

"Don't worry about him. Just work stuff. Let's go enjoy dinner."

We eat a delicious meal of steak and lobster while listening to the mayor go on and on about the future of Tampa Bay. The final speaker is the head coach of the Tampa Bay Buccaneers, and he gives a motivational talk about a player who was destined to be a star. One day at practice, the athlete took a hit wrong, and his career was over. The coach's message is to enjoy today because life can change in an instant. I look around the room at all the blessed people and wonder if everyone understands his message. I vow to enjoy every minute and kiss Lia on the cheek. I want to bury my past and move on.

The night ends with an auction. I am three Mules in and feeling the energy of the night. When a one-week stay at the Treasure Island Beach Resort comes up, I raise my hand. The bidding goes on for a few minutes, but my table cheers me on. In the end, I am the winner and probably paid double what a week would cost.

On the way out, Terrance puts his arm around me and says, "Charge the trip to the bank. You deserve it. Are we going to see you at the parade tomorrow?"

"I wouldn't miss it for the world."

After picking up our car, I set the Tesla to romance mode. A cracking fireplace appears on the screen, the seat heaters warm up, and a romantic playlist begins. Lia groans, but I sing along to "Let's Stay Together" by Al Green.

As we drive home, I think maybe I am the king of the world, but the coach's words ring in my ears—life can change in an instant.

CHAPTER 11

"How do I look?" I ask Lia, as I walk out of the bathroom in my pirate outfit. I spent a week growing out my beard and have a multicolored shirt underneath a bedazzled vest with shiny black boots. On my head, I wear a black pirate hat with a skull and crossbones in the middle that I spent more money on than I want to admit.

She looks me up and down and laughs. "This is what successful grown men do in the United States? Dress up like pirates and give away beads to pretty girls? Remember, I am a sniper, so you better behave."

This is my first year as a member of Ye Mystic Krewe of Gasparilla. While it seems silly to Lia, it is a big step for me. The YMKG is a civic organization inspired by a fictional pirate. Founded in 1904, it is made up of successful lawyers, politicians, and bankers. More importantly to me, many Safe Harbor Bank executives are members, and Terrance personally asked me to join.

This is my first year taking part in the invasion of Tampa Bay known as the Gasparilla Pirate Festival. We gather at the Tampa Yacht & Country Club and have makeup applied as we enjoy several pre-invasion cocktails. We board the world's only fully rigged pirate ship and sail through Tampa Bay surrounded by hundreds of smaller ships.

My best friend and Tampa's own movie star Oak Williams is the grand marshal this year. He will lead one hundred parade floats, fifty krewes, and several marching bands down Bayshore Boulevard.

The morning is beautiful with a cool breeze and lots of Florida sunshine. Lia drops me off at the staging area to get makeup applied by volunteers. I promise to behave, and I kiss her goodbye.

The bank's lead attorney is a longtime member of the Krewe and is surrounded by several pirates. He waves me over and hands me a drink.

"Jason, have you met the mayor?" he asks, as he puts his hand on the shoulder of the man I had listened to the previous night and see regularly on the news.

"No, I don't believe we have met," I say, shaking his hand.

"Nice to meet you, Jason. I'll see you in a few hours when I turn the key to the city over to you plundering marauders."

After several drinks, we make our way onto the pirate boat. It is over one hundred and fifty feet in length with three huge masts that tower more than one hundred feet above the deck. The bravest pirates scale the masts for the best views, holding on tight to the crow's nest. Having consumed my share of rum and Coke, I choose to stay down below. The boat is pulled through the water by tugboats among a gauntlet of booming cannons. We wave to other boats and to people lined up on the streets.

After taking the key to the city, we begin the four-mile walk down Bayshore. The best guess is that there are three hundred thousand revelers, but it looks like a million to me. The route smells like stale beer, sweat, and carnival food. The young pirates walk the route handing out necklaces to kids and flirtatious women, while the older pirates ride our float enjoying drinks and flinging beads. It is Tampa's Mardi Gras and a wild time that gets rowdier as the day goes on. I feel like a rock star as thousands of people beg for our trinkets.

We pass the Safe Harbor Bank tent, which is halfway down the route. I stop and say hello to inebriated co-workers dressed as silly as me. I see one of my employees waving his arms and yelling something at me. It is my deputy security officer Scott Kowalski. He is wearing a tank top that reads "Aaaarrrgggghhhh."

"Jason, I need to talk to you," he screams over the crowd.

"If you haven't noticed, I am a little busy right now," I yell back. "We'll catch up Monday."

"It's important," I hear him say, as I am swept away to the next tent.

By the end of the day, the parade route is filthy. Trash and beer cans litter the streets everywhere, and the cleaning crews move in. Those who attend the parade move on to drink more at Jackson's Bistro on Harbour Island, while the more adventurous head to Ybor City.

I meet up with Oak, who is surrounded by hundreds of fans, all in various stages of pirate dress. The majority are scantily clad women with many strands of beads around their necks from a hard day of smiling and, in some cases, flashing their "treasures." He has a YETI tumbler filled with an unknown libation in one hand and a Cuban sandwich in the other. He is dressed in a black T-shirt with a white skull that reads "Give Me Your Booty."

"My man," he yells as he pulls away from the crowd. He gives me a big hug, and we walk away from his admirers. Security guards do their best to keep the groupies a safe distance away. Nearly all of them have their cell phones out and are taking videos or pictures. Oak is oblivious as always.

"Looking good, Oak. How is the king of the parade?" I ask.

"Just another Saturday in the life of Oak Williams," he says, taking a big bite of the Cuban. Mustard runs down his cheek, and he uses his arm to wipe it away.

"We're pretty blessed, aren't we?"

He looks around and smiles. "We've come a long way from two kids living with your grandparents. Let's get out of here. I have the second floor of Ulele rented out for us and a hundred of my friends.

My agent got a fleet of limos, and one can take you home after we eat—unless you want to head out with me for the night."

I know better than that. Oak and I are playing golf the next day, and I do not need to be around the craziness that surrounds him. I also miss Lia and am already buzzed, bordering on drunk. "Let's go eat, and then you are on your own."

He takes off a strand of beads from around his neck that has miniature pictures of himself. He places it over my head and says, "Suit yourself, but you know there is no party like an Oak Williams party."

I nod and smile. As we walk to the waiting limo, I can't help but wonder what Scott needs to talk about.

****

My ringtone plays The Temptations' "My Girl," signifying Lia is calling. "Hey babe, we are just finishing up."

"Did you finally beat him?" she asks.

"We are on eighteen, and I need to make this putt."

"Good luck, but Scott from the bank is here and says he needs to talk to you. Apparently, you guys are working on something important."

I rub the pinky with the missing nail. "Will you put him in my office and tell him we'll be back in twenty minutes?" I hang up the phone.

"A thousand bucks says you miss that putt," says Oak, as he grips his neck with his massive hands and makes a choking sound.

I ignore him the best I can and continue to go through my routine. Read the green, set the line on the ball toward the cup, take a practice putt and a deep breath. It is a warm day in Tampa with plenty of humidity, but a strong wind blows occasionally.

"I will bet you twenty bucks," I reply, as I step away and start my routine again.

Oak rolls his eyes. "Jay-Bird, I won't even get out of bed for twenty bucks, but I know bankers have limited funds, so I am happy to take your money."

It is an eight-foot putt with a little break right to left. I have been making them all day and feel confident. I pull my putter back and then push smoothly forward. The putter connects with the ball, and I keep my head down waiting to hear it drop before I look toward the hole. I never hear the sound.

"Pay me, sucker," yells Oak, ignoring the staff and other golfers who have come out to see the movie star at their club.

I pull a twenty from my money clip and hand it to him like it is my last in the world. Oak is the star of six *Rage* movies and has a net worth north of two hundred million. He takes my twenty as we walk off the green and hands it to a member of the staff who is raking the practice sand trap.

"Thank you for being a fan," he says to the man. "Go see all my movies."

I play most weekends, hit balls at the range, take an occasional lesson, and have the best equipment. Oak never practices and is still wearing the Gasparilla shirt from yesterday with the addition of a bright green bucket hat. The snooty club pro tried to get him to change, but Oak just laughed. Despite all of this, he wins every match.

After graduation from college, Oak and I moved to Florida from the Midwest. I started my career at a large regional bank, while he worked as a bouncer at night. During the day, he sat by the pool writing a screenplay he called *Rage* about a college dropout who took on the Mafia.

Oak was always special. The son of a black father who came in and out of his life and a white mother, his skin is mocha and his eyes are green. He is six foot three and was all-state in three sports. He has great genetics and the ability to talk to anyone. He is also half crazy but the best friend a guy could ever have. He is loyal and generous, and he always has my back. I view him as the brother I never had but always needed.

While I worked my way up at the bank, Oak sold his screenplay and convinced the studio to let him have the lead in the first *Rage* movie. He moved to LA and became the star of a movie franchise. When he left, I was crushed, but I wanted him to live his dreams. It felt like he was another person leaving me behind.

After golf and a quick trip to the store, we walk through the door of my house, and I kiss my wife hard. I know it makes her uncomfortable, but I don't care. Even though we are very different, I feel like Lia is my soulmate.

"When are you leaving this clown and running away with me?" Oak asks as he struts in. Somewhere between my Tesla and the door, he removed his shirt. He kisses her cheek and hands her a bottle of Willamette Pinot Noir and a grocery bag of filet mignons.

"Sorry, I don't really care for tall, rich, gorgeous men. I'll stick with Jay."

"That's great," I grumble as they both laugh. "Why don't you two start the grill and open the wine? I need to talk with Scott for a few minutes."

In addition to being my deputy security officer at Safe Harbor, Scott Kowalski is also my IT expert. Since Terrance acquired it, the bank has grown to one of the top thirty in the country. It is headquartered in Tampa and has grown very large in the last five years, primarily by acquiring other banks, adding an international department, and focusing on private wealth management. With stock options, I estimate that I will be wealthy when they all vest. Not Oak-rich but play-golf-every-day rich. Scott has been with me since I accepted the job, and I trust him like family.

My job at the bank is amazing. I like and respect the people I work with and those I work for, not to mention I am paid a high salary. I find the work stimulating, with a new challenge to overcome every day. Lia and I live a dream life in a McMansion set in paradise. We'd both grown up very differently, so I am grateful every day. I have the woman of my dreams, and my best friend is a famous movie star. Not sure how life could get much better. There are days like today that I can almost—but not quite—forget about my past failures.

"Hey," Scott says, as I walk into my home office.

The room has plush tan leather furniture and a bookcase holding all my favorite books, with a ladder that rolls on a track so I can reach the highest shelves. There are two televisions mounted on the wall for those days I need to watch the stock market and a game. A large window allows in natural light and a view of my neighbor's front yard. A small built-in beverage fridge holds some craft beers, water, and soda for visitors. I love my house, and this is my favorite place to relax.

Scott is fidgeting and moving around the room. He always seems nervous and sweaty no matter how cold the room is. He is short and stocky with thick glasses and unruly brown hair. I count on him to understand the latest technology, and he is head and shoulders above most at the bank.

"I am really sorry to bother you, but you said no cell phone calls or texting on Project Cardinal."

No one besides Lia, Oak, and Avner knows about my time in Israel. No one knows why I have a burn on my right forearm and a missing fingernail on my left pinky finger. They don't understand why I am so paranoid about some things. Only Lia knows about the nightmares.

"You did the right thing, Scott. I don't trust technology."

He clears his throat. "Something is very wrong at Safe Harbor Bank."

CHAPTER 12

"Okay, slow down," I say. "You are kind of freaking me out."

We started Project Cardinal many months ago, after noticing some strange activity in the bank's Executive Banking Division. This group only deals with high-net-worth individuals who can deposit more than $1 million. It is a highly competitive segment of the banking world and a very profitable one for Safe Harbor. Rich people tend to need brokerage accounts, second homes, and financing for boats. They also have a lot of spare cash.

"What have you found?" I ask.

Scott continues pacing the room, drinking a bottle of Mountain Dew. He slams back what is left and spills a little on my carpet. "Ever since they hired that guy from Switzerland, we've seen some large swings in money deposited in and then out of the bank."

That guy from Switzerland is Eric Gruber, the one who confronted me at the charity event. He is a forty-year-old former citizen of Switzerland who runs the Executive Banking Division. He is the epitome of a Swiss Banker—tall, only wears custom-made suits, and has thick blond hair. Over the years, his suits have grown a little tighter from him consuming too much wine and expensive food while entertaining rich prospects.

Most of our employees find him arrogant and obnoxious, but he is beloved by Terrance. They are often seen sitting together in Eric's spacious corner office drinking coffee and talking in hushed tones. Lately, the door has been closed, and no visitors are allowed.

"That is not so strange. The rich transfer money all the time. They vacation, buy cars, and whatever else the privileged do."

Scott stretches his neck to each side, resulting in two loud cracks. After removing his glasses, he says, "Jason, I've been poking around a little and looking at a lot of data."

I don't love where this is going. Rocking the boat at Safe Harbor is not a great way to grow a career. Whistleblowers and complainers find their way out of the bank. If they try to sue, they are crushed by high-cost attorneys on retainer.

"I hope you have not been poking around anywhere you are not supposed to be," I say. "We need to stay in our lane."

He puts his glasses back on and seems to contemplate his next words carefully. "Jason, I went deep into the company's systems and found something I am sure I'm not supposed to see. The bank has thousands of accounts with only account numbers, no names."

"That's not so strange. High-net-worth customers want privacy and pay a price to get it. That's why the Executive Banking Division has its own technology group. They keep information separate from the rest of the bank. You can't have a teller pulling up some famous athlete's account."

I am feeling better. Maybe this is not a big deal. I'm sure we can discuss the issue with some of the data nerds and put Scott's concerns to rest.

Scott shakes his head and runs his hands through his hair. It sticks up at odd angles, and his eyeballs dart frantically around the room. "I don't think you understand. These are secret balances being kept in shadow accounts. They do not roll up to the bank's official books. Thousands of accounts owned by people throughout the world. Athletes, actors, and business titans."

"Wait a minute. I thought you said they were accounts with no names attached."

"That is what I am telling you, Jason. I found it all. There is a hole in the system. I read everything—account numbers, names, and balances. There are specific relationship and management notes for each account. And there is something else."

My head is spinning. I try and understand the implications of what I am hearing. Not only has Scott broken company rules, he also may have done something illegal. As his supervisor, I am now also in the soup.

"Scott, you shouldn't have done that. There is separation of departments for a reason. Your actions have put our careers at risk."

"This isn't about our jobs. This is something bigger. These are secret accounts that are being hidden to avoid paying taxes. It is tax fraud. But that's not all."

"Jesus, Scott, what more could there be?" I ask, rubbing my left pinky.

"There are huge outflows from these accounts going somewhere, and it is being directed by the bank's executive management. Money is skimmed from these accounts and sent somewhere. It is like a fee for the illegal service."

I need a drink. I can't believe what I am hearing.

"Let's calm down. You need to stop looking at this information. We'll get together tomorrow morning and figure out what to do. I am sure there is a reasonable explanation for this."

I am breaking out in a sweat, and my chest feels tight. It's been a decade since I've had an attack.

This can't happen again. I've done everything to build an amazing life. I don't think I can handle another Israel situation.

"Jason, I didn't just find it. I also downloaded it all. I have proof, and it is all right here." He holds up a laptop he has been gripping in one hand. "We can take these guys down. We can be fucking heroes."

I have trouble concentrating after Scott leaves the house. Lia, Oak, and I eat steaks and drink expensive wine until after midnight. The steak tastes bland and the wine rancid as the conversation replays in my mind. Oak tells great stories of working in Hollywood and traveling the world with other rich and famous people. Usually I enjoy it, but my mind keeps going back to Project Cardinal and Scott's laptop.

When we go to bed, Lia says, "What is wrong with you? You seemed distracted all night. Did something happen with Scott?"

I never keep anything from Lia. I trust her with every secret, but this is a real bombshell, and I don't want to make her complicit if a crime is being committed.

"Scott and I have been working on a project, and he found some troubling things. I don't know if it is a big deal or not, but it is a Monday problem. Nothing for you to worry about."

"Is it that Project Cardinal you mentioned?" she asks nonchalantly.

Her comment makes me sit up straight in bed. I know I have never mentioned anything about Project Cardinal to Lia or anyone else besides Scott. "How did you know that name?"

She looks at me, smiling her dazzling smile and flashing the little gap between her front teeth. Then she turns out the bedroom lights. "Baby, you told me the name a while ago. No big deal. Let's get some sleep."

There is no way I am going to sleep. I toss and turn as the sheets twist around my legs like snakes and then I fling them off. I am hot and then cold and finally give up. I pace through the house thinking of Scott's laptop and accusations. I am sure I have not told my wife, the former Israeli agent, about the project. I don't know what is going on, but I have a bad feeling my life is never going to be the same.

CHAPTER 13

I decide to approach the Project Cardinal situation with calmness and reason. Thinking back, I probably mentioned the code name to Lia, and I am sure there is a reasonable explanation for the secret accounts. Scott needs to delete the information he stole from his laptop.

I am dressed in a gray suit with a light blue shirt and no tie. Covid officially killed the tie, and even stuffy bankers and lawyers now go without. I still make it a point to dress to impress each day, following the lead of our top management. I want to be part of their inner circle one day. Only the people in the Executive Banking Division wear ties every day, as mandated by Eric. They don't even take off their jackets when they go to the bathroom.

"Come on, Scott, let's go get a coffee," I say when I arrive at work early Monday morning. I am yawning and feeling kind of cranky, but I need the situation under control.

"Didn't you sleep last night? You look like shit," he responds.

We walk a few blocks to Buddy Brew Coffee, which is located on the first floor of Tampa's tallest building. The aroma of freshly brewed coffee combined with the scent of cinnamon makes my mouth water. The baristas steam milk and rush around clinking cups and wiping down the counter. Other customers chat while soft indie music plays. We find comfortable seats in the back and talk about last night's football game. The waitress brings me a black coffee and Scott two pastries and a cold brew with extra sugar.

"Listen, Scott," I say, "I've been thinking a lot about Cardinal, and I am sure there is an explanation."

With his mouth full and crumbs in his beard, he responds, "Yes, the explanation is tax evasion." He reaches into his backpack and pulls out a paperback book. He holds it in the air like a prize.

"There are books on the subject. It is all right here. The same scam has been done at several Swiss Banks over the years, but ours is like Banque Suisse," he remarks, turning to a chapter in the middle of the book. "This Italian guy discovered it, just like I did. No one knows if he was a crook or a hero. They were doing the same things—unnamed accounts for tax evasion. This is 101 for fraudulent Swiss Banks, but Banque Suisse was one of the most corrupt in the world, not to mention one of the stupidest."

I hold up my hands. "Slow down. You're saying Safe Harbor Bank is running the same scam they did in Switzerland?"

"Similar, but different. The secret accounts and tax evasion are the same, but there is a twist. SHB is taking a percentage of the money saved, and it is being moved offshore. It's like a corrupt partnership between the bank and thousands of individuals."

I sit back and sink into my chair. My calmness and reason are melting away. I try and respond, but the words don't come out. I reach for my coffee and spill it all over the table. The waitress rushes over with napkins, and I apologize.

"This sounds crazy, Scott."

He finishes off his first pastry, wipes his mouth, and washes it down with a high-octane caffeinated cold brew. "You think it is crazy? Guess where Eric Gruber came from?"

"He was an executive at UBS and Credit Suisse," I reply confidently.

"Look a little deeper, Jason. It might not be on his resume, but he was also at Banque Suisse in their Private Bank. This asshole brought the scam to Safe Harbor," he says, his volume rising. He is speaking so fast that his words run together.

A couple of young ladies at a table nearby glance our way and frown.

"Drop your voice. You never know who is listening," I whisper.

He hands me the book. "We need to get back to work, but you need to do a deep dive on this. When you are ready, I am going to show you the spreadsheet. I've got it all, but they have no idea I found the secret. I just need a little more time, and I can trace the outflow of cash. It goes offshore into shell accounts and all over. Lots of financial gymnastics. Mentions of family offices and complicated trusts."

My stomach clenches, and I feel sick. I want to find a reasonable explanation, but Scott is right. The evidence is starting to mount up. I am trained to identify issues, and I know we have uncovered a potential shitstorm. I want to run and hide, but I'm not going to be that person.

I lean in and drop my voice even lower. "Scott, you need to stop digging until we get our arms around this. Promise you will give me some time to think about what to do."

"Do the research, and we'll talk about it later in the week." He looks around, his eyes darting from person to person. "We need to pick somewhere safe."

I grab my half-filled coffee and stand up to go. "Hey, one more question. When you came over to the house, did you mention the name of Project Cardinal to Lia?"

CHAPTER 14

I am confused and conflicted. Scott confirms that he did not mention Cardinal to Lia or anyone else. I walk down to the park at lunch, eat a hot dog, and skim the book he gave me. It is time to admit, he's onto something big. Eric's background in Switzerland and the secret accounts are compelling. Now I must decide what I am going to do about it.

There is only one way for me to relieve the amount of stress I feel. Krav Maga Tampa is my go-to for training. It is time to work out and forget about the craziness going on at the bank. Monday night is always a busy class, which makes it more fun. I ignore the smell of sweat and ammonia, and stretch my tight muscles.

Upon returning from Israel, I sought out a gym to keep up my training, and the owner is the real deal. We connected from the beginning, and I attend class once or twice a week. I have skills, but Instructor E can still make me submit any time he wants.

The final minutes of class are "bull in the ring." It simulates the real-world situation of being jumped by a group of bad guys. We take turns in the middle with aggressors coming from every direction. Krav Maga is a self-defense and fighting system. It allows you to address attacks under any scenario. It is about avoiding the fight if you can. Instructor E says, "The best way to win a fight is not to get into a fight. You must stay calm under pressure and use anything you can to neutralize your attacker. But always run if you can."

If there is no way to avoid a bad situation, the idea is for quick and extreme violence to remove yourself or your family from risk. I love it, and it gives me confidence that I can handle most situations.

Tonight, I am the bull, and I've got three attackers to deal with. We are in full gear including protection for our mouths, heads, chests, hands, and, most importantly, our groins. This is not a sport, and there are no rules. We are aiming for speed and attacking the most vulnerable parts of the body.

The first attacker pushes me to start the fight. I keep my distance as his friends circle me like vultures. Once the conflict starts, it is full speed and violent. The closest attacker receives a kick to the groin, dropping him quickly. Attacker two grabs me in a bear hug, and number three moves in. I pull my knees to my chest and kick the man in front of me with as much power as I can. I stomp on the foot of the attacker behind me, which loosens his grip, and I land a fist to the crotch. I finish off each attacker with simulated throat strikes and knees to the chin. The battle is less than a minute, and none of the three would have walked away if it was in the street.

After a great workout, I go home and shower. Lia and I planned a nice dinner out, and I want to stop thinking about Cardinal.

Lia looks amazing as always. Her dark hair is pulled back, and she has her favorite blue topaz necklace on. She's been designing jewelry for many years and has built a nice little business selling online and to the ladies of South Tampa who have money to burn.

We have reservations at On Swann, our favorite restaurant located in Hyde Park Village, just a few miles from our house. The village is busy with a lot of people shopping at high-end international chains and indie boutiques. Women move in packs, giggling and drinking iced coffees. Couples hold hands while waiting in line at the ice cream shop.

It is a nice night with a cool breeze and no humidity, which is rare for Tampa, so we sit outside. The sun is setting, and joggers pass by on their way to Bayshore. The hostess leads us to a small metal table pushed up against a railing with green vines that cover the iron. I feel blessed to be in my situation, with a great career, plenty of money, and the woman of my dreams, but Cardinal keeps invading my thoughts. I try and block it out, but it won't go away. It sits in the back of my mind and springs forward every few minutes.

I order two Kentucky Mules along with appetizers, then sit back to enjoy our good fortune. I didn't grow up going to fancy restaurants with beautiful people, especially after my parents passed away. A big night out with my grandparents was Red Lobster.

In my early years, I felt like an imposter when we went to nice places. Over time, I've tried to fit in and enjoy it. The truth is, I am still more comfortable at Red Lobster.

"You look great tonight," I say.

My compliments make Lia uncomfortable. I assume it has something to do with her childhood. Her dad was an alcoholic who spent much of his life in the military and then bounced around from job to job. Her mom did her best to avoid the chaos of the house, but Lia said she was sweet when she was around. They've been dead for many years, and she rarely speaks of them.

Lia joined the military as soon as she turned eighteen, primarily to escape her life, but also because it is mandatory in Israel for every citizen to serve. She excelled due to physical strength that allowed her to compete against the men and a lack of emotion that kept her calm under pressure. The combination made her a perfect sniper. I've asked many times about those years, but she always changes the subject.

After the military, Shin Bet recruited her, and she was mentored by Avner. They worked together for years, living the motto of the division, "The Unseen Shield." She describes these times as a combination of intense adrenaline rushes and excruciating boredom.

"Do you miss your former life?" I often ask her.

She just shrugs and says, "Life is a journey; that time is over."

The drinks arrive, and we raise our glasses in a toast. "Lehayim—to life."

After the team saved me in Israel, I was whisked away to a safe house. A doctor and a nurse were waiting, and they placed me in a bedroom made up like a hospital room. They sedated me and then started to work on the burns and the missing fingernail. My face was also puffy, and I looked like a raccoon because of two black eyes. Lia held my hand and stroked my hair while my injuries were being attended to. I was in a drug-induced, dreamlike state, and she would never tell me what I said, but Avner often laughs about my declarations of love. I was embarrassed, but drugs or no drugs, it was how I felt.

The physical wounds were easily treated, leaving faded reminders, but the mental scars still stick with me today, like an undertow below calm water. The shame never goes away. I let my parents down, and I failed under pressure with Dr. Levi. Avner and Lia assure me that I am a hero, but I know it isn't true. I can see it in their eyes. If they hadn't saved me, I would be dead.

I met with the senior officers of Shin Bet and their lawyers as they worked on the case against the Bank of Israel. Uri was arrested but well-connected enough to avoid prison. They blamed it all on David and some other low-level bankers, who all went away for a decade. The bank was fined, but otherwise, business went on as usual.

Finally, it was time to come home. I felt like a shell of myself but dared to ask Lia to come with me. She agreed to a short vacation. That turned into a marriage of ten years. I don't know if she was running to me or away from something else, but it doesn't matter as long as she is with me.

I immediately relax as the bourbon slides down my throat. The concoction goes down effortlessly, delivering smoky and sweet flavors. Tables are packed close together, and the chatter is relaxing, like cicadas in backyard trees. At times like this, my heart feels full of happiness and gratitude.

The waitress returns, and we order dinner. After another sip, I reach out and take Lia's hand, but it feels cold. She gives me a brief squeeze and pulls away. "How is your business going?" I ask.

Lia rotates her drink in circles, and I can hear the ice cubes moving through the whiskey. "It is fine. I have been designing new items, and orders come in every day."

"What do you think about opening a brick-and-mortar shop? Some place like this would be great. We've got the money, and you are so talented."

She takes a small sip and frowns. "I don't think I could deal with all these uppity women. I like being online where they buy if they like the jewelry, or they go someplace else. It is easy. Anyway, what if we decide to move? We don't need a lease to trap us here."

I shift in my seat trying to hide my frustration and feel the vines from the railing poking my arms and legs. "We've talked about this. Why would we move? We have the perfect life right here."

As always, she changes the subject. "How is work going for you? Anything new?"

"Work is good. We're busy with the usual, checking out suspicious activity reports, looking at large wires—same old, same old. We've got a big project going on with compliance to train employees in *Know Your Customer rules*. The government requires us to know who owns every account so that we can stop fraud and money laundering."

"Did Scott finally calm down? He looked very stressed when he came over."

It is my turn to change the subject. I don't want to talk or even think about Cardinal. "He's fine. You know Scott: he is an odd duck who drinks too much caffeine."

"Why did you name your project Cardinal?" she says, looking around the patio.

Again with Cardinal? What the hell is going on?

"I name all our projects after birds. Must be a flashback to Israel. How did you say you found out about Cardinal?"

"I already told you. Scott mentioned it," she maintains, leaning back in her seat and crossing her arms. A vein pulses on her forehead.

Someone is lying to me. Either my friend and co-worker or the love of my life.

I feel my phone buzz in my pocket and ignore it. I want to get dinner back on track, but the buzzing continues.

"You better take that," Lia says.

"How do you even hear my phone? It is on vibrate."

She shrugs and looks away. Lia is always tuned in to her surroundings, even now, a decade after her career has ended. She notices people and has incredible hearing. She's always on the lookout for danger, even though we live in a bubble of high society.

I curse under my breath and pull out my phone. I've missed two calls from Scott, and there is a text.

"I have proof that Cardinal is real. Meet me tomorrow, ten-thirty at Daily Eats on South Howard. We are going on a field trip."

CHAPTER 15

Dinner had been going downhill, and Scott's text ruined the night. I am pissed. This is getting out of control. I want to go back to my life before Cardinal, but it is time to find out what Scott knows. It is only Tuesday, and I am already exhausted.

I dress in business casual because Scott said we are going "undercover." I don't know what he has in mind, so I wear tan pants with a white shirt and dark brown loafers. I switch out my Rolex for a Shinola with a brown strap and a white face.

When I arrive, Scott is already sitting outside in Daily Eats' patio area drinking iced tea. A half-eaten waffle with whipped cream sits in front of him. It floats in maple syrup like an inner tube in the ocean. The smell of vanilla and nuttiness hangs in the air. He is wearing a black hoodie with black-and-gray military fatigue cargo pants and a pair of black Chuck Taylor high-tops. A cheap, black baseball hat sits on his head and wraparound sunglasses cover his eyes. He looks ridiculous.

"I told you to dress undercover, not like a South Tampa yuppie. Want something to eat? You're going to need your energy."

I sit down and order water from the waitress. Lia had given me the cold shoulder after dinner, and I'd had another restless night. By the time I arrive to meet Scott, my hands are already trembling from too much coffee.

"Scott, what is this about? I told you to stand down while I try and figure out what is going on."

He shoves an oversized piece of the waffle into his mouth. "Did you read the book? The one about Switzerland and tax evasion?"

"Yes, I finished it last night after you ruined my dinner. No way this is going on at Safe Harbor."

He looks around, even though we are the only ones outside. He leans forward and says, "Not only is it going on, I am going to prove it today."

"What are you talking about? We should be at work focused on real issues, not playing detectives."

He pulls out his laptop, takes off his sunglasses, and stares at me with his eyes wide. "Once I show you this, you can never go back. Are you ready?"

The hair stands up on my arms, and I notice I am rubbing my missing pinky nail. I want to say "no" and run back to my perfect life, but I don't. I must know what is going on.

"Show me what you have."

He moves his chair next to mine and puts his hand on my shoulder. Looking around, he powers the computer up. "I downloaded everything and put a bug into the system that updates it every day. I have the account numbers, the associated names, and the relationship manager notes. Most importantly, I can track the inflow and outflow of the money."

I feel sick inside. I am sure Scott has broken the law by downloading this information, and now I am a co-conspirator. Even if it isn't illegal, we could both be fired for it. Scott is positive we are heroes, but I am not so sure.

"Here is the thing—this is laundered money. It comes into the bank off the balance sheet, and there is no record of the cash. These are all hidden accounts to avoid paying taxes. Let me give you an example, and then I'll prove it today. Have you ever heard of Sebastian

Keller?"

"Of course, he is one of the South's largest property developers. He banks at Safe Harbor and lives on the water in Culbreath Isles. I have been to parties at his house. Seems like a nice guy, and he's very rich. He can afford to pay his taxes."

"Guess which group handles his accounts?"

"As I said, he is rich, so I assume the Executive Banking Division."

"Correct! So we should not be able to pull up his accounts."

"Yes, for privacy, only certain people can do that. We don't have access."

He starts working on the keys of his computer and swings the screen my way. It looks like a rudimentary Excel spreadsheet that he can search by name or keyword. He types in the name "Sebastian Keller." What comes up is a balance and a history of the account along with notes that have been exported from a customer relationship management system, or CRM. It is not what I am used to seeing in the SHB system.

"What am I looking at, Scott?"

"What you are looking at is Sebastian Keller's dirty account, or his dark money. Look at this example."

He highlights several transactions.

He shows me where the customer deposited several hundred thousand dollars one month ago. He then points to a section that details the bank's cut and ten percent moved out of the bank. Now I am looking around the patio, shifting in my seat with my eyes darting around. I wave off the waitress when she comes back.

"A few questions. How did the money make it into the bank? He couldn't deposit it at a branch. There would be a record of it." I twist my watch back and forth on my wrist and scan the Excel document. "What happened to the bank's cut? Where did the other cut move to?"

Scott takes a large sip of iced tea. Half of it misses his mouth and ends up on his hoodie. His hands are shaking, and he is speaking very fast.

"The bank's cut gets laundered back in as revenue, making Safe Harbor look more profitable than it is. The other ten percent is moved offshore. I have not been able to trace it. It just goes poof. I've seen a couple of references to *The One* and something called BCD Investments, LLC. Any idea what the hell either of those are?"

I consider what he is saying. It sounds like the rambling of a crazy man, but it is right in front of me. The mention of *The One* feels like an itch in the middle of my back that I can't reach. It sounds familiar, but I cannot remember why.

"There is also terminology that I don't understand. Family offices, shell companies, offshore accounts, and synthetic trusts. You need to figure out the financial and legal mumbo jumbo. I am just an IT guy."

"Scott, this sounds insane, but how does the money physically get into the bank, and how does the customer know his balance in this dark or dirty account?"

He shuts down his computer, takes the last bite of his waffle, and packs everything up. He stands and starts walking away.

"Come on, that is what I am going to show you today."

CHAPTER 16

We are sitting in Scott's car across the street from the Tampa Yacht & Country Club, the same place I prepped for Gasparilla. It is a warm and humid day, and he keeps the air conditioning on high. His car smells like pine air freshener and marijuana.

Scott opens his backpack and hands me binoculars. They look several years old. Something you would use to watch birds. He pulls out a camera and reaches into the back seat for a long telephoto lens.

"In the notes on Sebastian Keller's account, the relationship manager—a douchebag named Barnaby Schultz—noted that he is meeting Mr. Keller today for a deposit of one hundred and fifty thousand dollars."

I know Barnaby. Everyone calls him BS behind his back. He is portly with slicked-back blond hair, and he wears large tortoiseshell glasses that frame his fleshy face. Like everyone employed in the Executive Banking Division, he dresses to the nines. He favors dark three-piece suits most days of the week. Every Friday, he wears a blue-and-white seersucker suit with a pink bow tie. Most employees roll their eyes as he strolls by with his chin in the air and hands in his pockets.

"Crouch down a little bit. Here comes BS's beamer," says Scott.

I slide down in my seat and watch Barnaby park his brand-new silver BMW i7. I must admit, it is a gorgeous car. He finds a spot in the back of the parking lot and passes by us without a glance before walking into the club. He carries a brown leather briefcase with a strap across his shoulder. Moments later, we watch as the hostess seats him on the deck with a view of the water. We have a ringside seat to watch his meeting.

"How did you know where he would be sitting?" I ask Scott while looking through the binoculars.

"BS comes here every Wednesday. He is a member of the club. He meets one of his rich customers, has lunch and cocktails, and then heads back to the office. He sits at the same table every time. I guess it is a benefit of membership, not that I would know."

We sit together in silence for a few minutes while I watch Barnaby through the binoculars and Scott fiddles with the camera. Motley Crue's "Wild Side" blares through the car speakers, and he bobs his head.

I have been to the yacht club many times and feel uncomfortable as we spy on the members. Some of them are my friends.

Scott sits up and points. "Here comes Keller. Grab your popcorn."

Sebastian Keller cannot be missed. He is six foot four, three hundred and fifty pounds, and drives a bright red 1969 Mustang Convertible. He looks like a giant driving a clown car down the street. He has black Ray-Ban sunglasses, and his hair is thinning on top but long in the back. He is not trying to be inconspicuous.

As he exits the car, he puts on a New York Yankees baseball hat and strolls toward the club. He carries a brown leather briefcase identical to the one Barnaby carried in earlier. He appears to be singing a song as he walks.

"Showtime," says Scott, as he starts taking pictures.

"What are we looking for?" I ask.

"Watch the briefcases. I guarantee they switch at some point."

We watch as they greet each other with a hug. They are opposites. Barnaby is well-dressed and short, with a thick mane of slicked-back hair. Sebastian is massive, dressed in cargo shorts and a colorful Hawaiian shirt, with his hair flowing out the back of the hat.

"What do you suppose those two have in common?"

Scott contemplates the question for a moment. "Fraud and tax evasion."

He reaches into his backpack and pulls out a pack of mini powdered donuts. He shoves two into his mouth, and a puff of white powder falls like snow. He turns to me. "Want one?"

"No, I am good."

"Suit yourself."

We sit watching the table for twenty minutes while they are served seafood salads. Sebastian drinks iced tea, and Barnaby sucks down two gin and tonics. As they finish, the hostess and a waitress pull two tables together blocking our view.

"Oh fuck," mutters Scott, sitting up. "I've been scouting this place for weeks, and that has never happened. We are going to miss the money shot."

"No, we're not. You stay here. I am going in," I say, as I grab his hat and exit the car.

I need to see this through. I'm taking a huge risk, but I must know if this is real. To be a hero, you need to take some chances.

I enter the yacht club with Scott's hat pulled low. I recognize several people and avoid eye contact. The hostess asks me for my member number, which of course I do not have.

"I'm meeting Terrance Browning," I say. "He asked me to get a table on the deck with a nice view of the water. Is that okay?"

She smiles and leads me outside. I point to a table with a great sightline to BS and Sebastian. She places two menus down and wipes away a couple of crumbs. "Your waitress will be with you shortly."

I sit with my back to their table and place my cell phone up against a condiment bottle. As I touch the camera icon, the screen turns live. I scroll to video and reverse the view so I can record behind me. I move the phone around a little until I have a perfect view of Sebastian and BS. I press the red button to record just as Barnaby pulls a book from his briefcase and slides it over to Sebastian, who peeks inside and nods. Barnaby pays the check, and they stand to leave.

Come on. Do it. I know you two are dirty.

Sure enough, they pick up each other's briefcases and stroll out the door. I press the button to stop recording and let out a long breath just as a heavy hand lands with a thump on my shoulder. I turn to find Eric Gruber staring down at me.

"What are you doing here, Miles? I am quite sure you aren't a member," he says.

I grab my phone and slide it into my pocket. "Hey, Eric. I was supposed to meet someone here, but I guess I got stood up."

"By the way, you shouldn't wear a baseball hat into the club. Have some class when you are representing the bank."

"Great tip," I reply, as I take it off and head out the door. I can feel his eyes burning into me, and I pick up my pace.

I slide into Scott's passenger seat with my heart pounding. "Get the hell out of here. I almost got busted by Gruber."

Scott turns to me and asks, "Did you see the exchange? Did you get proof?"

"Not only did I see it, I have a video of it. Cardinal is real!"

CHAPTER 17

I can't concentrate on work the rest of the day. Scott is right—Project Cardinal is real. Now we just need to figure out what to do about it. One thing is for sure: we can't stop this alone.

I dial a number I know by heart.

"This better be important," grumbles Avner.

It is midnight in Israel, but I know he is awake. He sleeps less than anyone I know.

Around five, I slip out of my office to go for a walk on Bayshore Boulevard, where we celebrated Gasparilla just a few days ago. On one side of the famous street is a long sidewalk that twists and turns along the water. On the other are gorgeous multimillion-dollar homes. Dark rain clouds are moving in from the west, and the water is choppy. The wind is picking up and blowing directly in my face, making it more difficult to move forward. The usual salty smell is replaced by the reek of dead fish.

I need to think. We are about to kick a beehive, and the implications will affect every part of my life and the lives of many others. The weight of the decision is like carrying a hundred-pound weight on my back as I fight the wind.

"You're not fooling me. I know you are on a stakeout or some private security job or maybe drinking at the Lion's Den."

"Guilty as charged. What's going on? Is everything okay with Lia?" he asks. "Where are you? It sounds like a wind tunnel."

It is good to hear his voice. Something about Avner makes me feel safe and that everything is going to be okay.

"I'm just going for a walk, and a storm is coming in. Lia's fine. I just have something else going on I need to process with you."

He pauses, and I think I hear some ice cubes in a glass. "Are you on a regular cell phone?"

"Yes," I say feeling warmth rush to my cheeks. I immediately know the mistake I've made, and a rap on the knuckles is coming from my teacher.

"You know better than to talk about anything important on a nonsecure cell phone. Don't you remember any of your training?"

"I wasn't thinking clearly," I admit. My time in Israel sometimes feels like a show I watched on Netflix. Another life that was someone else's. I need to transform back into the Shin Bet agent.

"How important is it?"

"I think it might be something big."

"You know what? I could use a little sunshine. How about I come to visit for a few days? I would like to see Lia anyway."

"I would love you to come to town, but I don't want to put you out."

"Jason, you've been putting me out for over a decade. You stole my favorite agent, dragged her to your old folks' state, and probably turned her into a Real Housewife of Tampa. I'll see you in a few days. I'll send Lia the info on a proper phone. And don't do anything until I get there."

As an employee of the government, I know money is tight for Avner. A flight from Israel to Tampa isn't cheap.

"Want me to wire you some money for the flight?"

There is silence on the other end of the line. I cringe, thinking that I've offended him. Lia told me that money has always been a tough topic for them both. Large raindrops start to pelt me in the face and dampen my clothes.

"Don't worry about me, banker boy. I will see you when I see you. Don't do anything stupid before I get there."

Despite the weather, I feel better as I walk away. Having Avner in town will be a step in the right direction, but I worry that I am just pulling him into my storm.

****

I wake up early on Wednesday morning with butterflies in my stomach. I am meeting Zeke Michaels, the head of the local FBI's Bureau of Financial Investigations. I want to tell him about Cardinal, but I am unsure how he will react.

When I enter the coffee shop at Hotel Haya in Ybor City, he is sitting at a table for two talking on his phone. The café is busy with a combination of locals typing away on their laptops and hotel guests preparing to investigate Tampa or enjoy day drinking by the pool. The storm moved through late last night, and the sun is shining bright.

My mood is not as sunny. I feel guilty for ignoring Avner's advice not to do anything until he arrives, but I am panicking. I'm scared about what is coming, and I feel like I'm keeping a secret from Lia. We've been a little off since our dinner out, and I need her on my side to make it through this mess.

I've worked with Zeke when we've needed expertise in financial records analysis or forensic accounting. He is in his mid-forties with thinning hair and a pooch belly. Even though he stands only five foot nine, he is one of the most intimidating men I know. He has lizard-like eyes that go from bulging to slit-shaped pupils when he is ready to strike. He has a habit of staring at you while making a point, and it feels like his brown eyes are staring through your soul. Twenty seconds feels like a lifetime. He also curses every other word and seems to enjoy the shock value.

He waves me over and covers the phone. "Get me a café con leche, will you? I'll just be a minute more."

I return to the table with his drink and a black coffee for me. I also order his favorite breakfast treat—Cuban toast with guava jelly. The corners of his mouth turn up upon seeing the toast.

He hangs up the phone. "Coffee and toast? You must need something."

"Can't I just want to catch up with my favorite FBI man?"

He stares intensely, causing sweat to form on my brow.

"No one wants to see the FBI," he says and bursts out laughing loudly, causing several people in the café to look up from their laptops.

Zeke is a former state prosecutor who also has his CPA license. He is smarter than everyone and lets you know it. He can be dismissive and condescending. I remind myself we are on the same side.

"Seriously, Jason, what's up? Is something wrong at the bank? Got some funny money being funneled through, or some South Florida drug money being laundered at good ol' Safe Harbor?" he asks as he grabs his combination of espresso and steamed milk and gets to work on the toast. He dips half of it into his drink and smears the pinkish-red jelly over the other half. "You know I don't trust those fuckers that run the bank. They are lucky they know some of the guys up the FBI ladder." He contemplates his food for a minute. "You know I'm trying to drop a few pounds, and you bring me carbs first thing in the morning. But damn it's good. You going to share it with me?"

I shake my head. I was stressed last night and still don't have an appetite. I am not sure how to broach Project Cardinal with Zeke. I don't know enough details at this point, but I know he has the expertise to point me in the right direction. I must also be careful. Zeke is a friend, but he is also an FBI agent first and foremost. He has a reputation for closing cases quickly and is very ambitious.

"I want to talk about a hypothetical situation off the record. Can we do that?" I request, as I look him in the eyes.

Zeke puts down his toast and cocks his head as he stares at me. I try and hold his gaze but look away.

"First of all, you know I am a lawyer and an FBI agent. Proceed carefully. Nothing is off the record. I am always happy to help you, but you know I don't play games. Strictly by the book, Jason."

Should I change the subject or take the leap? My next few words could change my life forever. I am standing on a cliff with one leg hovering over the edge. Time to jump. I know it is the right thing to do.

"I know who you are, Zeke. Here is the deal. A co-worker and I came across some strange activity."

He sits up straighter and licks jelly off his finger. "Strange activity at the bank or with a customer?"

"Both."

He looks around the café, checking out every face and looking for anyone within earshot. He says, "Follow me."

We get up from our table and move through the hallway into the lounge. The bar is not open early in the morning, but there is a private room in the back known as the Roosevelt Room It is decorated like a giant library with floor-to-ceiling paintings of the former president and renowned big-game hunter, Teddy Roosevelt. There are stuffed replicas of many of his favorite prizes, including buffalo and antelope.

I hope my head is not tacked to the wall when Zeke is done with me.

He closes the door and chooses a seating area with small, white leather sofas facing each other and a glass table in between. A bighorn sheep stares down at us.

"Jason, talk in generalities. Generic explanations that do not cause me to act or report this up the chain."

Sweat is dripping down my lower back, and I take a deep breath. I am rubbing my left pinky but quickly stop myself.

"Someone may have stumbled upon a scheme set up by a bank that allows high-net-worth customers and entities to avoid paying taxes."

He chews on this information like the guava and toast. He doesn't say anything, just closes his eyes. When they pop open, he nods for me to go on.

"And that's not all. I think this bank is taking fees, pushing some of it back in as revenue, and sending a portion somewhere."

"Sending it where?" he asks.

"I have no idea. That is where someone may need some help. They have tried to follow the money, but it gets lost in a maze of trusts, shell corporations, and international wires. Also, have you ever heard of anything called *The One* or BCD Investments?"

He puts down his coffee, and a thin smile crosses his face. "No, but now you have my attention. This could be a fucking bombshell, buddy. Count me in."

CHAPTER 18

One part of me feels like things are spinning quickly out of control. I'm in the middle of a hurricane, and now I am sucking Avner and Zeke into it along with Scott and me. The other part feels energized, like this could be my chance to put Israel behind me, do the right thing, and be a hero.

Zeke promised to call me after doing some research. I drive to work, hoping that he will find some new information and join our cause. I know the FBI needs to be involved, but the thought scares me a little. I also need to wait until Avner arrives before making any further moves.

I go into Scott's office and nod for him to follow me. We walk to the elevators and press the button for the lobby.

"Okay, Scott, I believe you about Cardinal, but I'm not sure what to do about it. I met with Zeke this morning to get his thoughts."

Scott's eyes grow wide. "You talked to the fucking FBI? This is insane. Shit, did you mention my name to Zeke? I'm petrified of that guy."

I smile at a co-worker walking by and look around for anyone who can hear our conversation. "Keep your voice down, Scott. I didn't give Zeke specifics, but we are going to need the FBI. We can't do this on our own. Sooner or later, this is going to blow up, and we need to prepare or just put our heads in the sand and move on."

He strokes his shaggy beard and runs his hands through his hair. He has dark bags under his eyes and is stepping from foot to foot. Cardinal is taking a toll on both of us.

"It's too late to move on. I've been downloading more and more information. This is big and involves a lot of people. It's even international. I know the money is going offshore, but it disappears like a fart in the wind."

"I am going to meet with Zeke again this afternoon to see what he's found out. I also have someone coming to town who can help us."

"Jason, you want to add more people to the chaos?"

"Trust me. This is someone we want on our side."

He reaches out and places his hand on my shoulder. "You know I trust you. I'm going home sick. My laptop has all the information. We can't let it fall into the wrong hands."

"You go home, and I'll deal with Zeke."

"Remember, Jason. The FBI is there to solve cases. They don't care about the collateral damage, which might be us. Be careful of Zeke. When you roll around with pigs, you always get dirty."

As Scott walks away, my phone rings. It's Zeke, and he tells me to meet him for lunch at Carmine's, a restaurant in Ybor City on Seventh Avenue. I agree and tell him I'll be there by noon.

****

On my way to meet Zeke, I park in a garage several blocks away, passing tattoo parlors, other restaurants, and many bars that won't open until dark. Old men are sitting outside of cigar shops smoking and drinking espresso. Their cigar smoke is rich and earthy and makes me crave a stogie. I love the gritty feel of Ybor and enjoy walking the streets. There is no need to be pretentious and pretend to be something you are not. Lia thinks it is dirty and smells like urine.

She is not wrong.

The restaurant is buzzing with activity, customers filling every seat. A line is forming at the hostess stand, forcing a pretty woman to apologize for the wait. The staff is running around delivering food and clearing tables as fast as they can. Somewhere in the back, a plate shatters, causing heads to turn. Carmine's is a popular spot for visitors to Ybor as well as the locals walking from their offices.

Zeke is sitting in the private room in the back. He attended the local Jesuit high school with some of the family who owns the restaurant, and they allow him to use the room whenever it is not booked for a party. The table is full of deviled crabs, stuffed potatoes, and pressed Cuban sandwiches. He is digging into a bowl of yellow rice and black beans when I walk in, but he is not alone. An unsmiling Hispanic woman is sitting next to him slurping garbanzo soup. She barely looks up to acknowledge me.

What the hell, Zeke? No one else is supposed to know about Cardinal. Who the hell is this lady?

"Let me guess," he says a little too loudly. "You want a salad. Too fucking bad, Sally. Enjoy some real food."

I sit down, and he slides a Cuban my way. The addition of an uninvited guest makes me lose my appetite, despite the aroma of the grilled ham, roast pork, and Swiss cheese sandwich.

"Hey, Zeke, who is this? I thought our meeting was just between us?"

He takes his knife and fork and goes to work surgically dissecting the deviled crab. Most people eat them with one hand, but Zeke cuts everything into small pieces. Even chicken wings and candy bars.

"I love the *croqueta de jaiba*," he says, rolling his tongue for extra effect. "Don't worry about her." He nods to the lady. "This is my partner, Agent Gloria Chavez. I filled her in. Say hello, Gloria."

Agent Chavez just stares at me. She has what they call RBF or resting battle-ax face.

"This was not part of the deal, Zeke. I agreed to work with just you on this," I complain, my voice starting to rise.

Zeke places his silverware on the table and stares at me with those eyes. They bulge and then close to a slit. "Like I told you, Jason. I don't play games. Everything by the book. If you have a problem with Gloria, you have a problem with me. Now have some food and let's talk."

I take a deep breath and then a drink of cold water. I'm starving, so I ignore the bile in my throat and take a bite of the Cuban. The warm crusty bread combined with the salty meat and tangy mustard is delicious. The crunch of the sour pickle is the *pièce de résistance*.

"Did you find anything on *The One* or BCD Investments?"

"*The One* is the stuff of silly fiction books. Rumors have been around for decades about a secret entity trying to take over the world. No proof of any such thing exists. Good subject for all those hoax freaks who don't believe we were ever on the moon."

Gloria stays stone-faced while Zeke takes several bites of his deep-fried crab croquette. "Now, BCD Investments is far more interesting. They were recently under investigation for that bank failure, Silicon Valley Bank. You know what I am talking about?"

"Of course, Zeke. When the regulators shut it down, it caused panic throughout the banking world. It was basically a run on deposits caused by large customers."

"But did you know an affiliate of BCD Investments was one of the massive depositors that pulled out and warned others to do the same?"

I choke on my sandwich. "Are you sure, Zeke?"

"Not only that, BCD was also shorting the stock. They made millions from the collapse."

"Isn't that securities fraud?" I ask. Suddenly the sandwich feels like a rock in my stomach.

"Let me take this," says Agent Chavez. "The SEC looked at it. Felt like a 'short and distort,' but technically, they did not do anything illegal. My guess is they will close that loophole. Honestly, no one thought a depositor could start a run on deposits, but with social media, it can happen. You're the banker; you know that any bank can be manipulated."

She is right. It is the dirty little secret of banking. No bank has enough capital to withstand a true run. We take deposits and lend them out or invest them. No bank has enough liquidity if everyone wants their money back at the same time.

"There's more, Jason," continues Zeke. You asked me about family offices and trusts and shell companies. One of the major investors in BCD is this conglomerate of family offices—basically unregulated investment vehicles for ultra-high-net-worth individuals." He reaches for some Cuban bread and dips it into Gloria's soup. She scowls and pushes the bowl toward him.

"These things have been around forever to pass wealth from generation to generation. Some are legit, but many are set up for tax avoidance. There is enough wealth in these family offices to move markets, especially when they are pooled together. Do you have any proof that Safe Harbor and BCD are associated?"

"No," I respond.

"Do you have any proof that your Richie Rich boss Terrance is involved?"

"No," I respond again as I sink in my chair.

"Then I think it is time to make a trip to the penthouse to find out what he knows. And you're going to wear a wire."

CHAPTER 19

I agree to talk to Terrance but refuse to wear a wire. I've worked with him for many years, and even though he can be cold and aloof, I still consider him a mentor. He is also a powerful person in Tampa and banking. I don't need to burn bridges before I understand what he knows. It is hard to believe that he is involved in the tax scam, but as CEO, how can he not be? It is time to find out.

I swipe my employee card in the elevator to take me to the building's top floor. When I arrive, I go directly into the bathroom. I try to stay calm, but my hands are slightly shaking, and a thin mask of sweat is forming on my face. I splash on some cool water and adjust my dark blue tie to make sure the dimple is just right. I can feel dampness forming under my arms. I take several deep breaths. Five seconds of inhaling through my nose and eight seconds of exhaling out of my mouth.

I've been a spy in Israel, trained by Avner and Lia to succeed. I can do this.

The executive floor is a special place most of us aspire to join. The carpet is plush, and there is beautiful art on the walls. A hint of music plays through hidden speakers, and it always smells like chocolate chip cookies.

Desks sit outside every office occupied by each exec's gatekeeper. The people in the offices are too important to be bothered. Each gatekeeper has a serious look and a defensive personality.

I've been to the top floor many times for meetings with Terrance and whoever else he has sequestered. He is always flanked by Clinton—a young guy Terrance calls his chief of staff. Clinton takes notes on an Apple MacBook and rarely says anything or makes eye contact. Rumor has it that he is the son of Terrance's neighbor.

Am I walking to my funeral? Is this career suicide? Should I turn around and go home? Can I stay calm and do this? Damn, I am all over the place.

Before I know it, I am in front of Terrance's corner office. Clinton rises stiffly from his desk and says curtly, "Follow me."

Terrance's office is modern and does not fit in with the rest of the top floor. It is minimalistic, with a large white desk that is bare except for his laptop. There is a conference table and a more casual seating area with stiff furniture. In the corner is a small bar, and he has a private bathroom. The floor-to-ceiling windows have sweeping views of the bay.

The strangest piece of furniture is a white egg-shaped chair. I was told that you lie down in it with your head inside and your legs sticking out. Supposedly, Terrance enters the egg for twenty minutes a day to meditate, think, and work out problems. I've never seen him in it, but super-rich and successful people do strange things.

Terrance rises from his desk and offers his hand. It is icy to the touch and somewhat limp. He immediately uses sanitizer and rubs it in.

"Nice to see you, Jason. I enjoyed spending time with you and Lia at the event last week and at the parade. They were both good times." He directs me to the seating area. "Do you mind if Clinton joins us?"

Terrance never takes notes, and rumor has it he has a photographic memory.

"Of course not. Nice to see you, Clinton."

Clinton just nods and takes a seat at the conference table.

On the coffee table sits one single book, *Japanese Death Poems:*

Written by Zen Monks and Haiku Poets on the Verge of Death. Rich people are weird.

Terrance smiles, showing off his perfect white teeth. "To what do I owe the pleasure? Hopefully not an issue in the security world. I know there are lots of threats we are faced with, but I sleep well knowing you are keeping an eye out for the bank."

I clear my throat and say, "I don't want to overreact, but my team has found something strange that revolves around the Executive Banking Division."

He leans back and his eyebrows arch. "What could be the issue with EBD? Eric runs a profitable and tight ship."

I consider my next words carefully. "It could be a mistake, but it looks as if there may be a tax evasion scheme at play."

Terrance sits up straighter and steeples his fingers in front of him. "Whoa, slow down, Jason. Tax evasion within EBD? That's impossible. You know we have one of the best compliance teams in banking, and Eric is an industry pro. There is no way."

"I know it sounds crazy, but we've seen some things." I try to keep my voice strong and confident.

"What types of things, and how is that even possible? Due to the client base, EBD is on its own system. You wouldn't even have access to that without my blessing."

If I was floating in the deep end previously, I am now being pulled under. Terrance's face is starting to take on a shade of red, and his fists ball for a second.

He stands and I follow suit. "Let's take a breath. I am going to investigate a few things, and we'll get back together this evening. Clinton will come get you when I'm ready."

"Thank you, Terrance. I don't want to upset you, but I felt like it is my responsibility to let you know."

He nods and the smile returns. The red has left his face, and his arms are at his side.

"You did the right thing. I am sure it is a misunderstanding. We'll get to the bottom of this."

As Clinton escorts me out of the office, I can see Terrance entering the egg out of the corner of my eye.

CHAPTER 20

I sit squeezing a stress ball in the shape of a giant penny until my hand cramps. Clinton finally peeks inside my office at six-thirty. Most of the floor is empty except for the cleaning company, which rushes around vacuuming and dusting.

"Terrance is ready for you. Follow me," he says.

And I am ready for Terrance. I am going to ask him directly what he knows and not be pushed around. Nervous or not, I am going to move the chess pieces until I have a checkmate.

We ride together in silence to the executive floor. I make a few attempts at conversation, but Clinton just stares straight ahead like a statue. The elevator door opens, and he walks ahead.

Why are the offices all empty? That's strange. Some of the top brass are always working late, and the cleaning crew is lined up, ready to come in. It doesn't even smell like cookies. It reeks of someone's rotting lunch shoved in the trash somewhere.

Walking into Terrance's office, I'm surprised to find a larger group. In addition to Clinton, Terrance, and me, Eric Gruber is present along with the bank's in-house attorney. There is also a man I don't know standing off to the side. It appears I am entering the wolf's den. Clinton slams the door causing a loud bang, and I jump a little.

Check your surroundings, and take note of everyone in the room and their proximity to the exit. One way in and one way out.

I glance at the stranger. He is looking down at me, so I figure he is about six foot three. His suit jacket strains to contain thick arms, chest, and back. His bald head reflects the overhead lights, and he wears glasses with no frames. Former military pretending to be corporate.

"Sorry to keep you so late, Jason. Please join us," says Terrance.

Everyone sits down in the seating area except Clinton, who stays standing. He is not taking any notes this time. No one is smiling, and no one shakes hands. I have been to more lively funerals.

"Jason, I think you know Eric Gruber. "

I greet him warmly. "Of course. Nice to see you, Eric."

He just nods, as cold as a long walk on a windy winter night.

Stay calm and confident. They are trying to throw you off.

"And this is Max Braun."

"Nice to meet you, Max. Are you an employee of Safe Harbor? I don't think we've met."

Terrance answers for him. "Max is part of my private security team. I've asked him to join us tonight, as he has special skills that might come in handy."

Why does Terrance have a private security team? What kind of special skills does this guy have? I have been trained to deal with difficult situations and dangerous people. I know there is only one exit, so I'll need to deal with the big guy first if it comes to that. Always be prepared for the worst.

"So, everyone, Jason and I met a little earlier today, and he mentioned that he and his team found an issue with the Executive Banking Division," states Terrance.

Eric speaks up immediately. I can see veins pulsating in his temples and in his neck. "For the record, this is a joke. I don't know what you think you've found, but you're confused. I think you should be fired for making these accusations."

"Calm down, Eric," says Terrance. "We'll get to the bottom of this as a team. Does anyone want a drink? It is after hours. Clinton, make everyone a Paloma. Use the good Patrón."

While Clinton mixes the drinks, everyone avoids eye contact. Eric is seething, and the attorney is doodling on a pad of legal paper. When I catch Max's eye, he stares at me without blinking. I realize I am rubbing my left pinky and will myself to stop.

Finally, Clinton breaks the tension by serving the drinks on the rocks in highball glasses. He places them on coasters in front of everyone. Eric drinks greedily, but everyone else ignores their cocktail. I have a sip, but the drink is as sour as the mood in the room.

I speak up first. "I wasn't blaming anyone, but my job is to protect the bank. I must bring issues to Terrance's attention."

"You are claiming tax evasion in my unit, you asshole. That sure as shit feels like blaming to me," retorts Eric, as he stands, towering over me.

I can feel a spray of spittle as he yells. I stay sitting with my hands folded in my lap as I was trained to do during stressful times.

Terrance holds up his hands. "Again, let's relax."

"Here is the problem, Jason," says Terrance, as he steeples his fingers and leans forward. "We've had our IT people investigate the situation. As you know, for privacy, the EBD is on a very secure platform that is separate from the rest of the bank. It is imperative to protect the high-net-worth folks from fraud and employees making a mistake with their accounts." He breaks the steeple and opens his palms toward me. "It is a competitive segment, and Eric's team provides exceptional service."

"Yes, I am aware," I respond.

"So getting back to the problem. Someone accessed that information without approval. After accessing it, they downloaded private bank information to some device. That is illegal," he declares looking at the bank's attorney, who nods his head in agreement. "We need to know who did it and where that information is being stored. We also need to know who else has seen it."

Max speaks for the first time. He has a slight German accent. "In time, we'll find out who did it. The hacker was skilled, but everything leaves a trail."

I inch up in my seat and lean forward, mirroring Terrance's body language. I did not prepare for an ambush, but I must take back control of the conversation. "Can we talk about the information on the tax fraud that was found? Why aren't we talking about that?"

"We have compliance looking into that, Jason. No longer your problem. But for now, we need to know who on your team hacked into the system and deal with that internally before bringing in the police. Hopefully, we can keep this in the Safe Harbor family."

I am the bad guy. Terrance has made that clear. The threat has been lobbed like a grenade. I need to get out of the room and figure out what to do.

"You have until nine tomorrow morning. I am adding Max to your team to help find the missing information. I assume you already know who the mole is. You shouldn't risk your career and everything you have built up here, Jason. We can discreetly solve this problem."

With that, he stands, ending the meeting. I am shell-shocked, and my legs are wobbly.

"Max, walk Jason to the elevator. Everyone else, stay here with me."

Max nods to the door, and I head out with my mind racing.

What the hell just happened? I went from reporting a crime to being charged with one. I should have waited until Avner was in town. Trying to do this alone was crazy.

He walks closely behind me but does not say a word until we get to the elevator. I reach out to press the button to call the elevator car, but he pushes my hand away. I square up instinctively.

He speaks in a hushed tone, his accent more pronounced. "I want you to listen very closely to me. I know who you are, and I know about your time in Israel." He points his finger very close to my face. "I know about your wife's military and government background and all the crap that went down there. I know you are a chickenshit who got interrogated, and you're lucky to be alive. At least for now."

I push his finger away and ball my fists. If this guy wants a fight, I'm ready.

"I know what you're thinking. You are considering using some of that Krav Maga bullshit. I guarantee that is the wrong move." He pulls back his jacket to show a gun holstered on his hip. "You have a lot to live for. I would hate for something to happen to you and that pretty lady of yours."

He moves a little closer until his chest is nearly in my face. He looks down, and I can feel his breath. "Remember, a big and skilled man beats a little and skilled man every time. See you soon, Jason."

CHAPTER 21

I drive straight home at top speed, weaving in and out of traffic. I ignore red lights and stop signs.

It is one thing to threaten me, but how dare they threaten my wife? I need to get to her and make sure she is safe. I am never going to lose someone I love again. I should have told her everything from the beginning. What was I thinking? We are a team.

I slam the car into park and run toward the front door. Through the shades, I see a big man standing next to Lia. I burst through the door, ready to kill if necessary, and scream, "Get away from her!"

"What the hell is wrong with you?" exclaims Oak, as he turns around.

"What are you doing here?" I ask, as my chest heaves up and down.

"Not exactly the welcome I was hoping for, Jay-Bird."

"Look who showed up," remarks Lia. "Are you okay?"

There have been very few times in my life that I'm not happy to see Oak. Unfortunately, this is one of those. The day was brutal, and I need to discuss everything with Lia. My life is unraveling, and I need help to put it back together. Max also threatened her, and she needs to know.

"Not only do we have Oak, but apparently you invited Avner to town, and he'll be here at midnight. I guess it will be a full house."

In all the chaos, I forgot to tell Lia about my call to Avner. It is time to come clean about this mess.

I walk over and give Oak a big hug. His powerful arms squeeze me back like a python. It reminds me of when we were kids. He was always looking out for me and had my back. "Sorry about that, Oak. I need to talk to Lia about something. By the way, why are you in town?"

"I don't know." He shrugs his shoulders. "I just felt like you needed me here. We're brothers."

"Thanks, Oak. Can I get you a drink?"

"How about rum and Coke? Not the cheap stuff. Some of that fancy rum of yours."

I go over to the built-in bar and grab a bottle of 1703 Master Select. I mix it with Coke and hand it to Oak.

"We'll be back in a minute. Lia, can I talk to you in the bedroom?"

"What's going on?" asks Lia after I close the door.

I'm not sure where to start, so I decide on the beginning. I take her over to a small seating area in the bedroom. "Do you remember Scott and I were working on something called Project Cardinal?"

I know she does, because she'd brought it up to me, but I no longer care how she found out. Maybe I did mention it. It doesn't matter.

She nods. "I remember that name and Scott coming over last time Oak was in town, but you never told me anything about it."

"Honestly, I didn't think it was anything, but over the last few days, it's become real."

Lia's face tightens, and she transforms from my wife to the agent I knew many years ago. She sits straighter, and her focus turns on like a light.

"Tell me everything," she says.

I lean back, blow out a big breath, and tell her the whole story—from Scott's suspicion to the evidence on the laptop to the meeting earlier in the evening. I tell her about Terrance, Eric Gruber, and the threat from Max Braun.

She takes it all in without changing expressions. The ultimate poker face. I pride myself on profiling based on body language and microexpressions, but Lia trained me in those skills. She can make me think whatever she wants. As her eyes look to the ceiling, I can see her considering possible moves. She is in her world, working on a puzzle in her mind.

"Jay, we knew something like this could happen. We thought it would be a ghost from my past, but we can handle this," she insists, then hugs me tightly. Her arms make me feel safe, and I breathe in her perfume.

She stands and goes to the walk-in closet, returning with a dark green backpack that's been hidden away in our custom-built safe for years. She empties the contents on the floor. Lying in front of me is an envelope full of cash, a fake ID for each of us, two Glock pistols, and a set of keys. It is what Lia calls our "get out" pack.

As an Israeli Shin Bet agent, she dealt with many nasty people. Lia and Avner worked on some high-profile cases. While their real names should never have been public, there were leaks, and retribution can go along with the job. We feel safe an ocean away, but we planned for the worst.

"Lia, I don't think we are there yet. Do you?"

She contemplates the question while picking up one of the Glocks. She is comfortable with it in her hand and moves it slowly, reacquainting herself with its weight. "Let's wait until Avner gets here. It sounds like you stepped in some serious shit with some bad people. He'll know what to do."

I can't help but notice a hint of excitement in her voice.

****

Oak and I pick up takeout Thai food. I don't have an appetite and just move my pad thai around the plate. I can't forget about the "get out" pack sitting upstairs and the thought of possibly leaving my perfect life behind. Life can change in an instant.

After dinner, we sit out by the pool and drink beer. After a few, I start to settle down. It occurs to me that I have not called Scott, but I decide it can wait until morning. I need a game plan first and hope we can come up with one tonight.

Around midnight, I hear a rustling in the bushes, and I see Lia turn her head. Oak is oblivious as he talks about an actress he would like to date. We both stand when we see a shadow in the moonlight.

"Go get the Glock, Lia," I whisper in her ear. "I'll hold them off until you get back."

Before she can leave, the shadow transforms into a man. "Guess who's in town?" Avner says.

I blow out a long breath. "What the hell are you doing, Avner? Where did you come from?"

"Well, originally my mom and most recently Israel. Is anyone going to hug me?"

I am first to give my friend a tight bear hug. Lia is next and they embrace warmly. Finally, Oak gives him a fist bump. They have been competitive since the day they met. Two alphas vying for my best friend status. Each has what the other wants. Oak craves the real-life excitement and street cred of a true superhero, not just a make-believe one up on the screen. Avner could use a little more money to make ends meet.

Aver looks exhausted from the trip. Over the years, he has kept his muscular build but gained a few pounds due to injuries and a couple of work-related wounds. He is wearing his customary black T-shirt, blue jeans, and a black baseball hat. He adds a sports jacket or vest if he is carrying a weapon. His beard is a little longer with some patches of gray mixed in, and the only new addition is a pair of Hey Dude shoes. He still looks like a badass and has added a few new tattoos on his arms. When talking about Avner, Lia always says it is good to be friends with the monster under the bed.

"Why are you creeping around instead of using the front door?" I ask.

"I got a rental car and parked offsite. It is called good tradecraft, Jason. You might start thinking that way. By the way, I scanned the area. You are being watched."

Lia jumps in. "A black Cadillac a block up."

"Yep," responds Avner.

"Why didn't you say anything, Lia?" I inquire.

"There is nothing to do. The guy is just keeping an eye on us and not being very smart about it."

We go back to the fire pit. It's a humid night, and the mosquitoes are actively attacking. I grab everyone a fresh drink, and we catch up for a while. It is nice to have all the people I care about in one place, but I can't stop thinking about someone watching our house.

"It is great to see you all—even Oak. But what is this all about? Is there really an issue, or did you just miss my handsome face?" asks Avner.

As always, he gets right to the point.

"You didn't mention anything to me about an issue, Jay-Bird. What's going on, and who would be watching your house?" Oak sounds a little offended at being left out.

Over the next twenty minutes, I explain everything about Cardinal. Almost word for word what I told Lia earlier. Oak interrupts often with questions, and Avner sits back taking in the information. Lia is also quiet, and she exchanges glances with Avner. They have always been able to communicate without saying a word, and it makes me jealous. I'm not sure if there has ever been anything romantic between them, and I don't want to know.

Finally, Avner speaks. "Didn't I tell you not to do anything until

I got here?"

I swat a mosquito and notice a small prick of blood on my arm. "Sorry, Avner. I thought I could handle this on my own."

"Well, you put yourself and Lia in danger."

"Back off, Avner," says Oak. "You don't make all the rules."

Lia steps in. "That's enough tough guy talk. We are all on the same team, and we'll figure this out together."

"First thing tomorrow, I am going to check out this Max Braun character. He is the only one who made a physical threat. He sounds like some sort of rent-an-asshole. Lia and I have dealt with lots of those types over the years," states Avner.

Oak stands and starts pacing. He takes a long pull of his beer and seems to be choosing his words carefully. "Maybe I am missing something. You guys stole the data or whatever the hell you were talking about, and now you are risking this awesome life you have built. Remember, Jay-Bird, we came from nothing. Why don't you just give the laptop back and say sorry? Why jump on this grenade?"

"I hear what you are saying, Oak, and honestly I'd like to do that, but you can't unknow what you know. There is something wrong going on here, and if I don't do something, I'm no better than the people involved. You know my parents always told me to do the right thing, and I want to honor their memories."

He walks over and puts his hand on my shoulder. "It's just some rich people not paying taxes. What's the big deal? Rich people get away with everything. Trust me, I know."

Avner stands. "It's late and these bird-sized bugs are eating me alive. This situation is a mess. Let's all get some sleep and decide what to do in the morning."

We clean up the beer bottles and head inside. When no one else is around, Avner says quietly in his thick accent, "Jason, I have a bad feeling about this. Call in sick tomorrow. When you threaten to separate rich people from their money, they will do anything to stop you."

CHAPTER 22

I roll around all night. Avner's words keep echoing in my ears. When *you threaten to separate rich people from their money, they will do anything to stop you.* I also didn't update Scott, and that is weighing heavily on my mind.

Getting up earlier than everyone, I brew some coffee. I breathe in the aroma, and it automatically relaxes me. After pouring a mug, I go out back and check my phone. There was a voicemail left at two forty-five AM, and I press play to listen.

"Jason, this is Scott. Someone tried to break into my house."

He is breathing heavily, and his words run together.

"I grabbed the laptop and ran out the back door. I think there were a few people. I don't know what is going on, but I am running away. I am going to the place we first met. Meet me there as soon as you can."

I immediately call him back, but it goes straight to voicemail.

What was I thinking? I should have called Scott as soon as that goon threatened me. I should have made sure he was safe. What if they hurt him, or even worse? I can't let someone else down.

I run upstairs and wake Avner. He is deep asleep but jumps right up.

"Come out back, I need you to listen to something," I say.

I play the voicemail for him.

"Do you know what place he is talking about?" he asks.

"Yes, there is an all-night coffee place about a mile from his house. It is where I first interviewed him. We laugh about it all the time because they literally have the worst coffee in town. I fucked up, Avner. I should have warned him."

He strokes his beard and closes his eyes. He always does this when thinking of what to do. I can see his forearms pulsating. The new snake tattoo looks like it is slithering down his arm. Finally, he says, "Let's go meet him. Do you have a gun?"

I dress quickly in jeans and a hoodie, trying not to wake Lia. I go into the closet and grab the Glock from the "get out" pack. There is no going back now, even if I want to.

Avner takes me out back and through the neighbor's yard to a side street where his rental is parked. It is still dark out, and he drives in the fast lane, passing the few cars that are out so early. We arrive at Cool Richard's Coffee in Carrollwood, and he spends a few minutes getting acquainted with the Glock. He checks the magazine and pulls back the slide to chamber the bullets before placing it against the small of his back.

It is six-fifteen on Thursday morning. The staff either burned the coffee, or a skunk got loose. Cool Richard's took over a failed Starbucks and did very little to change the layout except add some beanbags and old board games that gather dust. It is basically an open space with tables throughout and a counter in the back.

Several people are looking at their phones or laptops, but one customer looks out of place. He is reading the paper and peeks at us over the page, then hides his face. Avner and I both notice. No one reads an actual newspaper anymore.

Scott is nowhere to be seen. I check the bathroom and call his phone again. Right to voicemail.

The barista approaches us. "Hey, are you looking for some dude with a scraggy beard?"

He is tall and skinny with a yellow apron. He has glassy eyes from waking and baking, and still smells like pot. He yawns and drinks from a mega-sized coffee cup. His name tag reads "Alexander the Great."

"Yes, have you seen him?"

"He was here at like four in the morning. I think he was all jacked up on something. He drank like three espressos and kept looking out the window. I asked him if he was okay, but he ignored me, so I went into the back."

My eyes are darting all around the coffee shop, and I am rubbing my pinky. Avner seems to be calmly processing the information but also keeps an eye on the guy with the paper.

"Do you have any idea where he went?" I ask.

"No, dude, not my business, but are you Jason?"

We look at each other. Avner nods at me.

"He said he had to go but gave me a computer bag and twenty bucks and told me to give it to you when you showed up. He told me it is important, and I promised to make sure you got it. He also said there was a note inside and that you would probably match the twenty. Do you want it?"

He walks into the back and comes out with Scott's backpack. I look around to see if anyone is watching, and Avner touches the small of his back to make sure the Glock is in place and accessible.

I hand Alexander a twenty, and we quickly walk to the front door. We both notice the man with the paper still watching.

"You go to the car. I am going to have a conversation with this guy," says Avner.

"No way. You're not my handler anymore. This is my situation, and we do it together."

"Fine," he says. "But what did I teach you about surveillance?"

I think back to Israel and situational awareness training. "There is never just one. There is a team here."

The corners of his mouth turn up for just a second and then the scowl returns. He instructs me to buy two coffees and sit in the booth next to the man with the paper. I have a good view of the other customers. Avner sits across from the man. I take a sip of my coffee. It has a strong and bitter taste that makes my face pucker up.

"Put down your paper and look at me. If I see you touch your phone, you're dead. I want to know who you are working for." Avner speaks in a low tone.

The man slowly places his paper on the table. He is nondescript and unremarkable. A perfect gray spy. "What the hell are you talking about?"

Avner slides the Glock out of his pants and holds it under the table. "I don't have time for this. I have a gun pointed at your crotch, and you have one chance to tell me what I want to know or Uncle Mike becomes Aunt Michelle. Again, who are you working for?"

The man looks around without emotion. "Contract job. I have no idea who is behind it. Hired on the dark web. Our team is spread throughout the area looking for a guy named Scott, and we have that guy's picture as well," he replies while nodding to me. "It's not personal. Just a job."

"Give me your phone."

The man hands it over without an argument, and Avner removes the SIM card. He pockets the phone, and without looking at me says, "Get number two's phone."

I have been observing the room and watching faces. Number two is a twenty-something woman staring at her cell. She wears glasses, has no makeup, and has her hair pulled back in a ponytail. Shapeless sweatpants and an oversized sweatshirt make it impossible to guess her weight. She avoids eye contact with everyone and slumps down to make herself look small. She gave herself up with one glance in our direction.

I approach her. "Give me your phone."

She continues to avoid eye contact. "I don't know what your problem is, weirdo, but I will scream and call the police."

Avner is in front of her quickly. "No, you won't. Call the police and we'll call the FBI and find out who you really are. We have them on speed dial. Your move, princess."

She turns her eyes to us and then flips the phone my way. I pocket it, and we exit the coffee shop, knowing we probably only have minutes until their backup arrives.

As we walk to the car, Avner says, "Well that was a cluster. Now they know you have the laptop and what my car looks like. Even worse, this isn't some Mickey Mouse operation. We're up against something big and coordinated."

Avner drives out of the parking lot, keeping within the speed limit. He makes three left turns in a row, finds the interstate, and then takes the first exit back to a main road. While he does this, I look inside the backpack. It has Scott's laptop, a notebook, and a short note.

Jason, I didn't know what to do. I'm freaking out. Someone broke into my house, and I'm worried they can track me by my phone, so I threw it in a lake on the way here. If something happens to me, I want you to have the laptop. I also put directions on how to look at the data and all of my notes. Be safe, and hopefully we'll see each other again.

– Scott

CHAPTER 23

Avner continues to drive in a complicated pattern to avoid being followed. He is concerned about the size of the net our adversaries have spread. After half an hour, we park at Dunkin' Donuts on Kennedy Boulevard. It is close to The University of Tampa, and there are several students eating donuts and drinking coffee. A long line is forming at the drive-through as commuters caffeinate for the day ahead. Their lives seem very simple.

Whatever is going on is much bigger and more organized than some rich people avoiding taxes. Whoever is behind this sent a team in the middle of the night to Scott's house and hired a surveillance team from the dark web to search for him and me. They have someone watching my house and have threatened me and Lia. What's next?

I need to formulate a plan. I can't keep putting my friends at risk. Most importantly, I need to find Scott.

Avner and I order coffee and a dozen glazed munchkins. The smell of the buttery, sugary treats makes my mouth water and my stomach rumble despite all the stress. We sit on the patio away from everyone else. I keep the laptop in the seat next to me.

"We need to go to Scott's house. I need to make sure he is okay. This is all my fault. I should have warned him about what was going on," I say.

Avner pops a munchkin into his mouth and licks his fingers. He is as cool as ever. "We can't go over there. Whoever broke in is watching the house. The last thing we need is a confrontation. I am not even legally supposed to have this gun."

I try to relax, but my heart is beating like a drum and the coffee isn't slowing it down. It is also piping hot and burns my tongue. "Avner, Scott could be in trouble. This is my fault. I will never forgive myself if he is hurt."

"You need to get your shit together, Jason. I know it's been a long time, but you are trained for this," he states as he cracks his knuckles and stretches out his hands. "I trained you myself. You, me, and Lia are going to think it through and come up with a plan, but you need to be thinking clearly." He points to his head. "Scott did the right thing by dumping his phone. He is probably on the run, hiding out at a friend's house."

It's true. I was part of a badass team, and I held my own. Time to bring the fight to these assholes. This could be my chance to right many wrongs. I always feel better when Avner is around, but it is time for me to step up.

"You're right. Let's go home."

We take another snaking path through South Tampa neighborhoods and park the rental a few blocks away. When we walk in, Lia is waiting in the kitchen. She has one of the Glocks in a holster on her thigh. The sight startles me. I place a dozen donuts and two coffees on the kitchen island.

"Where have you two been?" she asks. "I was worried sick. You took one of the Glocks. I was about to come looking for you."

I give her a big hug and whisper an apology. I walk to the window, pull back the curtains, and scan the neighborhood for anything nefarious. I wonder if they are watching us right now or if a team of assassins is on its way. I rub my shoulder blades and feel stress balls growing on both sides. For a moment, I feel dizzy.

Just then, Oak walks out of the spare bedroom wearing only a pair of basketball shorts. He looks as tired as I feel.

"Why in the hell are you people up so early?" he asks, yawning. "I haven't been up this early for a decade. Is that coffee for me?" He looks at Lia. "What's with the outfit, G.I. Jane?"

She looks down at the gun and states, "We have someone outside our house and these two disappeared. A good operative is prepared for anything."

Lia seems to be enjoying this. Her eyes are shining, and she reminds me of that woman I knew a decade ago. I hand them both a coffee and point to the living room. "There have been some developments. Let's sit down."

The main floor of the house is a large open space with a kitchen, living room, and dining room. There are two bedrooms downstairs and two bedrooms upstairs, plus my office. I lead everyone to the seating area and turn off the television. Lia and I sit on the couch, and Avner and Oak face us in a couple of comfy beige chairs. I sit close to Lia and hold her hand.

"I received a voicemail this morning from Scott. Someone broke into his house, and he escaped out the back. He told me to meet him at a coffee shop, so I woke Avner up, and we went to try and find him."

Oak interrupts as he takes a bite of a chocolate éclair donut. "Why'd you take him instead of me?"

"Probably because I am an actual law enforcement agent and not some fake tough guy," responds Avner.

"You guys can have a pissing contest later. This is important," says Lia. "Tell us what happened, Jay."

"Like I was saying, we went to the coffee shop and Scott was not there, but he left the laptop with all the information for me. There was also a surveillance team, but we slipped them."

Lia's eyes grow wide. "You have the laptop everyone is looking for?"

"Dude, this is getting out of control," remarks Oak. "You need to give it back before you end up like your friend Scott."

"Everyone needs to chill out," instructs Avner, raising his voice. "For all we know, Scott is somewhere safe and sound."

I get up, bring the laptop bag over, and place it on the coffee table. It's hard to believe that anyone would kill for something so ordinary.

As I sit back down, my cell phone rings. I hope it is Scott, but the caller ID reads "Terrance Browning."

I look at Avner. "It's Terrance. Should I answer?"

He nods, so I answer and press the speaker.

Here we go. Another step down this staircase to the unknown.

"This is Jason."

Everyone in the room turns to me.

"Jason, this is Terrance. Have you thought about our conversation?"

"Good morning, Terrance. I need to talk with one of my employees, but I can't locate him."

There is a pause and whispering on the other end of the line.

"I am sure he will turn up. I am going to send Max over to pick you up so we can work through this situation."

"That won't be necessary. I am not feeling well, so I am not going to be in today."

Another pause, and I hear him whisper again.

"I thought I was clear, Jason. I want that laptop now. You are risking your career and your freedom, not to mention millions of dollars in stock options. We can do this any way you want. The hard way or the easy way."

He knows about the laptop. Terrance sent the team after Scott and now they are coming after me.

"That sounds like a threat, Terrance," I respond with a shaky voice.

"You are damn right it is a threat," he yells before hanging up.

We all trade glances, and Oak buries his head in his hands. I stroke my left pinky, and Lia strokes the Glock. Avner just sits quietly with his eyes closed. I am in the deep end, struggling to breathe.

"I need to go check on Scott. I have a bad feeling about this," I say.

"Here is the problem, Jay," says Lia. "Whoever broke into his house is going to be watching it. You need to let a little time pass, and if he doesn't contact you, we'll send Avner in. He knows how to navigate a property under surveillance."

She goes to the window and does her own scan. "They may be on their way here right now. We might need to leave."

Oak stands up quickly. When he is upset, he talks with his hands. "Why is no one listening to me? Jason, it is time to give that damn laptop back, say you are sorry, and keep your damn job. This isn't your fight."

I understand where Oak is coming from, but I am surprised by his passion. He generally loves a good fight, but something about this situation has hit a nerve.

"Trust me, Oak. I wish I could go back a week and choose to never go down this path. Unfortunately, I know what I know, and I am going to do the right thing." I stand and place a hand on his shoulder. "I need to go dark and figure out what to do. I'm not putting all the people I love at risk."

"You are not Jason Bourne. You are Jason Miles," screams Oak. "What the fuck do you know about going dark?"

"He knows plenty," says Avner. "I agree it is time to take that laptop someplace safe and figure out what to do. I'll go with Jason, while you and Lia work here. We'll all communicate with burner phones. Do you have any weapons besides the Glocks?"

Lia laughs out loud. "You know me, Avner. I have enough firepower close by to hold off an army. If you two need to run, you might want more than a couple Glocks if these are really bad guys."

I can see thoughts turning in his head. He grabs a pencil and a notepad from the kitchen. "I'll make a list of what we need."

Oak speaks up again. "Maybe I should go with him. I've known

Jay-Bird the longest."

"That's the stupidest thing I have heard in a long time. Let's send one of the most famous people in the world with someone going on the run. That would be the shortest undercover mission ever," responds Avner.

Oak moves quickly to confront him. He stands inches from him stretching to his full height, some three inches taller than Avner. "You want to go, tough guy?"

Lia and I move rapidly to separate them. We know how quickly Avner's fuse can be lit, and he is the most dangerous man I have ever met. Lia pulls Oak back, and I stand between the two.

"Guys, the only way we will get through this is by working together. You are all my team. One rip and everything comes apart. I need us all to be on the same page, or I might not make it out alive."

CHAPTER 24

"This should be interesting," Zeke says to Gloria, as they enter the lobby of the Safe Harbor Building. He places his badge over his head.

"What are we doing here, Zeke?"

"The director called and said to drop everything and get over here. He said to find out what Terrance Browning needs and what he knows."

They are met at the security desk by a young man who identifies himself as Clinton. He asks to see their identification and takes his time reviewing each one. Satisfied, he says, "Follow me."

In the elevator, he scans his employee card, which gives access to the executive floor. Once they arrive, he places them in a conference room and tells them Terrance will join them when he is available.

The conference room is even more plush than the rest of the floor. It has glass walls on two sides and a small refrigerator in the corner. Elegantly dressed employees walk by carrying files or iPads. They peek out of the corners of their eyes at the two wearing FBI windbreakers and look away quickly.

Zeke and Gloria take seats at a marble table that is long enough to fit twenty or more. There are two flat-screen televisions on the wall. One display is broadcasting MSNBC and the other Fox News. Both have been set on mute, and quiet symphony music plays from hidden speakers. A spread of bagels and assorted cream cheeses sits in the middle of the table.

Zeke grabs a bagel and chews several times before spitting the bite into a napkin. "Stale. Probably been here since yesterday."

"We look a little underdressed," says Gloria, as she stands up and walks around. "I feel like a goddamn fish in a tank."

"Relax, Gloria. You know the director is friends with Terrance Browning. And when the boss says jump, we ask, 'how high,'" responds Zeke, leaning back with his hands on his belly.

"He just likes these rich assholes because they take him to all the places he can't afford as a government employee. You know, golfing at Old Memorial and dinner at Bern's Steak House. I'd rather eat at Chick-fil-A myself."

Zeke brings his finger to his lips. "You know every word is probably being recorded."

"What are they going to arrest me for? Telling the truth? You're the hotshot lawyer. Are you telling me you couldn't get a jury to convict these guys of being arrogant snobs?"

On cue, Terrance enters the room, followed by several serious-looking, gray-haired men. They follow him like baby ducks following their momma. He is wearing his usual pink shirt with a blue blazer and khakis, while the other men all wear expensive dark blue suits. Clinton follows behind avoiding eye contact with everyone.

"Agent Michaels and Agent Chavez, thank you so much for coming," Terrance says without shaking hands. "Please let's take a seat. I only have a few minutes. We always have board meetings on Thursday morning."

Terrance sits at the head of the table. The FBI agents sit on one side, the old men on the other, and Clinton sits ten seats down, away from everyone.

"Make sure you thank the director for me. I appreciate him

sending you over on such short notice. I'd like to introduce you to my legal team. We have our in-house attorney and several folks from outside counsel."

Each attorney nods solemnly to the agents.

"What can we do for you, Mr. Browning?" asks Zeke as he takes out a yellow legal pad.

"Call me Terrance. We have a very troubling situation at Safe Harbor Bank. One or more of our employees breached a private system and stole important data. We need the employees located and the data returned."

Zeke stares at Terrance for several seconds. "What type of data?"

Terrance looks at his legal team, who shake their heads in the negative. "I am sorry, we can't get into detail about the data that was stolen, but we believe it was transferred to a laptop."

Gloria speaks before he finishes the sentence. "How would you like us to locate this information if we do not know what it is?"

"We'll provide you with the details you need to know," responds one of the attorneys, as he adjusts his red polka-dot tie.

"The important thing you need to know is that there has been a theft committed by an employee named Jason Miles and one of his staff members, Scott Kowalski," explains Terrance as he leans forward and steeples his fingers. "Jason oversees the bank's security division, and Scott is his IT expert. I gave Mr. Miles the opportunity to turn in the stolen data this morning, and he refused."

One of the attorneys hands him a file, which he quickly reviews. "We have since fired them both and would now like them arrested. We've found troubling background issues, and there might be mental problems."

"Let's slow down, Mr. Browning. We don't know if a crime has been committed in the first place. Our technology folks will need system access. Who can provide that?" asks Zeke.

Terrance stands, as does his flock of legal ducks. "We'll get you some access, but only what is prudent. I am sure the director will understand. Thank you for coming by."

Zeke and Gloria also stand and start walking to the door when Zeke stops and turns to Terrance. "Mr. Browning, are you aware that we've worked with Jason Miles on several occasions? He brings us in for our financial crime expertise."

"I know we've used the FBI, but the details are a bit below my pay grade."

Zeke pauses for several long seconds and then smiles. "Well, there is something that you should know. Jason contacted me a few days ago with concerns over money laundering and tax evasion taking place at Safe Harbor. Would that be something in your pay grade?"

Terrance does not skip a beat. "Jason Miles had the access and skill set to fake whatever he needed to. I assume this is a blackmail play." Before he leaves the room, he turns to them. "Agents, just do your job. I want Jason Miles apprehended and our property returned. Now, Clinton, show the agents out."

****

Avner paces the room, squeezing a tennis ball he found in the garage. Lia draws lots of circles and arrows in a notebook Oak is talking to his agent, telling him that he will be in Tampa for a little longer. I'm sitting off to the side working through scenarios in my mind.

"Okay, everyone, we need to focus. It is time to come up with a plan of action. Max may be on his way over right now, and I'm not sure exactly what I would do," I admit.

"Let's go through the options," suggests Lia. "Jason can go to the FBI. He can make a deal with Safe Harbor. Or we can all go dark. Go somewhere safe as a team and figure things out."

"You know my vote," states Oak. "Make a deal and keep your job."

There is a part of me that wants to do that, but the horse is out of the barn. There is no going back to Safe Harbor ever again. That reality hits me like a brick.

Where will I work? Can I get another job, or would Terrance make sure I never work in this field again? Would Lia stay with me if I'm unemployed? I can't be alone. I've got to figure this out.

My cell phone rings. I'm hoping to see Scott's name but remember his phone is at the bottom of a lake. Instead, it's the FBI. Even in normal times, a call from Zeke makes me sweat. I answer quickly and press the speaker.

"Hey, Zeke, I was going to give you a call. There have been some new developments."

"I'm aware, Jason. I just left a meeting with your buddy, Terrance Browning, and his legal beagles. He said you've been fired for stealing company information and wants the FBI to bring you in."

I feel like someone is holding my head underwater. Zeke's words sound muffled, like I am listening with earmuffs on. My legs buckle slightly, and my heartbeat accelerates. Lia puts her hand on my shoulder and squeezes lightly. I should have expected this, but hearing the words out loud is still shocking.

"You know that's bullshit, Zeke. I came to you and told you about the tax fraud. What other lies did he tell you?"

"I mentioned that we'd talked and you'd made accusations about something not being quite right at the bank. He started talking about your background and suggested that you might have some mental issues. Claims you and Scott stole the data, and he expects you to blackmail the bank for them to get it back."

Avner reaches over and puts the phone on mute. "You need to get off this call ASAP. It's being recorded, so state your innocence and tell him you'll be in touch."

I take a deep breath and steady myself. The information is coming like a fast-moving train. "Zeke, I haven't done anything wrong. I have proof, and you need to believe me."

"Of course I believe you, Jason. Come into the office, and we'll sort this all out. You and Scott should bring that laptop with you."

Lia shakes her head and signals me to end the call.

"I'll be in touch, Zeke," I say and hang up.

Avner reaches over and powers off the phone. He removes the SIM card, and we return to the seating area. Avner's square jaw is set, and he is stroking his beard slowly. I can see Lia rubbing the small gap in her front teeth with her tongue, and her eyes are moving from me to Avner and back again.

"Okay, it's game time," Avner says. "Time to go to dark. Both these assholes at Safe Harbor and the FBI are probably on their way. They both want you and that laptop."

"Why not go to the FBI?" asks Oak. "Tell them what you know and let them deal with Safe Harbor. Or throw the laptop into the ocean."

"It is too late for that, Oak," I say. "These guys are sophisticated and are setting me up as the fall guy. I need some time to figure out what to do."

Avner turns to Lia. "Will you grab the 'get out' pack?"

When she returns, she places the backpack and a duffel bag on the coffee table between us. They add Scott's laptop bag to the pile.

Avner places everything on the table. He removes the Glock from his lower back and puts it carefully next to the other Glock Lia has been wearing. There are four spare magazines, each holding fifteen rounds. Next, he removes an envelope of cash.

"How much cash do you have in here?" he asks.

"Five thousand in dollars and an equal amount in pesos," responds Lia.

"That's good. Oak, do you have any more cash on you?"

Oak's eyes are glazed, and he is slowly bobbing his head. He looks like he might be in shock. He reaches into his wallet and pulls out an additional $800 and places it on the table.

"I can get him as much as he needs," he declares.

Avner then looks at the two fake passports and matching Georgia driver's licenses. Mine reads "Thomas Smith," and Lia's is "Mary Smith." He hands Lia's to her and places mine in the pile.

Digging deeper into the duffel bag, he pulls out ten prepaid burner phones. He gives everyone a black square phone and places the rest in the pile.

"Everyone needs to activate these things. They are the only way we are going to be able to communicate for a while."

"What's wrong with his iPhone?" asks Oak.

Avner responds, "That thing is a tracking device. How about the laptop, Jason? I am sure they can track that." He reaches for the computer and examines it closely.

"Scott's note said he disabled Safe Harbor's tracking mechanism. We should be good."

Avner pulls out a set of keys. "Where is the car?"

"We keep it in this shitty storage place over on Gandy Boulevard. I prepay every year in cash, and I drive the car around occasionally to make sure it starts. It is old and ugly but dependable and will get the job done," states Lia.

Finally, he pulls out a thin black vest.

Now it is getting very real.

"Might as well get used to wearing this thing now. Take off your shirt, Jason."

I do as he says, and he slips the vest over my head. It has Velcro straps that go around my waist and over my shoulders. It has some weight to it, but the technology has come a long way since Israel.

"Remember, Jay," explains Lia. "This will stop most bullets, but they will still knock you on your ass and probably break a rib. Some bullets will go right through."

It will also not protect me from a direct shot to my head or legs.

"Why do you have all of this stuff?" asks Oak. "I know you played a soldier in Israel, but why do you have all of this a decade later?"

Lia speaks up. "It is for me, Oak. Avner and I put away some very dangerous people. We must always be prepared. We figured someone could come after me, and of course, Jason and I would go dark together."

He shakes his head in disbelief and sits back heavily on the couch. "This is more unbelievable than one of my movies," he mutters to himself.

Everything is happening so fast. I'm most concerned about the safety of those I love, especially Lia. I could never live with myself if something happened to her.

It is my turn to speak. "Listen, everyone, I am sorry to pull you into this mess, but you are all I have. You are my family, and I need you to help me through this."

"We'll figure it out, Jason," says Avner as he stands. "But we need to get going."

I shake my head. "I'm going alone. You are the one who taught me that it is easier to track two than one. I am going deep, and you guys can't know where I am. That would just put you more at risk. I can do this."

I'm trained for this. It will all come back. It has to.

"No way in hell," objects Avner. "This is what I do for a living. You need me with you."

"Sorry, Avner. My mind is made up."

I stand and go upstairs to fill the duffel bag with some toiletries and extra clothes. All very generic items to help me blend in wherever I am going. I put on a black-on-black golf hat and pull it low. I haven't shaved, so my beard is already getting dark.

I go downstairs and give Oak and Avner a quick hug. I ask Lia to join me outside. We hold hands and stand in silence for a few minutes. I don't know what to say. I just want to be with her.

She breaks the silence. "You don't have to do this. We could run away together. No one would ever find us. Oak has access to huge wealth, and the world is a big place. It might be a fun adventure."

I shake my head. "What these people are doing is wrong. I think I can prove it and get us out of this mess. I also need to find Scott. I'm really worried about him."

We both have tears in our eyes, and I feel her trembling. I hold her tighter and breathe in her scent to try and imprint it in my memory. I realize this might be the last time I ever see her. I wipe away the tears and walk away.

CHAPTER 25

Avner, Oak, and I leave in the Tesla. Avner drives with Oak in the passenger seat, and I lie down in the back. We need to get clear of all surveillance and threats so I can get my vehicle. We pass the car that has been parked down the street overnight. The driver starts his engine and then realizes he has a flat back tire, thanks to Avner. To rub it in further, Avner rolls down the window and gives him a middle-finger salute.

We drive for about twenty minutes, scanning for a tail, and stay off the main roads to avoid security cameras. When Avner is sure we are free, he moves through residential neighborhoods to get to a fast-food chicken restaurant across the street from the storage facility.

It is called Gandy Storage, and it has seen better days. There is a rusty chain-link fence around the perimeter and a keypad to enter your security code for entrance to the facility. The storage units are gray and un-air-conditioned. There are high-end storage facilities all over Tampa, but this is for someone who wants something cheap—primarily for junk. Years ago, Lia and I rented a unit and a parking spot out back.

"Jason, keep your hat low and pull your hood up. There are cameras everywhere, even in that shitty place. When the bad guys and FBI realize you are on the run, they will access security footage. We were clean coming over here, so if you can get to the car without anyone tracking you, you will be in the wind," Avner observes, handing me the keys to the backup car.

I grab the duffel bag and backpack. They hold everything I will own for the next few days. I am going from a life of luxury to something quite different.

"Love you guys," I say as I slip out the back. "See you on the other side."

I pull my hood over my head and run across the street. I walk up to the keypad and enter our code. There is a long road in the middle with units on both sides. The even numbers are on the right and the odd on the left. At the end of the road is an uncovered parking lot with cars, boats, and RVs. All are older models and not in great shape. No one with money would ever come to this place.

Our dark-colored Honda Accord sits in spot number 3131. I have not seen it or thought of it in years, but Lia said she drives it occasionally and changes out the gas. I press the unlock button, and it acknowledges with a chirp. The interior is tan with cloth seats, and there is a layer of dust over everything. Lia hung a car freshener in the shape of a tropical drink that smells like piña colada on the rearview mirror. It is a far cry from my Tesla.

The car's only upgrade is dark-tinted windows. When we initially bought it, I argued with Lia about the need to spend any money on such a junker. As usual, she was right.

I attempt to start the car, but the motor will not turn over. I try several more times with no luck. The engine just makes a buzzing sound.

What the hell am I going to do now? I don't know anything about cars. This was the shortest escape from civilization ever.

"Looks like you have a problem," says a deep voice.

I freeze. I didn't notice anyone else in the parking lot, and I curse myself for not checking out my surroundings. Maybe Avner was not as clean as he thought. Could be Max or the FBI. I reach for the duffel bag and put my hand on the Glock. It is cold and heavy to the touch.

"You need a jump? Your battery is dead. I have cables," a man offers, stepping out of the shadows.

I release the weapon and breathe out my nose. I wipe sweat off my forehead and respond, "That would be great. Let me pop the hood."

A few minutes later, the Honda roars to life. I thank the man without making eye contact, and when he leaves, I vow to be more diligent.

The temperature is rising, but I don't want to roll down the windows, so I crank the air. A strange smell escapes. Something between dead fish and sour milk. I place the Glock under the driver's seat and put the backpack and duffel bag in the trunk for safekeeping.

I need to be smarter if I am going to be a hero.

I adjust the seat and put the car into drive. I need to find a place to stay that will accept cash and not ask questions. But first, there is something else that I must do.

****

"What now?" asks Oak.

Avner pulls out Jason's cell phone, reinserts the SIM card, and turns it on. The phone beeps and whoops, signifying a bunch of e-mails and texts.

"Let's go for a ride and see if we can catch some criminals. Do you know anywhere private that we can have a potentially violent conversation with someone?"

Oak considers the question. "I know the perfect place."

They drive back through the neighborhoods and turn north on Dale Mabry Highway, a major north and south thoroughfare in Tampa. It is late morning, and traffic is heavy. Avner swears under his breath as a Ford F-150 cuts him off.

After turning right on Bay to Bay, they continue straight until they reach a fork in the road on Bayshore Boulevard. Avner rolls the window down and puts his elbow out. He breathes the crisp, clean air through his nose and exhales loudly.

"This is a pretty sweet area," says Avner. "You live around here?"

Oak points as they pass a condo building named the Virage Bayshore. "I own the penthouse in that one."

"Of course," responds Avner, shaking his head. "You ever feel guilty for having so much when so many have so little?"

"Not really. I earned it and so can they. I came from nothing. Actually, less than nothing."

They take Bayshore through downtown Tampa and exit near Ybor City.

"Do you see that construction site over there?" Oak says as he points at a half-built building with no work being done. "Pull up to where those orange cones are. I'll move them out of the way. We can go to the back, so we have privacy."

Avner drives to the end of the development and turns around so they can see if another car enters. He and Oak exit the Tesla and look around. Several buildings have been started, and heavy machinery is parked haphazardly. The air is full of dust, and the sun is hidden by a large grouping of clouds.

"What is this place?" Avner asks.

"It is a multi-use property. It is going to be retail, apartments, and offices. Something happened with the city, and the construction was halted."

"How do you know about it?"

"I invested in it, and one of my guys got an e-mail update about the delay. Now it is the perfect spot for quiet. If I am in town, I park over here—drink a beer or smoke a joint to get away from all the chaos of my life."

Avner rolls his eyes and reaches around his back to grab the

Glock. He checks the magazine and releases the safety.

"Looks like we have company," states Oak nodding toward the entrance.

"Like I said, a cell phone is basically a tracking device, and this is Jason's company cell. We need to know who is tracking it, and we're about to find out. Let's get back in the car so they don't run away."

CHAPTER 26

At FBI headquarters, Zeke and Gloria take seats in the director's office. The chairs are small and hard, clearly not meant for guests to stay long. The room smells of hair tonic and coffee.

Their supervisor initially ignores them as he types an e-mail. He is lanky, and his clothes hang off him. He has an old-school comb-over of dyed brown hair that is turning a bit red. Reading glasses sit on the end of his large hooknose. He worked his way up in various field offices across the country until being named director in Tampa. Zeke thinks he is more of a politician than a leader and is more concerned about his place in society than fighting bad guys.

When he finishes his e-mail, he says, "I just got a call from Terrance Browning, the CEO at Safe Harbor, and my good friend. He is not happy."

"Let me explain," offers Zeke.

"I sent you two over to assist the bank in finding Jason Miles and this other guy. Not to have you accuse one of the most upstanding citizens in Tampa of tax fraud and money laundering."

Zeke can feel his face reddening and his hands clenching. His lizard eyes are starting to bug out. He takes a deep breath. "Director, Jason Miles called me days ago and told me about what he found at Safe Harbor. We need access to their systems to figure out what is going on. Jason's a good guy. We've worked with him several times."

The director stands. "Good guy or bad guy, it doesn't really matter. I want an arrest and to close this case. Am I making myself clear?"

As Zeke is about to respond, a junior agent knocks on the door. "I apologize for interrupting, but we have a ping on Mr. Miles's cell phone and the location."

"Great, now go do something productive and bring this guy in. That is all, agents."

****

A Cadillac CT5-V Blackwing moves slowly down the construction site road. It is black with heavily tinted windows. It is kicking up dirt and gravel as it moves forward. The driver parks, blocking the Tesla in. A tall, thickly built man with a bald head and glasses exits the driver's side. He is joined by a massive man with a long black beard and several facial tattoos.

"Come on out and say hello, Jason," he yells.

Instead, Avner and Oak exit the Tesla.

"Surprise," says Avner.

The overcast skies start to spit large drops of rain. The breeze turns into wind and the dirt into mud.

"Who the fuck are you two?" asks the bald man. His hands form into balls, and he moves forward.

"I am guessing you are Max Braun, the asshole Jason mentioned." Avner closes the gap between himself and the two men. "And who is your friend?"

Oak does the same, moving toward the larger man. He isn't used to looking up at many people. The man smiles at him and grunts something in a foreign language.

"I want to know where he is. This is not your problem unless you make it so," says Max as he reaches into his jacket.

With incredible speed, Avner points the Glock at Max's head.

"Get your hand out of your jacket, or it is lights out. Tell your man to do the same thing."

Max slowly moves his hand back to his side and says, "Arrêter, Orsu. You fools have no idea what you are fucking with."

At that moment, three black Suburbans turn down the street. Avner slowly puts his weapon back into his pants and covers it with his jacket. Everyone turns to see the new guests.

The rain starts to come down harder, and a flash of lightning is followed by a loud rumble of thunder. The raindrops make a dinging sound on the cars.

The lead vehicle pulls over, and a short, somewhat portly man with lizard eyes exits wearing an FBI windbreaker. A Hispanic woman with a permanent scowl follows closely behind holding an umbrella.

"Who the hell are you four and where is Jason Miles?" Zeke yells as he looks around. "Hey, aren't you Oak Williams?"

Zeke and his agents separate Avner and Oak from Max and Orsu. They take IDs from everyone, and Zeke examines each one carefully. Avner watches him closely as he looks at each ID, then looks at each person and then down again. His eyes expand and then contract. He exchanges glances with the female agent, who is looking over his shoulder. *This guy is trouble*, thinks Avner.

"My name is Agent Zeke Michaels, and this is Agent Gloria Chavez. Can someone explain to me why a movie star, an Israeli citizen, and two guys from New York are trespassing on a construction site?" Zeke asks as he looks at each person. "This sounds like the beginning of a bad joke. And why do you have Jason Miles's car and cell phone, but no Jason?"

When no one says a word, Zeke offers, "We can do this at FBI headquarters if no one wants to answer me."

Avner steps forward. "Oak and I are friends of Jason. I am in town visiting him and his wife. We're old friends."

"That's a good start. Now why do you have his car, and where the hell is he?"

"That is what we are wondering," answers Oak. "We had some drinks last night and when we woke up, he was gone, but he left his cell phone at the house. His wife was worried, so we are out looking for him."

Zeke looks Oak over suspiciously. "Sounds like bullshit, but we'll accept it for now."

He turns and looks at Max Braun, who has his arms crossed and is leaning against the Cadillac.

"How about you two?" he asks, looking down at the IDs. "Max and Santoni."

"You can call him Orsu, which is Corsican for bear. He doesn't speak much English, but he is fluent in French if you happen to speak the language," responds Max condescendingly.

"Don't think I speak the language? How about poly-vu fuck you."

Max ignores the comment. "We are independent contractors hired by Safe Harbor Bank. We are looking for Jason Miles also. The phone is the bank's property, and we are hoping to have a word with him."

Zeke walks over to Avner with a plastic Ziplock bag. "Go ahead and drop the phone in here."

"I must object," barks Max. "As I said, the phone is the bank's property, and we need it."

Zeke fixes him with a hard stare for nearly a minute. "Your CEO called the FBI, dumbass. The search for Jason Miles is now an active case, and we'll take whatever we want, including your ass to headquarters. If you want to be an asshole, we'll tow that pretty car, and you can walk home. That includes your French-speaking pet Corsican bear."

Max just nods. Avner notices the veins on the bank henchman's temple pounding and a pronounced eye tick that seems to be getting worse. He enjoys the reaction.

"Now, I don't know what is going on, but I'm going to find out. We've got pictures of your IDs, and for the moment, you can go. But stay out of our way. If you hear from Jason, have him give me a call, or you call me."

Everyone nods and moves toward their cars. Avner stares at Max until the moment is broken, when Zeke asks Oak to join him by the Suburban. Avner hears him say in a hushed voice, "Do me a favor—sign this piece of paper, and make it out to Samantha. She's my kid and is a big fan."

As the cars pull out, Zeke motions Agent Chavez and the other agents over. "Those four are not telling us what they know. I want two of you on this Avner guy and the movie star, and I want two of you on the goons. Keep a distance, but I want to know where they go."

Still standing in the rain, Zeke and Gloria watch the agents move out.

Gloria says, "What do you think is really going on?"

Zeke considers the question. "Sooner or later, Jason is going to resurface, and I want him first. I don't know who is guilty and who is innocent, but I do know one thing. This is the kind of case that makes careers, and I want to be sitting in the director's office, so someone is going down."

CHAPTER 27

Step one when going dark is to alter your appearance. I don't have access to the kind of specialists that intelligence agents use, but there are some simple things I can do. The hats, hoodies, and glasses help, but I know what needs to be done. My hair is part of my identity, but it must go. I can no longer be a preppy banker. You don't just try to look like someone else; you become someone else. Create a cover story and live it.

One place that does not have cameras is The Cut Barbershop on Busch Boulevard. It is a classic old-school barbershop specializing in fades, designs, and beard trims. When Oak is in town, he stops by to see his personal barber. He loves the place and spends hours there laughing and talking shit with the fellas. There is a picture of him on the wall, along with several local professional athletes and an *American Idol* contestant. It is Thursday afternoon, so the place is empty.

I've been here with Oak a couple of times, but his personality eclipses everyone else. I feel comfortable that they won't recognize me or remember me if someone comes asking later. These are also the kind of guys who don't talk to the police.

"What you need, brother?" asks a man sitting in a recliner watching ESPN and reading a magazine.

I take a deep breath in. The smell of the barbershop reminds me of hanging with Oak. The fresh and clean scent of the talcum powder mixes with aftershave and hair tonic. There is also the strong and sharp smell of Barbicide, which is used to disinfect.

"Time for a buzz cut," I say as I remove my hood and hat.

He directs me to a black leather chair that swivels one hundred and eighty degrees. He places a cape over my clothes that is tight around my neck. He takes a moment and examines my hair. After running his fingers through it a few times, he says, "You sure? You got good hair and lots of it. We could just buzz the sides and keep the height. You know, gel it up a bit. That's called tight with height."

I shake my head. "Time for a fresh look. Buzz it with a number two trimmer. All the way down."

"Your hair and your money," he says as we bump fists. "You also want a shave, Jason?"

I freeze and feel my heart skip a beat. "I think you have me confused with someone else."

As he pulls out his gold-plated trimmers from the drawer, he responds casually, "I never forget a face, Jason. You're Oak's boy. I am in the people business, and Oak makes an impression."

Should I stay or get up and walk out? At this point, the damage is done. I just need to get the cut and then get the hell out. Fading into the dark may be harder than I thought.

He takes the first chunk of hair off, and it floats to the ground like ash. "Guilty as charged," I admit. "You have a good memory. No need for a shave, I am going to grow out the beard. Business on top and party on the face."

The rain tapping on the roof is calming until we hear a loud clap of thunder and the electricity flutters. He stops cutting. "I hear there is a storm coming our way. Could turn into a hurricane."

Twenty minutes and thirty bucks later, there is a pool of hair around the chair. I stare in the mirror and realize I am becoming a different guy. Now for step two.

****

After changing your appearance, the second thing to do is find a place to hide where no one will think to look. I drive fifteen miles to the Sunny South Motel on West Hillsborough Avenue. The entire time, I am paranoid that the team from the dark web might be expanding their surveillance net.

There is no way they can find me. I have a different car and a different look. But what if they have technology I've never heard of? Am I going crazy already?

Years ago, we joined the Tampa Police Department as they followed up on a tip about a bank robbery suspect who was staying at the motel. I remember thinking, Who stays in a place like this?

The motel is peach with a brown roof and brown doors. It is one story and built in an L shape. Guests park in front of their door and have a short walk in. It is perfect if you must get out quickly.

The office is underneath a fluorescent light that reads "*VACNY.*"

I enter to find a young man behind the counter with a name tag that reads "Charlie." He has a patchy beard and dark skin. In front of him is takeout Chinese that smells greasy with too much soy sauce. He is playing a game on his phone. There is protective glass keeping him safe from the customers.

I smile and say, "I need a room for a few days."

He barely looks up. "ID and credit card."

"I have cash."

He ignores my comment. "ID and credit card, or no room."

"How much is the room?" I ask.

"Seventy-five bucks a night."

"How about if I give you two hundred bucks and you can keep the difference for your trouble?"

This gets his attention, and he finally looks up and studies me. "No drugs or company in the room, got it?"

I reverse my car into the spot in front of the room and take my meager possessions from the trunk. It is a long way from The Ritz, where I recently stayed with Lia. There is a decent-sized bed in the middle of the room with a green-and-orange flowery bedspread. Above the bed is a picture of a rooster. I lie back, but the mattress feels like granite.

Against the wall is a dresser for clothes, a mirror, and an unevenly hung TV. There is also a small fridge with a microwave sitting on top. The floor covering is cheap tile, but overall, the room is clean. As I walk by the mirror, I catch a glimpse of myself, and I'm shocked by what I see. A successful banking executive transformed into some guy with buzzed hair, a darkening beard, and bags under his eyes.

I walk one block to the convenience store, which is simply called Food Mart. It smells like fried chicken and body odor. I purchase cheap black sunglasses, a six-pack of Modelo, and cheese burritos that are on sale.

Back in the room, I open a beer and pull the drapes across the window. Instead of using the dresser, I keep my clothes in the duffel bag and set up the laptop on a small table. I double-check the dead bolt on the door and place the Glock close by. The last item I fish out of the bag is one of the burner phones.

I have to figure this mess out. Life has changed in an instant.

The best place to start is the laptop. I power it on and take out the notes Scott left behind. In typical Scott fashion, he made the password long and impossible to guess. I follow his instructions and press enter. I receive a message that reads:

Incorrect Password. Access Denied. Try 1 of 3.

I curse to myself and look closer at Scott's scrawled note. His handwriting is horrible, and I can't make out the difference between some of the letters and numbers. They all seem to run together. I squint closer at the instructions and try again.

Incorrect Password. Access Denied. Try 2 of 3.

"Fuck!" I yell. One more wrong attempt and I'm locked out of the computer. My only chance to prove the criminal scheme will be gone. I put my head in my hands and rub my throbbing temples. I realize how tired I am and start pacing the room. To get my blood flowing, I perform twenty push-ups. I get a whiff of lemon deodorizer every time my nose gets near the carpet.

If you do this wrong, you're screwed. So much for being a hero; you can't even log in to a computer.

I squint again at the password. I am sure I have it right, except for a digit that looks like either a five or an S.

Mom and Dad, please give me some help. I just need to know which one it is.

I type in the password one more time using a five and then erase it. I then type it in with an S. Here goes nothing and everything. I hold my breath and press enter. The screen opens, and I am looking at several documents.

Thank you, Mom and Dad!

After slowing my thumping heartbeat, I decided to work on the data all afternoon, have a burrito, and take a nap. When darkness sets in, I have something I need to do, and I know it will be dangerous.

CHAPTER 28

The day in the Sunny South Motel has been fruitful. After three beers and two burritos, I completed a deep dive into the data from Scott. It is unbelievable. Thousands of wealthy people are in on the fraud. They deposit money, which is laundered, and ten percent is sent off to an unknown destination. Their balance is kept in a private journal. It all takes place on a separate system that Scott somehow found.

There are names and notes and balances. It is searchable in several ways. Athletes, politicians, and high society from all over the world. This is a powder keg. As Scott said, references to trusts, family offices, and shell companies are everywhere. This appears to be a well-organized scam for the top percentage of the wealthy, but the end point for the excess funds continues to be a mystery.

Once the sun sets, I change into black jeans and the same black hoodie and hat from earlier. I hide all my belongings under the bed and place the Glock in the back of my pants, as I've watched Avner do many times. It feels heavy and awkward. I worry that I might accidentally shoot myself. I lock the motel room door and start up the Honda. The rain is coming down harder, and the lightning flickers across the dark clouds. The wipers make a screeching sound on the windshield and do a poor job clearing the water.

First, I grab the burner phone and call Lia. She answers right away.

"Baby, is that you?"

Hearing her soothing voice with the light Israeli accent makes me ache for her even more. Her flat but caring tone is a perfect balance for my emotional state. "Yeah, it's me. How is everything there?"

"Well, Avner and Oak had a run-in with that Max character, and when things were getting interesting, they were interrupted by your FBI buddy."

"Zeke showed up? How did they all come together?"

"Avner had your cell phone. Everyone was tracking it. He said Max is a real-deal asshole. He's upstairs working on his computer to find out more about him. Are you okay?"

"Yes, I'm doing okay, but I miss you. I went way off the grid. Staying in a total shithole motel and shaved my head."

She laughs. "You shaved your beautiful hair off?"

"I look like a meth addict."

"I bet you look sexy. When can I see you? You know I can lose any tail."

I think about it. I want to see her, and I know she is an expert at escaping surveillance. On the other hand, if Zeke is involved, everyone is being followed. He is smart and relentless.

"Maybe tomorrow. I need to do something tonight."

"What are you doing? Can I help?" she asks softly.

"Don't tell anyone, especially not Avner, but I need to check on Scott. I feel so guilty. I should have told him what was going on."

"Jay, this is risky. Are you going to his house?"

I am breaking every rule of going dark by confiding in her, but there is no one I trust as much as Lia. "That's the only place I can think of to check. I'll be careful. I just need to know he is safe. You know I can handle myself."

"I know you can, but I am going to meet you. You need someone to watch your back. I need to get out of this house. Sitting here doing nothing is driving me crazy."

"No chance, Lia. I've already put enough people in danger. All I am going to do is sneak in and then out. No one will even see me. Plus, Zeke has people all over you. He knows how much I want to see you."

She is quiet for a few moments. "I don't like it, but take the Glock with, just in case. Promise me you will be careful, and call me when you are done. Love you, Jay."

I cannot stop thinking about Lia as I drive to Scott's house. The thought of running away with her is making more and more sense. She is probably right about Scott. He is just on the run—but if so, why wouldn't he call me?

Scott lives in an older neighborhood known as Carrollwood Oaks in North Tampa. His house backs up to a park, so I can enter the backyard undetected. No one in his neighborhood has visible cameras.

I cruise down his street looking for anyone who seems out of place. The street is dark, with old oak trees that block the light from the streetlights. There are cars parked on the street, and Scott's Camry is in his driveway. No one is out in the horrible weather. I drive out of the neighborhood and into a park. There are signs posted that read "Closed After Dark," but no gates at the entrance.

I park in one of the spots and look around. The parking lot is deserted, and the few lights they have are burned out. It is dark, and a chill goes up my back. I should've had Avner meet me.

I pull the Glock out and make sure the safety is off. I grab a pair of black driving gloves out of the glove compartment and pull them on tight. A bad feeling follows me around like a shadow. I am nervous and can feel the convenience store burritos grumbling in my stomach. I exit the Honda and pull my hood over the hat to keep me a little drier from the driving rain.

The house is only a three-block walk through the darkness. I move past picnic tables, old grills, and kids' toys. I can see the back of Scott's house as I move slowly from tree to tree. Stepping in large puddles, I realize I am rubbing my missing fingernail.

I stop behind a large tree before entering his backyard. I listen for what seems like an hour but is only a few minutes. My heart is beating out of my chest. I can hear an owl hooting somewhere in the distance.

Seeing no one around, I creep to the back of his house and crouch down next to a cheap patio set sitting on a ten-by-ten concrete pad. I inch up to the sliding glass doors and look in. The house is pitch dark, and I can't see a thing. I try the door, but it is locked.

I've been to a couple of barbecues at Scott's house, so I know there is a side door that leads into the garage. I crouch down and move around the house. The door is unlocked, and I slip into the garage.

Blackness engulfs the space, and I take a moment to let my eyes adjust. I can make out a couple of old rusty ladders, some paint cans, and a disassembled Harley motorcycle. It is Scott's dream to rehab the old bike and take a ride across the country. I hope he has the chance when this is all over. I will go with him.

I am shocked to find the interior door already open about five inches. My Spidey Sense is going off big-time. I should run back to my car and call Zeke, but instead, I push the door farther open and walk quietly into the kitchen.

Scott has all the shades pulled down, making it dark, and it is very warm. I turn my phone flashlight on to navigate the room and that is when I smell an acrid stench that fills the air, making me want to throw up. I know what I am going to find, but I must know for sure. I move through the kitchen and into the living room. Lying on the floor in a pool of blood is my friend Scott.

I gasp and move toward him. I check the side of his neck for a pulse, but there is none to be found. Salty tears of sadness and rage drip down my face. Someone has killed Scott, and I could have stopped it. I failed again.

As I stand staring at the body, I am suddenly unable to move. What if whoever killed him is still in the house? I reach back and feel the cold butt of the Glock. Suddenly, a bright light shines through the window. There is a loud knock at the door that sounds like thunder in a church.

A voice booms, "Scott Kowalski, are you in there?"

I turn to run and hear the voice say, "Police! Don't move."

CHAPTER 29

The door nearly bursts as someone attempts to kick it in. I run full speed through the kitchen, out the garage, and into the backyard. I trip over an old rake and land in mud but jump up and keep going as fast as I can. I hear voices behind me, which propel me even faster.

Nearing the car, I realize I am not going to be able to get into the vehicle and get away. Instead, I head for the park entrance. I am counting on being able to outrun my pursuers and hopefully not get shot.

Out of nowhere comes a red Mustang that I assume is part of the group trying to catch me. I keep running full speed, but then I hear someone shout, "Get in the car, Jason!"

I have no choice. I am about to be arrested and charged with who knows what, so I grab the handle, pull it open, and jump in. The car takes off toward the exit of the park and enters the street at seventy miles per hour. With the wet roads, the back wheels slide before the driver can regain control.

I look at the driver, and Avner smiles back at me. "Did you call an Uber?"

Completely out of breath, I mutter, "How did you know?"

"I'll tell you the story in a minute—after I take care of something."

He drives to a nearby Walmart and parks next to a green compact car. "Come on," he says as he exits the Mustang. "And keep your head down. A few people are looking for you."

"Whose car is this?"

"Don't worry about it. I borrowed it. The green one is my new rental that I picked up this afternoon. Lie down in the back seat. We need to get out of here in a hurry."

I lie down and close my eyes. Things have gone from bad to awful. Not only am I on the run, but Scott is dead, and the police are after me along with the FBI and the Safe Harbor thugs. I feel tears welling up in my eyes.

"Do you have anything to eat and drink where you are staying?" asks Avner.

"I have three beers and a microwave burrito," I respond. I am still trembling and feel sick. My clothes are soaked and muddy. I smell like I stepped in dog shit.

"That isn't going to do. I've got some pretzels and bourbon in the trunk. I need to get you hidden as soon as possible. Give me the address to your place."

I tell him the address, and he throws the car into gear.

He continually looks in the rearview mirror as he is driving and makes a quick U-turn. "Hang on, I don't like that SUV a couple of cars back. I investigated that dark web group we ran into at the coffee shop. It is a special surveillance group for hire," he explains as he takes several left turns and then increases his speed. "They blanket the area in cars and on foot. They're not usually armed but report in what they see. You must assume they are everywhere."

Still looking behind us, Avner presses down on the gas pedal again. He swerves through three lanes of traffic. "They are still there. We have a tail."

He suddenly slows down and nearly collides with a pickup truck. He curses under his breath and whips into a residential neighborhood. The SUV is still behind us when he throws the car into park and jumps out. The SUV is caught off guard, and the driver slams on the brakes. Avner pulls his weapon from under his coat and fires a bullet into each front tire.

"These guys are like cockroaches; we may only see one, but I guarantee there are more. We need to get the hell out of here before the neighbors call the cops."

Half an hour later, we arrive at the Sunny South Motel. "You checked this place for cameras?" he asks, looking around.

"You think this dump spends money on cameras? The vacancy sign doesn't even work."

"Good point. Regardless, pull your hood over your hat, and I'll do the same."

We enter the room, and Avner lies down on the bed. "This place isn't that bad. When Lia and I were on stakeouts, we stayed in places where the bedbugs battled the rats as soon as the lights went out. You need to change your clothes."

"Avner, Scott is dead. I saw him in a pool of blood. They killed him, and it is my fault."

He stands up and walks over to the dresser. He opens the bottle he brought in from the car and pours two fingers of bourbon each into a couple of cups. He hands one to me. "Let's toast to your friend." He raises his cup and mutters, "Aleha ha-shalom, peace be upon him."

I raise the other cup, and we both drink. The warm liquid feels good going down my throat.

"I am sorry about your friend, but it's not your fault. You couldn't have known how serious this was when it started." He eats a handful of pretzels and chases it with a gulp of booze. "We'll make them pay, but we need to be smart. You are a popular man. Lots of people want to find you."

He tells me about his day with Oak and the run-in with Max Braun that was interrupted by the FBI. "That FBI guy is a character, and so is his lady partner. They only let us go so they could follow us.

Don't trust him."

"Zeke is very intense, but don't underestimate him. He is very smart. How did you get away from his tail?"

He gave me his best "*Really?*" face. "They never had a chance. I slipped away, rented that little car, and checked into a motel over by MacDill Air Force Base that is even shittier than this. I researched Max Braun and his pet ape Orsu and then touched base with Lia. She told me what you were up to."

Even though Avner saved my life, or at least kept me out of jail, I am hurt that Lia betrayed my trust. I know their bond is deep, but it has always made me a little jealous.

Avner pours two more drinks. "I can see what you are thinking, but she was worried about you."

I nod and sip the bourbon. My head is pounding, and my heart is broken over Scott's murder. I cannot believe they killed him over Project Cardinal. I vow to make them pay if it is the last thing I do.

"I need to get going," he says, grabbing the pretzels and pouring more liquor into his cup.

"Where are you going?"

"You need a shower and some sleep. You look horrible."

"Avner, pick up whatever you need. It is time to bring the fight to them."

CHAPTER 30

Terrance Browning lies down in his custom-made egg, waiting for his burner phone to ring. He feels safe in the small space, like a bird in a nest, out of harm's reach. But he knows he is not safe. He needs to make up for this mess with Jason, or his time on Earth will be short.

Only Clinton and Max are in the room with Terrance. Even though he trusts them with his life, he thinks about sending them away but knows they are loyal and disposable if necessary.

After what feels like an eternity, the phone gently buzzes. Terrance exits the egg and sits rail-straight in his desk chair. He reads his social security number backward—*5555 24 905*.

"Terrance," says a familiar voice without preamble. "I don't think you understand the seriousness of this situation."

Terrance takes a deep breath. "I assure you that I do, and we are managing it. I have my best people on it."

There is silence at the other end of the line. Finally, the voice instructs, "You need to find Mr. Miles before the FBI does. They can never have the information that is in his possession. If they do, much of our work could be at risk. This is decades in the making, and your mistake could ruin it all. You don't want to do that, do you?"

Terrance walks to the window farthest away from the others. "Of course not, sir. I won't fail you."

"We have made you a very rich and powerful man, Terrance. Let's get this taken care of so we can get back to the cause."

A cold chill runs down Terrance's spine, and he closes his eyes. "I am appreciative of all you have done for me, and we'll have this taken care of by the next time we speak."

He is about to hang up when he hears a quiet voice hiss, "You better—or we'll be coming to visit you."

Terrance swallows deeply. "I understand that, but I need something from you, if possible. Miles has an Israeli working with him. A Shin Bet agent named Avner Cohen. He pulled a gun on Max. I think I can leverage him to find his friend, but Avner's gone dark as well."

"We have contacts everywhere. You'll have his location in twenty-four hours or sooner."

Terrance tries to say thank you, but the other end of the line has already gone dead.

He screams at Max, "Double the number of men looking for Jason Miles. I want him caught and that computer in my hands. I don't care what it costs."

Max nods. "What about those other two, the Israeli and the movie star?"

"We'll find the Israeli, and we already own the movie star. We'll turn the wife against him in time, but the FBI is all over her. If we can isolate Jason, he'll give up. But understand, if we don't get this problem solved, we'll be the ones on the run—and trust me, there is nowhere to hide."

****

I am sitting in the motel room organizing the data into alphabetical order on Scott's computer while drinking a large coffee from the convenience store. I couldn't sleep and finally gave up around five AM. I kept seeing Scott's lifeless face and that pool of blood. The smell continues to fill my nose.

The names and the amount of money are staggering. The notes associated with each client are scandalous. Scott unearthed a massive fraud and gave his life to do so. I am not going to let him down. We will bring these animals down together. I was already dedicated to doing the right thing, but now this is personal.

The television is playing a local news show in the background as I work. I hear the news anchor say, "We now go to the scene of a murder that has rocked the North Tampa neighborhood of Carrollwood Oaks."

I spin around quickly, and my blood goes cold. A pretty, young woman is standing in front of Scott's house holding an umbrella. She is wearing a dark suit jacket and has a serious look on her face. Long yellow tape keeps people away from the crime scene, and police officers are moving in and out of the house.

Her voice is grave as she reports. "Thank you, Bethany. Neighbors woke up this Friday morning to a horrible scene in this quiet family neighborhood. A local IT expert, Scott Kowalski, was found dead last night, the victim of an apparent gunshot." She pauses for effect. "Police are not giving many details except to say that this may be associated with data theft at Mr. Kowalski's employer, Safe Harbor Bank. The police did confirm that they were searching for a person of interest named Jason Miles. Mr. Miles was Mr. Kowalski's manager and a security executive at the bank. They will not confirm that he is wanted regarding the data breach and the murder, just that they want to talk to him. He is considered possibly armed and dangerous. They ask that if you see him, please call the number below."

The screen cuts to an 800 number and my press picture of me smiling in a dark blue suit and red tie.

"We'll keep following this story. Now back to you."

"That is a troubling report," the news anchor responds. "Now let's get an update on the tropical storm that may turn into a powerful hurricane."

As soon as the news story ends, my burner phone starts to vibrate. I answer tentatively after muting the television. "Yes?"

"Jay, it is Lia. Is it true? Is Scott dead?"

"Yes, it's true. I went there last night and saw him with my own eyes. I think it was a trap. The police showed up as soon as I did. They are trying to pin this on me. I barely got away and lost the car. I'm sorry I didn't call you, but I was a mess."

"I know, I was watching the local news when it came on. Did you see the report?"

"Unfortunately, I did. Don't worry about me. I can handle this," I respond, trying to convince both her and myself.

"I know you can. I checked the local news websites, and your picture is everywhere. You need to keep a low profile. I'll work on getting you another car."

I rub my temples aggressively, trying to get rid of the pounding headache. For once in my life, I'm not sure what to say to Lia, so I just tell her the truth.

"I miss you so much. We're going to make it through this. I just need to figure out my next move."

Lia is quiet for a moment. "Like I told you, Jay, the world is a big place. You say the word and we'll run. No one will ever find us."

"To be honest, I would like nothing more than that, but when things fell apart in Israel, I swore to myself I would always do the right thing. I will always stand up to bad people, and these are some of the worst. Now they have killed my friend. I'm going to make them pay."

"We're going to make them pay, Jay. Me, you, Avner, and even Oak. We need to figure out how to get together and make a plan. It's got to be at night and somewhere secure. I will handle it, but promise me you will stay hidden for now."

"I promise," I lie. "I love you, Lia."

I have no intention of staying hidden. There is someone I know who can tell me more about this scheme, and I am going to make a house call.

I take a long swig of coffee and place the Glock on the bed. It has been a while since I've cleaned one of these, but it is time to bring back that guy from Israel I knew a decade ago. The brave one who wasn't scared to go undercover and expose a corrupt bank. The one who trained side by side with Avner and Lia before my world and confidence was rocked by Dr. Levi.

A knock on the door startles me. I grab the Glock and peek out the curtain. Avner is standing there with his hood pulled tightly over his head. The brim of his hat is sticking out and rain is dripping off it. He is wearing the same clothes as yesterday and holding a bag that reads "Waffle House." He is balancing two large coffees in his hands.

I move the furniture I had piled up against the door and open it quickly. He slips inside and hands me the coffee.

"This is a shit storm, Jason. They are trying to pin Scott's death on you."

"I know, I saw the news. Where's your car?"

He removes his vest, which covers a shoulder holster and his weapon. He takes it off and places it on the bed. "I parked a couple blocks away, just in case. Things are getting too hot. You need to move out of this place. Can't stay anywhere too long."

"I would like to move, but I left my car last night."

He opens the bag and starts to place the food on the dresser like a buffet. There are waffles, bacon, eggs, and syrup. He hands me a plate and nods at the food. The smell of the sweet syrup and the sight of the greasy bacon causes bile to rise in my throat.

"I'm not hungry," I mutter.

"You need to eat to keep up your energy. I know you are not sleeping and last night was messy, but you need your strength."

"It wasn't just messy, Avner. Scott is dead. And what do I need my strength for? I have no car, the entire world is looking for me, and I'm living in a shithole motel."

Avner piles food high on his plate and sits down in a cheap chair. He ignores me, pours syrup over his waffle, and cuts it into large pieces.

"Now you're going to ignore me?" I ask.

"Let me know when your pity party is over. I get it. This sucks, but sometimes doing the right thing sucks. I've worked with a lot of good men and women in my life who lost their lives doing the right thing, so grab some food, and let's figure out how to get you out of this mess."

I realize I am rubbing my missing fingernail, and I try to hide it.

"You don't need to hide your finger. You earned that badge."

I feel tears welling up in my eyes. All this time has passed, and we've never really talked about Israel. I am embarrassed that I let the team down and had to be saved by Lia and Avner. I've spent years packing the memories as far back as I could, but at night, in my dreams, my bravado always fades away.

"Yeah, I earned that badge of weakness."

He gives me an incredulous look. "Badge of weakness? That is a badge of courage. You were some ordinary banker, and you made the decision to do the right thing. Lia and I always talked about what a hero you were."

I am shocked. Avner is a lion who deals with things I cannot even fathom. His words fill me with pride, but I don't feel the same about myself.

"I was no hero, Avner. Dr. Levi said it himself. I was a soft American who gave in before he even did anything."

"Dr. Levi was a psychopath who got what he deserved. I told you, sooner or later, everyone breaks. You, me, Lia—it doesn't matter. You held out long enough so we could wipe those assholes off the Earth."

He puts his plate down and faces me. "You need to understand what a hero is. To the ancient Greeks, it meant a protector. Someone with enough strength for two."

"Now you are a stoic warrior?" I joke.

"Just because I shoot people doesn't mean I don't think about life. Seriously, Jason. You need to stop being a victim. Be a creator of action, and then you will become a hero. And that happens every day. Let all the shit from the past go. It is history, and we have a job to do. We need to decide on our next move."

He's right. Time to stop feeling sorry for myself. I need to be the best version of myself. The life I had is over. It's over because bad people are breaking the law, and they killed my friend to hide their crimes. Scott's blood is on my hands. I failed him just like my parents, but never again. I can stop them and start to make amends. Creator to hero. Game on.

"Avner, I need your help finding the man I was in Israel before Dr. Levi. Can you work with me to bring it all back?"

While shoving bacon into his mouth, he says, "That's the spirit. Let's spend today focused on your training."

I grab the laptop and bring up a picture from Google.

"Thanks, Avner. When we are done training, this is our next move. We're going to make a house call on this guy," I say pointing at the screen.

CHAPTER 31

"Excuse me, can I have a word with you, Mrs. Miles?" Lia hears a man say as she walks to her car in the Publix parking lot. She ignores the voice and keeps rolling her cart of groceries. It is overcast, and the forecast calls for heavy rain. Despite the gray weather, she is wearing oversized black sunglasses with large square lenses that cover half of her face.

The man is flanked by two of his agents, who are dressed in dark suits and sunglasses. He is wearing olive dress pants and a white golf shirt. His attire makes it clear he is in charge. The suits are for newbies. Around his neck hang his FBI credentials. She notices how he struts, exuding confidence and maybe compensating for his lack of height.

Lia has been expecting them to make contact. She thought it would be at night, which is when she and Avner would have done it. The goal is discomfort. A public place like this makes sense. Trying to keep her off-balance. They have no idea who they are dealing with. She just needs to decide which role she wants to play.

Worried wife? Clueless spouse? Cold Israeli? Maybe all of the above.

Lia presses her key fob to unlock the doors and pops the hatch of the white GMC Yukon. One by one, she slowly places each bag in the back.

"Lia Miles, do you have a moment?" he asks.

Lia turns and closes the hatch. She looks the law enforcement agent up and down. "Who are you, and what is this about?"

"My name is Agent Zeke Michaels; I am with the local office of the FBI. We need to talk with you regarding your husband Jason."

"Have you found him? I've been so worried."

"No, not yet. We'd like to talk at FBI headquarters. It is not far from here. Please come with us. We'll bring you back after we talk."

"Am I under arrest?" questions Lia as she crosses her arms.

"Why would you ask that? Have you done something wrong?" he inquires.

Lia takes off her sunglasses and tilts her head. "Well, a professional intelligence group would generally schedule a time for a concerned spouse to give a statement. Maybe things work differently in this country."

He smiles briefly and then purses his lips. "We didn't mean to startle you; we just want to ask you some questions. We believe your husband is in danger."

His expressions do not match his words. But those eyes are interesting. Be careful of this one.

"If he is in danger, shouldn't you be out looking for him? I will follow you in my own car," says Lia as she walks to the driver's door and opens it.

"That's fine. I am going to send one of the agents with you so that you do not get lost."

Lia shakes her head. "I am not letting some stranger in my car. I have no idea who you are. If you want to talk, I will follow you. If you want to harass me, I will call my attorney, and we'll go from there."

Zeke stares at her, and a thin smile crosses his face. He holds up his palms and says, "Have it your way. We're in two dark SUVs. I suggest you follow closely. I would hate for you to get lost."

Lia takes a deep breath and starts her car. Before backing out, she quickly removes her Ruger Compact Pistol from her purse and places it in the glove compartment. She can feel her pulse quicken and a tingle moving throughout her body.

Finally, some excitement! This might be fun.

She follows one dark Suburban while the other pulls behind her. They box her in, just in case she changes her mind. Lia laughs and thinks about losing them just for fun, but sooner or later, she'll have to talk with them. She needs to learn what they know anyway.

It is a short drive to the local FBI office on Gray Street in South Tampa. The building is Spanish-style with orange clay roof tiles and a tan façade. A handsome black fence surrounds the building. A light rain begins to fall.

Inside, they walk through a metal detector, and Lia signs in. A female agent looks through her handbag and waves her through. Zeke leads the group to an elevator, which they take to the second floor. No one says a word or makes eye contact. Once they arrive, they walk to an interview room, and Zeke asks Lia to take a seat. Without another word, he leaves the room. The chair is made of metal and is hard. Lia begins a breathing routine to slow her heartbeat. She considers some microexpressions of her own to give them the impression she is nervous and confuse them even further.

Fifteen minutes later, Zeke reenters, along with a female agent. Her badge reads "Gloria Chavez." She wears stylish red-frame glasses, and her hair is pulled back into a tight ponytail. She stands while Zeke takes a seat.

Serious look and nice appearance. Clothes are well taken care of but not high-end. Hard to dress fancy on a government salary. No ring on her finger. Probably divorced. Hard to meet a man with a permanent scowl on your face. Must splurge for Botox a couple times a year. Supposed to intimidate me.

"Sorry for the wait. Can I get you something to drink?" asks Zeke, suddenly a gentleman.

"Yes, how about a nice chardonnay," responds Lia.

Zeke laughs. "Sorry, that is not an option. This is Agent Chavez. We like to have two agents in the room every time we interview someone. Do you mind if we record this?"

"Not at all," answers Lia. "Did you say interview or interrogate?" She sits perfectly still and makes eye contact with both agents. She pulls out her phone. "I will record as well, so there is no confusion on what is said."

Time to see what they know.

Zeke starts the camera and sits. He has a pad of paper in front of him and a cheap ballpoint pen. "My name is FBI Agent Zeke Michaels," he begins, "and I am joined by FBI Agent Gloria Chavez. We are interviewing Mrs. Lia Miles regarding the search for her husband Jason Miles." He turns his focus to Lia. "Mrs. Miles, I'd like to ask you a few questions about your background. It is our understanding that you have dual citizenship. You are a United States citizen and an Israeli citizen. Is that correct?"

"Yes. I am proud to be a citizen of both great countries."

"You were in the Israeli military for four years and then recruited by Shin Bet, the Israeli general security service—basically, conducting internal counterintelligence focused on sabotage, stopping terrorists, and similar activities."

"If that was true, and I am not saying it is, that would be classified." Lia gives him a direct look.

Zeke pauses and scribbles something on his pad. He has terrible handwriting, and all Lia can make out is several words and a circle.

He is thoughtful and a game player. Starts out kind, but sooner or later, he will turn on me.

"That's fine. Can you confirm that you came to America ten years ago with Jason Miles and married him shortly thereafter?"

"Yes, we have a wonderful marriage, and I love him very much. I'd like to know if you've got any idea where he is. I am very worried."

"We're asking the questions, Mrs. Miles. Our sources tell us that you worked together in Israel. Is that true?"

"If that was true, and I am not saying it is, that would be classified," repeats Lia as she folds her hands in her lap. "Why can't I ask questions?"

"Your husband is a security officer at Safe Harbor Bank?"

"That's right."

"Can you tell me when he disappeared and why?"

Lia shifts in her seat and considers the question. "Two days ago, I woke up and he was gone. I have no idea why. Can you help me understand what is going on?"

"That seems strange, Mrs. Miles," states Agent Chavez as she leans in. "Does your husband usually disappear?"

No emotion in her face or voice. A control freak.

"He is often gone early in the morning when I get up. I didn't realize he was missing until later in the day when I found his cell phone. We don't talk much about work."

"We also understand that you have two house guests." Zeke looks at his notes. "Oak Williams, the movie star, and Avner Cohen, a current Israeli agent."

"Yes, both are staying with us, but I can't confirm Avner's occupation, and Oak being a star is debatable," Lia says with a weak smile.

"So you are saying that you and your friends have no idea where your husband is? Or is that classified also?" asks Agent Chavez, her voice rising. A slight Puerto Rican accent emerges as she gets louder.

"I can only speak for myself. I do not know where Jason is. Do you?"

"Are you aware he is wanted for questioning in a murder case? The death of Scott Kowalski?" The kindness in Zeke's tone is slipping away. He is stern and direct.

"Yes, I saw that on the news. It is ridiculous. Scott was Jason's co-worker and friend," replies Lia, letting some irritation into her voice.

"How about something called Project Cardinal? Do you know anything about that?"

Lia slowly shakes her head. "I don't know anything about a Cardinal. What is it?"

Agent Chavez leaves the room and returns a minute later with a folder. She hands it to Zeke. He has readers hanging around his neck, which he places on his nose and then takes his time browsing through the pages, his eyes expanding and then narrowing.

What do you have there, agent? This must be the smoking gun.

Without looking up, he says, "I'm going to be straight with you, Lia. We think you know more than you are letting on. Do you know what it is called when you are dishonest with the FBI regarding an open case?"

Lia does not answer at first. Then she says, "How would I know such a thing? I am from Israel and sometimes struggle with your terminology."

"It is called obstruction of justice. It is a felony, and I think you are aware of a lot more than you let on," snaps Agent Chavez, nearly yelling now.

"We have here a history of your internet searches and cell phone calls," states Zeke as he makes eye contact. His eyes are now a sliver, and the corners of his mouth turn down.

"That sounds illegal, but go ahead," responds Lia.

"Can you tell me why you have been searching for flights to South America, Mexico, and Israel?"

"That must be from a computer in our home. I am not sure who was searching for what. Oak travels the world for his movies, and Avner may need to go back home."

Zeke's thin smile returns. "That's fine. How about calls coming and going from overseas? You have a security blocker, so we cannot ascertain who you are calling and who is calling you."

Time to go. These two are pros and aren't going to tell me anything

I do not already know.

"Classified, and I would like to leave now," says Lia, as she stands. "I have told you the truth and find your suggestions of guilt offensive. I want to find my husband more than anyone."

Zeke stands as well, and Agent Chavez moves to block the door.

"You know your husband is in danger," Zeke comments. "We need you to actively work with us to find him. We're not the enemy." He turns off the camera. "We think there are some bad guys looking for him. Together we can find him. We need you to convince him to come in."

"I appreciate your concern," Lia says. "You should stop harassing innocent people and start looking for him."

Zeke looks to the ceiling and turns the camera back on. "One more thing, Mrs. Miles. Are you okay if we follow you back to your house and search for anything that might help us find Jason? I'd hate for you to be found complicit in any illegal activities."

"If you want to search our house, get a warrant," says Lia moving toward the door. "And Agent Chavez, you need to get the hell out of my way."

CHAPTER 32

Avner and I spend the day an hour north of Tampa at a shooting range in rural Ocala. During the drive, we discuss tradecraft strategy and devise a risky but necessary plan for tonight. There is a brief break in the rain, which gives us a chance to shoot hundreds of rounds with the Glocks. We wear camo jackets and neck gaiters that cover our faces, just in case someone might recognize me from the recent media.

It is nice to escape the pressure of being hunted for a few hours. By the end of the day, much of my training in Israel is coming back to me, and I feel ready to bring the fight to the bad guys. Avner's intelligence experience is priceless, as is his friendship. Unfortunately, the wind and rain pick up on the drive back, which is going to make a tough mission even tougher.

Culbreath Isles is a beautiful waterfront community in South Tampa. It is one of the city's first high-end neighborhoods and continues to be one of the most exclusive. It is also where we are going to find and snatch the man who can tell us more about the tax scheme.

The only entrance is a guarded security gate, and a full-time security service drives the streets looking for anything or anyone that looks out of place. The only way to enter the neighborhood undetected is by boat.

Avner uses another one of his fake IDs to rent a twenty-four-foot, white Bayliner Trophy boat from the marina less than a mile from the neighborhood. It's a good size for what we need to do. The name of the boat is *Seas the Day*, which is what we are planning. The man warns him not to go too far out, as the water is choppy and bad weather continues to roll in ahead of a tropical storm.

I wait, crouching down in the back seat of Avner's car until dusk sets in. When no one is around, we move quickly to the slip and get in the boat. Avner starts it up, and we move slowly out of the marina and along the coast. The boat has a light on the front, which we use to guide us until we can see the outline of Culbreath Isles.

Sebastian Keller, the real estate developer that Scott and I observed at the yacht club, lives in a house on the end of a canal that leads to the bay. It is a six-thousand-square-foot newly constructed mansion with big palm trees out front and gorgeous uplighting that highlights the house at night.

He is the guest speaker tonight at a charity event at the Straz Center for the Performing Arts, so we know we'll have time to pull up the boat and wait for him. Assuming everything goes well, we figure we'll be home by midnight.

Avner cuts the motor as we arrive at Keller's dock. We sent a drone ahead to get a lay of the land and know that he has two lifts, one for his Yellowfin 42 Offshore and the other for a pair of high-end Jet Skis. We maneuver to the dock that separates the two lifts and tie our vessel firmly in place. We jump onto the wet dock and huddle together.

The rain feels like unrelenting bee stings on exposed flesh. We have our gaiters on and switched the camo out for rain gear. The smell of the water is like a warning sign, sharp and pungent, which makes my nose crinkle. It is as if the sea is cautioning us of impending danger, but we don't care. The mission is taking place.

Avner says, "From what I can tell, he has motion-detecting

floodlights and cameras. If we stay on the edge of the property, we can get to the garage and take him when he comes home. Are you sure he will be alone?"

"I'm not sure, but he's been divorced three times, and as far as I know, he is single," I whisper.

We move along the fence past a beautiful pool with several fountains and colored lights. The garage is built for three cars and set off from the main house. We crouch down in some bushes and wait in silence.

Twenty minutes later, Sebastian Keller pulls up in his classic Mustang. The top is up due to the weather. He is dressed in a tuxedo with a Yankee hat on. The car speakers are blasting Bruce Springsteen.

He opens the garage door, and we creep closer. After he pulls in, we slip in like ninjas. He is singing "Born to Run" somewhat off-key and doesn't notice us until it is too late.

He instinctively raises his hands and says, "Who the fuck are you guys?"

"Sebastian, we just want to talk," I insist.

He slowly lowers his hands and tilts his head. "How do you know my name?"

I pull down the neck gaiter. "My name is Jason Miles. I work at Safe Harbor Bank—or I did work at Safe Harbor Bank. I've been to parties at your house."

"You are the one they are looking for who stole some information from the bank and killed some guy. I heard all about it on the news. Why are you at my house, and who's the tough guy with you?" he asks. He is trying to sound confident, but I can hear the quiver in his voice.

"I didn't kill anyone. I just need to ask you a few questions, and then I promise we'll leave."

Sebastian removes his jacket. He is a large man but out of shape, and he's been drinking. He takes a step toward me, and Avner punches him hard in the stomach. He doesn't go down but throws up all over the garage.

"What the fuck?" he croaks, wiping his mouth with his sleeve and rising to his full height, towering above us both.

Avner pulls the Glock from his holster and points it directly between Sebastian's eyes. I have forgotten about the speed and viciousness Avner possesses. He always says that violence is a currency that everyone understands.

"You need to calm down, fat-ass," Aver says. "Your only chance of surviving the night is telling us what we want to know. Jason is going to tie your hands behind your back and put a rag in your mouth. If you try anything, I will not hesitate to put you down. Got it?"

Sebastian nods, and I tie his hands with Avner's zip ties as he scowls at me. I stuff an old rag in his mouth, and we lead him into the backyard and onto the boat. We place him on the bench seat in the stern, and we sit in two soaking wet white leather swivel chairs. The boat has a center console with additional room in the bow for seating. I pilot to deeper water, as Avner keeps his gun pointed at Sebastian.

The boat rocks violently, and the wind howls. I grip the wheel, steering through the angry water. The boat smells like gasoline, and the motor rumbles. I cut the engine when we are a couple of miles out. Far enough that no one can hear him scream. I feel sick as the vessel bobs up and down.

This is crazy. We just kidnapped a man, and we are out in the middle of a storm in a boat. No turning back now.

Avner roughly removes the rag, as Sebastian coughs and spits.

"What the fuck is wrong with you two? We could have just gone in the house."

"And let you trip a panic button of some sort? I don't think so," responds Avner. He puts down his gun and pulls a bucket of chum from the front of the boat. It smells fishy and rancid. He starts shoveling the bloody mixture into the water.

"What are you doing?" asks Sebastian, his eyes growing wide. "You can't put that shit in the water. We have bull sharks all over the bay."

Time to take on a new persona. Part of tradecraft is becoming new characters. I need the information.

"That's what we are counting on, Sebastian," I say. "I am going to ask you some questions, and if you don't answer or I think you are lying, I am going to throw you in. You will be a nice meal for several of them."

We can feel the powerful creatures start to bump into the boat. At first a light thump and then ramming the hull. The storm has spun them up, and they are hungry.

"Do you guys want money? I've got some cash and jewelry in the house. Take it all," begs Sebastian.

"We're not here for money. I need to know about your secret account at Safe Harbor," I say.

Sebastian tries to look confused. "Secret account? I have no idea what you are talking about. I bank with the Executive group, some jerk-off named Barnaby. There is nothing secret about that."

I stand up and move quickly to Sebastian. With all my strength, I pull him up and over to the side of the boat. I do my best to keep my balance so we both don't go overboard. "I have already warned you. If you play games with us, I will toss you over the side, and either you drown or some of those big ol' bull sharks get a tasty snack."

"Okay, okay," he screams. "I have an account with Safe Harbor that they said no one would ever know about. Basically, a way for me to avoid some taxes. No big deal. You guys know that rich people never pay taxes."

"How did you find out about Safe Harbor offering this tax evasion?" I ask.

"My CPA is a member of a group called the Wealth Defense Network. It is a group of accountants and consultants who help the rich stay rich. Real cloak-and-dagger shit," he replies as he looks in the water and then back at me. "I don't care about that, but hiding a few million from the tax man seemed like a good idea. At least until now."

"We watched you trade briefcases at the Yacht Club with Barnaby. Is that how you deposit the money?" I probe.

"Yes, I bring him the cash, and he gives me a book with a bank statement hidden in it. No big deal."

"What about the fee Safe Harbor charges that is sent abroad? What do you know about that?" I give him a slight shove toward the edge.

"Nothing really. My CPA just said it is the price of doing business, and at the end of the day, I am still ahead. I don't know where it goes, and I don't really care." He looks anxiously over the side as a large gray fin glides by.

Sebastian is just a clueless pawn in the game. He is happy with his tax avoidance and doesn't care about the larger picture.

"One last question. Has anyone at Safe Harbor or your CPA ever mentioned a group called *The One*?"

CHAPTER 33

We bring Sebastian back to his house and leave him on his dock. He smells like he might have whizzed in his tuxedo, and Avner makes it clear that if he says anything to anyone, he will take him on a voyage of no return. Sebastian swears he will never say a word and is so pale that I believe him. He also swore he has never heard of *The One,* even when I held his head a little closer to the water.

After dropping off the boat at the marina, we set off toward the motel. Two hours have passed, and I am exhausted but exhilarated. Avner parks across the street from the motel, and we watch for twenty minutes to make sure no one looks out of place. It has been a good night, and we have some new clues that bring us closer to solving this puzzle.

Avner and I agree to meet again in the morning to move to a new location, where I will take a deep dive into the laptop data. Avner will research the Wealth Defense Network and how it might fit into the Safe Harbor Bank scam. I also need to touch base with Oak to make sure he is doing okay.

I exit the car and dash across the street. I enter my room and do a quick sweep to make sure I am alone. I move some furniture in front of the door and place the Glock close by.

I take a cold beer from the small fridge and look at myself in the mirror. My beard is longer, and the hair on my head is starting to grow out. Knowing Sebastian can identify me, I change my appearance again. I grab my razor and some shaving cream and rub it on the sides of my head and the sides of my face. Five minutes later, I have a very short mohawk and a goatee. I finish the look with dark-framed, nonprescription glasses. I look like a forty-year-old wannabe skater, and I kind of like it.

Still amped up from the Keller interrogation, I take a long pull of the beer and look through the backpack for one of the burner phones. I review my list of numbers and dial Oak.

"Hello," he says cautiously.

"I can't believe it. You answered the phone."

"Jay-Bird, are you okay? I've been worried since you took off. Plus, you left me with that lunatic Avner. You know the guy is seriously nuts. He pulled a gun on those fools from the bank, and we were lucky the FBI didn't arrest us all."

It is great to hear Oak's voice. He always makes me feel better, and the thought of those two driving around together makes me smile for the first time in a while.

"He may be a lunatic, but he is *our* lunatic. Maybe you can use him in one of your movies. How is Lia doing?" I ask.

"You know Lia, always calm and unemotional. I want to go kill someone, and she barely has a pulse."

I know exactly what he is talking about. Lia's lack of emotion is tough for me, but I don't really care. She is all I want. I tell her all the time that she makes me a whole person, and she says that she can't fill my empty holes, only I can do that.

"Just please keep an eye on her. I think her lack of emotion is from her training with Avner. She's calm to balance out his crazy."

He pauses, and I can tell there is something more.

"She didn't want me to tell you, but she got picked up by the FBI today. Your buddy Zeke and some chick put the press on her. Made it seem like they cared about you and then suggested that she might be involved."

I can feel a throbbing in my stomach, and my hands ball into fists. I rub my left pinky and throw the glasses across the room.

"I can't believe Zeke did that."

"Jay-Bird, you only have three people in the world you can trust," he warns. "By the way, I need to talk to you about something."

"Not now, Oak. Whatever it is can wait."

"I mean it, Jason. We really need to talk."

****

Avner drives back to his motel after stopping for a drink at a shitty little bar known as The Dive Bomber. The small crowd is a mix of military guys and some old drunks. The lights are low, and the floor is sticky. George Thorogood's "One Bourbon, One Scotch, and One Beer" is playing on an old jukebox. Avner follows the advice from the song and has two shots and a beer but then stops, knowing he needs some sleep.

He parks the rental car a few spots down from his unit and walks slowly, enjoying the cool night air. The alcohol buzz feels nice, and they made progress on the case earlier. They now have a lead on who is funneling dirty clients to the bank and confirmation the scheme is actually happening.

As he nears his unit, two men with guns jump out from a car and four more come around the corner. He is outmanned and outgunned.

"Open the door slowly, asshole. We know who you are, and if you make one move toward your weapon, we will blow your head off," threatens one of the thugs.

I can try and run or fight, but if I do, I am probably dead. I've faced worse and somehow am still alive.

Avner uses his key to open the motel room door and walks in. He is immediately thrown against the wall and frisked. They remove his Glock and two knives before spinning him around to face Max, who walks out of the bathroom with a big smile on his face.

"Is he clean?"

Orsu, the large man from the earlier altercation, nods yes, and Max punches Avner hard in the jaw. Avner goes down on one knee but refuses to give him the satisfaction of going all the way down.

"That is for putting a gun in my face," states Max.

Avner stands despite being shaky. "I can't wait to get you alone and kill you slowly."

Max looks at his soldiers, and they all smile—some laugh uncomfortably. He then delivers a knee to Avner's crotch. This time, Avner goes down hard.

"Pick him up, search him again, and then tie up his arms and legs. This asshole is former special forces, so be careful. Throw him in the car and put the bag over his head," Max instructs. "Tough guy, you are going to go see the boss. If it was up to me, we'd stay in this room until you tell me where your little friend is. Unfortunately, Mr. Browning has more patience. But act up and you'll find yourself at the bottom of the bay with a slit throat."

CHAPTER 34

Avner is shuffled into a room with the black bag on his head and his hands and legs still bound. He can only take small steps, and there is a man on each side holding his elbows.

After leaving the motel, they drove around in circles to further disorient him. He can't be sure, but it must be two or three in the morning. The punch and knee to the groin, along with the booze, has his head spinning, but he is still working through scenarios to escape—or at least survive.

I'd already be dead if they didn't need something from me. Look for ways to escape and stay alive, or at least take a bunch of them with me.

One of the men rips the bag off his head, and it takes a moment for his eyes to adjust. It looks like the card room of a men's club. The paneling is dark wood, and the carpets are plush. There is a full bar against the wall and several card tables throughout. A strong smell of soap and lemon fills the room.

Terrance Browning is sitting in a padded wood chair playing with a deck of cards. He looks up and frowns. "What have you done to my guest?" he asks in mock surprise.

He points to a chair that has been set up opposite him. He continually shuffles the cards and then brings them to a bridge. "Give him a seat, and free his hands and legs."

Max cuts the ties off and pushes Avner down hard into the chair. He takes out his gun and stands between the two men.

"So you are the infamous Avner Cohen. I've heard a lot about you from Max and some friends of mine in Israel. They say you are a dangerous man."

Avner examines the room for exits and potential weapons. "And you are...?"

"My name is Terrance Browning. I am the CEO of Safe Harbor Bank."

Avner nods. He realizes there must be a mole in Shin Bet who was able to track his company phone to the motel. He makes a mental note to find the mole and kill him, along with first destroying the phone.

"Nice to meet you, Terrance. You didn't have to send these idiots. I would have come on my own."

"Would you like a drink? Maybe a nice Paloma?"

"Sure."

Terrance snaps his fingers, and Clinton appears from the corner to mix the drinks. He hands one to Terrance and one to Avner.

"To finding common ground," toasts Terrance, lifting his glass in the air.

Avner plays along and clinks glasses. He takes a long drink and contemplates the possibility of moving across the short space and snapping Terrance's neck without being shot.

I might be able to kill him, but I will die also. Might be worth it.

"Do you like to play cards?"

"Sure. I've been known to play a little poker."

"This situation is much like a game of cards. If you play your hand well, you win. If you play poorly, you lose. Do you understand what I am saying?"

Avner nods. *This guy is a lunatic.*

"I know you are in contact with your friend Jason. We need what he has, and sooner or later, we will get it. If you deliver him to us, he will remain alive and can move on with his life. If we are forced to search and find him, we'll take what we need and kill him."

"What makes you think I know where he is?"

"Avner, do not underestimate me and my people. We found you and we'll find him. He does not have the skills to stay hidden without you. A year of training doesn't make someone a pro."

"What is this all about? Just some scam to make rich people richer?" asks Avner.

The corners of Terrance's mouth turn up, but there is no joy in his eyes. He takes a dainty sip of his drink. He places his Paloma down and puts his hands out in front of him, steepling his fingers.

"This is much bigger than some rich people getting richer," he says, as he grabs a playing card and holds it up. "It is just one card in a very large deck. What you don't understand is that I am a patriot working with other heroes to make a better world. You can help us do that."

"What's in it for me, Terrance? Besides my own survival. Why would I turn on my friend?"

Terrance snaps his fingers, and Clinton hands him a folder. He opens it and licks his finger to separate each page as he slowly examines them.

"Can we talk about your childhood, Avner?"

Avner's eyes harden, and he leans forward. "No, we cannot."

Ignoring him, Terrance says, "We thought you were just another poor kid who joined the government because he couldn't do anything else. Turns out, you come from money, Avner. You aren't that different from me."

"I would proceed carefully, Terrance," warns Avner, moving another inch forward.

Sensing danger, Max moves closer as well. Orsu takes a position behind Avner.

"You come from immense wealth, but you were disowned by Mommy and Daddy. Totally cut off. What happened?"

"Let's just say they were corrupted by wealth, and I've made it my goal to stop people like them and you."

"Well, that's a shame. I guess we can't fix all your childhood problems tonight, but we can fix some current ones." He looks again at the file. "We know you have financial difficulties. Working for the government is not a great way to attain financial security. They use you and then discard you. You appear to be behind on your bills, and your bank accounts have slim balances."

"I'm doing fine," Avner insists, as he attempts to let go of the anger.

Get back into character. Don't let this asshole bait you. Survive tonight and kill them all later.

"No, you are not. I can offer you financial security and an invitation to work for us. A million dollars for delivering Jason Miles. Max could use a man of your skills for many things after that. What do you say?"

"A million dollars for Jason and the data?"

"That's right, Avner. It can be bitcoin, cash, shekels, or Skittles for all I care. Tax free, of course. I know a bank that can handle that for you," he touts, handing the file back to Clinton. "Do we have a deal? We need him fast. We have people who are getting anxious, and we do not like them to be anxious. Understand? Max will give you a phone so we can communicate with you."

Avner contemplates the situation and then offers his hand.

"Deal."

CHAPTER 35

I am so upset about Zeke hassling Lia that I decide to blow off a little steam by walking to the convenience store, despite it being late and in a shady part of town. The small motel room is starting to close in on me. It feels like the furniture has expanded, and I am gasping for oxygen.

I can't leave the laptop, so I strap the backpack tightly around my shoulders. I consider packing the Glock also, but it is only a two-block walk.

This is probably not a great idea, but I need to get out of here and clear my head.

The rain has stopped, but the wind is blowing hard. A few cars pass by, but there is no one else on foot. It is very dark, which makes me feel anonymous but also a little anxious. I am invisible but also easy prey for the creatures of the night. I pick up my pace as a chill moves through me.

The parking lot has large overhead lights, but many are burned out. The only vehicle is an old motorcycle weighing heavy on its kickstand. A voice from behind pulls me from my thoughts and makes me jump.

"Hey, man, do you have a cigarette I could bum?" the voice calls.

I spin quickly with my hands in a defensive position. The man is a couple of inches taller than me with a baggy shirt and jeans. He reeks of alcohol and has a large black gun pointed at my face. His hand is shaking, and the gun is held sideways like he is a character in an old gang movie.

"I want the backpack and all the cash you have," he demands.

I put my hands up to try and defuse the situation.

I am not going to die in this parking lot, but I also can't give him what he wants. Is this guy part of the surveillance group or just some druggie?

"I have a little bit of cash, and you can have it, but please put the gun down."

"Fuck you, bitch. I am in charge and making the rules," he says as his eye tics uncontrollably. "You have two seconds to give me the backpack and cash or you're toast."

I consider going for the gun, but he is a little too far away. We worked on disarming enemies in martial arts class, but it feels a lot different when it is real. My hands ball into fists as I hand him the backpack and the wad of cash from my pocket.

He greedily grabs both and smiles. "Nice doing business with you. You get to live another day. You're welcome."

I just stare at him, and he starts to laugh. It is a snorting foul sound from deep in his throat. He walks backward, still pointing the gun in my direction, and disappears behind the building.

I am not going to be anyone's victim ever again, starting now. I would rather die than live with more regret.

I move silently around the property to sneak up on him before he slips away into the darkness forever. As I round the corner, I see him leaning against a wall counting the cash. There is another man with him who is shorter but wide across the shoulders. They both turn to me.

"Look who decided he wants a fight," the first man says, as he pockets the cash. "You should have left while you had the chance. Let's mess this guy up."

He pushes the backpack out of the way, and they move toward me. They have the confidence and swagger of bullies used to brawling. The smell of sweat, booze, and urine is strong, and I want to gag.

"I'm not looking for trouble. I just need my stuff back. You can have some of the cash, but it is all I have."

The taller man makes the same gruesome laughing noise as before, looks at his partner, and says, "What do you think? Should we give this pansy-ass his things or give him an ass-kicking?"

"I say we kill the motherfucker," slurs the other man as they circle me.

Escape is not an option. Speed and violence are my only choices. Fast, fearless, and fuck 'em up.

There are two of them, but they are inebriated and unsteady. I swallow my fear and muster all the confidence I have. With speed that surprises even me, I move toward the thicker of the two men. I rain down a combination of punches, kicks, and knees just like I would in Krav Maga class, but this is real. No pads and no holding back. I go for the tender spots that can permanently disable, but I don't care. It is them or me. A knee to the crotch lands hard and a punch to the throat causes a gagging sound. I don't stop. I can't stop. I kick the side of his knee and hear a snap, then use my elbow on the back of his head as he goes down. His face crunches into the gravel and concrete.

The taller thief punches me from behind, but in my rage, I don't even feel the blow. I stomp on his foot and land an uppercut that sends him sprawling. As he comes forward again, I land a palm strike to his nose and feel it break. There is blood everywhere, a mix of his and mine. He goes down on one knee, and I kick him as hard as I can, sending him into the ground in a heap.

I am out of my mind with anger. All the frustrations and failures from the past scream at me—the death of my parents, Israel, and Scott in that pool of blood. The larger man is up on his knees, and

I mount him from behind, using the inside of my elbow around his throat to cut off the oxygen and choke him out. It only takes seconds for him to lose consciousness, and I am not sure whether he passes out or dies.

It is them or me. I'm not going to be a sheep anymore. This is my baptism.

As I turn to finish the job and gather my possessions, the lanky man stands on shaky legs. He pulls a switchblade from his pocket and releases the blade. Blood is pouring from his broken nose, which is now sideways on his face. Whatever these guys are on has made them resilient, but even though the fight is now one-on-one, it's much more dangerous. When you fight a man with a knife, someone is getting stabbed. My training tells me to run, but tonight I am not going anywhere.

If he knows what he is doing with the blade, I am a dead man. Instructor E would talk about timers and switches. A timer is a vital target that will end the fight—like a cut into a major artery, such as the carotid in the neck or the aorta in your chest. Within thirty seconds, you will lose consciousness and then bleed out. A switch will have an immediate effect like cutting a nerve or eyeball. All of these options are bad and will probably result in my death. I need to get the knife away from him.

I can hear Lia's voice telling me to end this quickly. He thrusts forward, and I realize he has no training. The next time he swipes at me, I avoid the blade and land my forearm just below his elbow pushing the weapon farther past his intended target. Unfortunately, the blade drops at an angle and cuts deeply into my thigh. Thankfully, it misses the femoral artery, or my thirty-second timer would have started. I grab his wrist and turn it sharply, ignoring the burning in my leg. The knife drops, and I slam him to the ground. I pin him down and pummel him with punches. One blow after another while I scream gibberish.

Pulling me from the slaughter is a voice that sounds far away and then closer. It is like an alarm clock going off while you are in a deep dream that it gets louder and louder.

"Dude, get off him. You're going to kill him," the store clerk yells.

I stand up, pulled from my hysteria. I realize I am crying and covered in blood and sweat. My jeans are torn where he stabbed me, and there is a deep wound. My knuckles are cut, and my heart is exploding against my chest. There is a pounding in my ears, and everything looks out of focus.

"I am going to call the police," the cashier alerts me.

I fish the cash out of the unconscious man's jeans and grab my backpack. "They stole my stuff. I was just defending myself," I mumble.

Instead of going back to the motel, I head in the other direction, assuming the police will be on scene soon. I double back a few blocks up, hoping the clerk will send the cops the wrong way. Walking is difficult, as my leg throbs and blood soaks my jeans. I look like a zombie limping down the road, but the cover of darkness is my ally.

I make it to my room without seeing anyone and barricade the door in case the police show up. I strip out of my clothes and take a hot shower. It takes forever to scrub the blood off, and I realize the knife wound is worse than I thought. I clean all my injuries with soap and water, and when I exit the shower, I hold a towel against my leg, which turns red quickly. I feel like I might pass out. I retrieve a first aid kit from my duffel bag. Lia was smart to include it in the "get out" pack. I rub antibiotic ointment over my wounds and some extra on my leg.

I think back to my training with Avner. In a monotone voice, he would explain, "If you have an open wound, you must avoid infection."

I pack the wound with gauze, use tape to secure the bandage, and elevate my leg. I drink bourbon directly from the bottle to ease the pain and calm my racing mind. I can hear police and ambulance sirens nearby and hope they are not heading my way.

The night was messy and violent, but I did not run. I didn't fail. I was challenged and stood up for myself without anyone's help. I know I can handle whatever is next. I smile despite the pain and drift off, holding the bottle and dreaming of lions and lambs.

CHAPTER 36

I wake up several times during the night. I can't get comfortable with my leg throbbing, and the stress weighs on me from the police sirens blaring up and down the street. I toss and turn. Hot and then cold. Blankets on then blankets off. The thought of the FBI interrogating Lia makes me so angry. I need to trust Zeke, but I don't know if I can. Maybe Oak is right that I only have three people in the world I can count on.

I agree with Avner that I need to change locations. I've been at the motel too long, and the incident last night makes it even more imperative. Another car is also a necessity. I'm a sitting duck with no way to get around. I still have plenty of cash along with the laptop and a weapon. My mind and body are slowly turning into the character in the mirror. I am looking and feeling harder and more desperate. The bags under my eyes are swollen and dark. I am bruised and bloodied from the fight.

I limp over to the window and pull the curtains back. The sun is coming up, and it looks like maybe the storm has passed. I know I need to make a call.

My options are growing slim. I need to know who Zeke is loyal to. Can I trust him, or is he just playing me, and I'll be another notch on his belt on the way up the ladder?

"This is Agent Michaels," says Zeke through the phone, sounding like he is already three espressos in.

"Zeke, it's Jason Miles."

There is a pause and some ruffling of papers. I hear him mumble something under his breath.

"Jason, are you okay?"

"I've been better," I confide, as I lightly rub my thigh. Blood is starting to show through the bandage.

"I can imagine so. Where are you?"

I know I must be on the defensive. Zeke is smart and tricky. I look at my watch to make sure I keep the call short. I don't think they can track the burner, but I am questioning everything at this point. Paranoia is invading every thought.

"I need you to leave my wife alone. She has nothing to do with this."

"How did you know we met with your wife? Are you talking to her or one of your other friends? Don't drag them down with you."

"Zeke, you know I haven't done anything wrong. For God's sake, I came to you about this. I need to know if I can trust you."

"I believe you, Jason, but you have to come in. Your friends at the bank have produced some fairly strong evidence that you stole data and money, and they claim you killed Scott because he knew too much. We also need to understand why you were at his house."

I am starting to sweat despite having turned down the air in the room. "Everything the bank gave you is fabricated, and you know Scott was my friend. I would never hurt him."

There is more silence and whispering, and I know my time is growing short.

"You know I believe you. Just tell me where you are and bring us that laptop. I will come to get you myself. Just you and me," offers Zeke.

I hang up quickly and drop the phone on the ground.

Sooner or later, I'm going to have to turn myself in, but I need to be able to prove whatever is going on first.

I spend the rest of the morning wiping down the motel room and packing everything into my bags. I think through my options. The list is getting shorter every day. I don't know if I can trust Zeke, but I am about to find out. I send him a text:

"Sunny South Motel. Room 19. Come alone like you promised. JM"

****

"I just got a text from Jason Miles. I have his location, and I'm going to bring him in," declares Zeke as he walks into the director's office with Agent Chavez following closely behind.

The director removes reading glasses from the tip of his nose and puts down *The Wall Street Journal*. "It's about time we have some positive movement on this. I get a call every day from Terrance Browning asking what the hell we are doing."

"You can tell him that we'll have Jason in custody today, and then we'll start unraveling this mess."

"I'm calling the Tampa Police Department SWAT team to go in with you. We own this case, but they want him too."

Zeke looks at Agent Chavez and then at the floor. He needs to control the rage that is building if he is going to be allowed to stay on the case. It is high-profile, and he wants the win. "Sir, I gave Miles my word that I would come alone. Agent Chavez will have my back."

The director stands quickly and tosses his paper down. He comes around his desk and closes the space between him and Zeke. Towering over the agent, he says, "This man is a fugitive and a killer. You have no idea what he is capable of. You think you know him, but we don't really know anyone." He backs up slightly. "Pull your head out of your ass, and stop thinking you two are best friends. Do your job and bring him in. Are we clear?"

"Crystal," responds Zeke, leaving the room.

They arrive at a closed-down fast-food location at ten in the morning. A SWAT team commander is pacing back and forth. He is Zeke's height but fifty pounds heavier. His arms look like thick legs, and his legs look like logs. He does not appear to have a neck but does have a serious case of cauliflower ears.

Tampa's Special Weapons And Tactics team is like most throughout the country, a collection of police volunteers who are highly trained and heavily armed. Much of their gear comes from military surplus and their weapons from arrested drug dealers. Each officer can carry the weapon of their choice, including handguns, submachine guns, and rifles.

The team is gathered around the commander. Each is dressed in black with a helmet and a Kevlar vest that reads "POLICE." Most wear their handgun on their leg for faster draws. They are physically fit, and no one has a smile. All of them wear black wraparound sunglasses to complete their look.

"Welcome to the command post," the team's leader says, waving Zeke and Gloria over.

"Gentlemen, these are our friends from the FBI. This is their show. We've been asked to help with the capture. Agent Michaels, would you like to give us a quick summary?"

"Thank you, commander. My name is Zeke Michaels, and this is Agent Chavez. The suspect is down the street at the Sunny South Motel. We have eyes on the room and a key from the manager. The suspect is a former banker named Jason Miles. He is wanted for data theft and for questioning in the death of a co-worker. We assume he is armed and possibly dangerous. This should be an easy one, fellas."

The team members look at each other, grumbling under their breaths.

"Did I say something wrong?" asks Zeke.

The commander gives a small shake of his head. "When you are part of a SWAT team you never say 'This is going to be an easy one' out loud. We go in assuming everything will go wrong."

The men pile into an angular bulletproof vehicle that looks like a black UPS truck. It has a siren bar on top and reads "POLICE" on the side. It is escorted by a police car and Zeke's SUV. Zeke looks in his rearview mirror and thinks that nobody wants to see this procession coming their way.

Once at the motel, the team parks on the side and exits the vehicle. An FBI agent hands over the room key, and the men form a single-file line known as a snake. The first man in line—the point man—holds a large black shield in front of him. It has a small clear section for him to see through.

"Okay, guys, let's take this man alive if we can," instructs the commander.

Zeke and Chavez will enter the room when it has been cleared. Despite all the heavy weaponry ahead of them, they still pull their handguns.

The snake moves past several rooms until it arrives at its destination. There is no speaking now, just hand signals. One of the team members quietly unlocks the door, and the team goes in one after another. They are prepared for resistance and willing to use violence.

CHAPTER 37

I leave the keys on the dresser and limp a half mile down the road to a diner that advertises a $4.99 special until noon on Saturdays. I check my watch and realize that I have plenty of time until the deadline. Inside it smells like grease and burnt muffins. One waitress runs from table to table taking orders and filling drinks.

The special turns out to be two eggs, two pieces of bacon, toast, and bottomless coffee. The coffee is bitter, so I add some cream to balance it out. The eggs are runny, but the bacon is delicious, so I mix everything together in each bite. I keep my head down and my belongings close to me.

I am anxious to find out if I can trust Zeke. On the one hand, we've known each other for years, but on the other, I know he is ambitious and closes cases quickly. It could go either way.

Avner arrives an hour later, driving an old Ford F-150 with rust on the doors and no hubcaps. It looks like it might have been red when it was new but is now just a combination of chipped paint and primer. He slides into the other side of the booth and asks the waitress for a coffee and water.

We examine each other and say at the same time, "What the fuck happened to you?"

I go first. "I was a dumbass and went for a walk last night. Got jumped by a couple of tweakers. I had the laptop, so I had to fight."

Avner's eyes move over me as he shakes his head. "Looks like they kicked your ass. What do I always tell you? Go for the balls, and ask questions later."

I laugh despite the pain radiating through most of my body. "You think I look bad? You should see the other guys. What's your story?"

"Stopped at a shithole bar and a biker took a swing. Caught one good one but ended it quick." He touches his nose and looks away.

"What's with the rust bucket?" I ask.

"That rust bucket is your new ride."

"Where did you get it?"

"Cash special at one of the Buy Here/Pay Here lots. It runs well, and no one will remember it."

Avner seems more withdrawn than usual. Something is bothering him.

"Is everything okay, Avner?"

"It's fine. Just finish eating, and we'll get you over to your new place."

Something isn't right. Avner is distracted and keeps looking at the door.

"Were you able to arrange for everyone to meet us?"

"Yes, I talked to everyone. We just need to pick a time. Lia will take Oak with her, and I'll come alone."

"That sounds good. We have something we need to do before heading to my new home."

We leave the diner and set up a mile from the hotel on the top level of a parking garage attached to a half-full corporate office complex. No one is parked on levels three or four, and no cameras appear to be active. Avner has two sets of binoculars, and we sit in the back of the pickup waiting for the action.

I placed the burner phone used to call Zeke underneath the wheel of the truck before we pulled out. It was crushed into a thousand pieces, just in case.

"You know they are coming with all they have, Jason," predicts Avner.

"What makes you say that?"

"Because that is what I would do."

"I've known Zeke for a long time. I think I can trust him."

Avner laughs and pulls out two long, brown cigars. We clip the ends off and light them up. Lia hates the habit, but seeing as I am halfway to prison already, I decide to indulge.

We sit in silence blowing streams of thick smoke up in the air. It is nice to be outside relaxing with my friend and not in the motel room.

"What happened to your leg?" he asks. "I can see some blood coming through."

I blow a smoke ring in the air. "One of the guys had a knife and caught my leg. No big deal."

"You get an infection, and it is party over. I'll get you some antibiotics. You need painkillers?"

"I would love some, but I need to be sharp. I'll stick with Tylenol."

Avner stands up and looks through the binoculars. "Showtime."

I hobble to my feet but don't see anything. I move my binoculars all around hoping not to see a procession of vehicles.

"Look about six blocks south of the motel. You can see a staging area in that closed Burger King parking lot."

I follow his directions until I see it. In the lot is a large SWAT vehicle, a police cruiser, and one black SUV. Zeke is walking the lot in his FBI windbreaker with the woman from lunch. He is drinking coffee and talking to a short but very wide man dressed in full attack gear.

"Fucking Judas," I hiss to myself.

Everyone jumps into their vehicles, and the police car leads the group down the street. They collect on the side of the motel, and the SWAT team moves into a single line. One by one, they move to the room with weapons fully drawn. Zeke and the woman are last in line. They also have their weapons drawn.

A thick black man with a heavy looking ram moves into position, but he first tries a key from the front desk. The SWAT team moves quickly. Several minutes later, one of the officers walks out holding pillows and blankets in the form of a man. Zeke stares at it and rips the pillow head off.

Avner looks at me and a huge cloud of smoke escapes as he laughs as hard and loud as I've ever heard him. Just the sight makes me start laughing, and within a few minutes, tears are streaming down both our faces.

"You knew that asshole wasn't coming alone," he says.

"I hoped, but I knew he would do his job. I know I have three people I can trust, and he is not one of them."

Avner nods and looks away.

CHAPTER 38

Oak pulls his hat down low and takes the elevator to the top floor of Two Tampa City Center. It is hard to be inconspicuous when you are six foot four and your face is on giant screens all across the world. He is used to selfies and people taking videos of him, but today he needs to blend into the background.

The Tampa Bay Club is one of Tampa's best business and social clubs and the kind of place Oak hates. It is a collection of rich old guys with enough token minority and women members to advertise themselves as a club that welcomes all. Despite his disgust, Oak will do anything to help his best friend.

You need to suck it up and do this. There must be some way to get Jason out of this mess. Maybe this Terrance clown will be reasonable. Pour on that famous Oak Williams charm.

"I am sorry, sir, you must have a collared shirt to enter the Tampa Bay Club," says the elderly woman at the desk dressed in a crisp white shirt with a black polyester vest over the top. She is propped up on a chair with her arms crossed and a frown on her face. She is clearly tasked with keeping the unwanted out and takes her job seriously. "And you certainly cannot wear that baseball hat."

Oak looks down at his gray hoodie and jeans. He thought he was dressed up for the trip downtown. He removes the hat. "Sorry, ma'am, I'm here to meet one of your members, Terrance Browning. He didn't say anything about a dress code. I'm sure you can make an exception."

"He is fine," says Max, as he walks in from the bar area and hands the woman a $20 bill. "Mr. Browning apologizes and will make sure Mr. Williams is dressed properly next time."

The old woman glares at Oak and nods for him to pass by. Under his breath, Oak mutters, "Old battle-ax."

Max leads Oak to the bathroom, where Orsu is waiting. They motion him against the wall to check him for weapons.

"Is this really necessary, fellas?" asks Oak as Orsu roughly searches his entire body. "I hope you are getting a thrill out of this. It is not doing much for me."

"Follow me, asshole," instructs Max. He leads Oak down a hallway with pictures of hundreds of former and current club members. All look about the same and many have last names that include Roman numerals such as II or III. The pictures are black and white, and most of the men have white hair and boring ties.

They pass through a room with a large marble-topped bar. There are several men drinking and playing dollar poker. The room is wood-paneled, and there is a recessed ceiling with a brass chandelier hanging down. A formally dressed bartender laughs with his customers, working hard for their spare change.

Max opens the door to a large patio with a sweeping view of downtown Tampa and the bay. Terrance is sitting at a table for two. The rest of the patio is empty. A charcuterie board sits in front of him with small pieces of cheese, meats, and nuts. Two cocktails with orange wedges and salty rims have been served but are untouched.

"I am so happy you called, Mr. Oak Williams, the famous movie star," says Terrance, pointing to the chair across from him. "I've taken the liberty of ordering you a nice Paloma and something to snack on. To what do I owe the honor?"

Oak sits down and takes a drink. He scrunches his face as the tart liquid goes down his throat. He grabs a fistful of prosciutto with his hands, causing Terrance's eyebrows to rise in alarm.

"I want to talk to you about Jason Miles. I'd like to figure out how to remedy this situation," Oak remarks as he chews on the salty meat.

"Do you like the view, Oak? I love to sit up here, have a cocktail, and watch the storms move in. You can see the lightning in the distance and the dark clouds approach like an army. Did you know a hurricane may be on its way?"

"Yeah, I heard something about that. Hopefully it misses us."

Terrance leans forward with his arms on the table. "Misses us? That is the last thing we want. Natural disasters are the universe's way of cleansing the earth."

Oak sits back in his chair, wishing he could get the hell out of here. This guy is a weirdo, and the two thugs sitting ten feet away are making him nervous. "About Jason?"

"Of course, but I want to talk to you about something else first. I understand your net worth is over two hundred million. Impressive."

"To be honest, I have no idea how much money I have. I've got people who handle those things. I even have some at your bank because of Jason."

"I know you do, and we appreciate it. Oak, I'd like to paint you a picture of how life could be."

This guy is a fucking loon.

Oak feels a surge of frustration and takes another sip of his drink, along with all the almonds on the board. "I'm sorry, Terrance, I don't have any idea what you are talking about."

"Do you know what the Gini coefficient measures?"

Oak shakes his head. "The what?"

Terrance steeples his fingers and smiles. "The Gini coefficient measures the spread between the rich—like you and me—and the poor. South Africa has the highest, with 10% of the wealthiest people controlling 70% of the wealth. Isn't that glorious?"

A bright streak of lightning fills the sky, followed by a loud thunderclap. Oak feels his blood starting to boil and looks out at the storm.

"What I am trying to say is that there is a storm coming our way, and we need people like you. Successful people with access to wealth to rebuild this mess of a world. I am offering you an opportunity."

"Listen, Terrance, I have no idea what the hell you are talking about. I was one of those poor guys you are talking about. I am trying to help a friend."

"Oak, we can build a world where education is valued, and the government spends less than it takes in. Where the superpowers work together. There is a war brewing throughout the world. The haves verse the have-nots. You need to be on the right side of it when it all goes down," declares Terrance, his voice rising and his eyes widening. He moves his seat closer to Oak's. "I'm offering you that opportunity, Oak. Join us in building the next great society."

Oak stands suddenly. Max and Orsu rush from their seats with hands in their jacket pockets.

"I don't know what the fuck you are talking about, but you are clearly insane," Oak responds, turning to walk out. "This was obviously a mistake."

Terrance raises his arms and calms his tone. "Please sit. I know this is a lot. Max and Orsu, return to your seats." He gestures to his two henchmen, then turns back to his guest. "Oak, do you know anything about technology?"

Oak sits and crosses his arms across his chest. His eyes narrow in annoyance and he says, "A little bit, yes."

"It is amazing what is happening. It is part of the revolution. Those who create artificial intelligence and artificial general intelligence will rule the world. Others will use it, but we have the men and women who create it." His voice drops low, like he is revealing a secret. "We own quantum computing and can use it all to change the world. Everyone thinks the technology is a decade away, but we already have it."

"I think you are nuts," proclaims Oak.

Terrance laughs. "All the greats were considered insane. Maybe I was wrong about you. I thought you might have vision, but instead, you just have money. Another poor kid who got lucky enough to obtain a few bucks and is destined to be poor again."

Oak stands quickly, tipping his chair over and causing the contents of the table to crash to the ground. Max and Orsu move toward the table. This time, Terrance does not stop them.

"Life is about choices, Mr. Williams. For instance, you can agree to help us and return Jason along with the stolen data, or we could simply throw you off this balcony. Seems like an easy choice."

Oak steps back and looks toward the exit. Instead, he grabs Terrance and hauls him over the railing, holding him in the air by only his belt. Max pulls his gun, but Terrance screams out. Heavy raindrops start to fall from the sky.

"Better step back, or I might lose my grip," Oak warns.

"Put away the gun," yells Terrance, as he dangles thirty-eight stories above the ground. "We don't need this. Oak, please pull me up. I was just giving you an example. I didn't mean we would physically throw you over the edge; we already own you and will figuratively throw your life over the edge."

Oaks jerks Terrance back over to solid ground but holds him close. "What are you talking about? I don't even know you."

"But we know you. You are going to do what we want, or you'll go down with us," threatens Terrance, pulling away. "Your career will be destroyed, and you'll lose all those houses and cars and everything you claim you don't need but secretly love. You are part of this already."

CHAPTER 39

Avner leased the new rental using one of his many sets of false identifications. He paid a month in advance and seemed excited to show it to me. My main concern is for my safety and the safety of the laptop. The minute-by-minute stress of knowing someone might break down the door at any moment is suffocating. The inability to sleep is debilitating. I am hopeful this will be better than the motel.

Upon arrival, I do not share his excitement. It was a thirty-minute drive to a mobile home in Thonotosassa. It sits on two acres in what feels like the middle of nowhere. It is white with two windows on each side. The roof is slightly pitched, and a set of wooden steps lead to a deck to access the front door.

The old deck slopes away from the mobile home, and the banister is falling. Vines are growing everywhere, and some cheap gray lattice runs along the bottom. The lot is heavily wooded, and the lane into the property is gravel and dirt. The heavy rains have turned much of the ground to mud.

"Are you kidding me?" I say, as I stare at the tin can masquerading as a home. The thought of staying in the dilapidated old box hurts almost as bad as the throbbing in my leg.

"It's perfect. There are no nosy neighbors, you can park your truck behind the property, and the trees give you good cover."

"I'm not the Unabomber, Avner."

He grabs my bag and steps out of the truck. I can tell he is hiding a smile. "The bad news is that you are wanted by the FBI and the Tampa PD for financial crimes and murder. You have no choice but to go deep undercover, banker boy. This will be good for you. See how normal people live."

The key takes a few moments to slide into the rusty dead bolt. When it finally turns, we walk into a long room with a kitchen at one end and a bedroom at the other. It is sparsely decorated with what looks like old lawn furniture. The smell of cat pee hits me like a brick.

"See, it even comes furnished," says Avner, as he walks to the kitchen and opens the fridge.

"You know what, I don't care. This is just a moment in time. I am doing the right thing, and I am going to avenge Scott's death—even if I must stay here all month."

"That's the spirit. I have been looking into the Wealth Defense Network, and I have some calls to make. I'll leave the truck and get an Uber back to town. We'll all come back, and I'll bring some groceries and something for that leg. Let's get it cleaned up before I head out."

I sit down and take off my jeans to expose the wound. Blood continues to soak through the dressing, and it feels like it has its own heartbeat. I am concerned it is infected, which is a problem I do not need right now. We work together to clean it and wrap it again. I change into shorts to avoid anything rubbing against it.

I unpack the rest of my bag and place the laptop in front of me. Avner tosses me his spare shoulder holster, so I can wear the Glock instead of letting it sit on the counter.

"You go. I am going to work on the data until you all get back, unless I get eaten by a bear or mob of hillbillies."

As he walks out the door, I hear him say, "You might clean up before your guests arrive. This place is a mess and smells like a cat. Meow."

I watch him walk off the premises and consider my predicament.

So far, I have a video of two guys exchanging briefcases and the confession of a man I threatened to feed to sharks. Not exactly a strong case to bring to the FBI. I also have no idea what Safe Harbor has fabricated to make me look guilty. I have no doubt the secrets are hidden in the laptop, and I intend to find them. Otherwise, I may be looking at prison—or something much worse.

****

"Mind if I join you?" asks Avner, after navigating his way through the busy cafeteria-style dining room. His tuna fish sandwich on pumpernickel and iced tea sit delicately balanced on the plastic tray. The scent of fresh bread and bakery treats fills the air. Avner knows he is taking a risk by asking Zeke for help, but his options are limited. He hopes he does not end the lunch in handcuffs.

Zeke looks up from his sandwich. "Do I have a choice?"

"That looks good," replies Avner, taking a seat.

"Wright's has been here forever. Everything is good," responds Zeke. He looks down at his half-eaten pastrami sandwich with mustard dripping off the sides. On the other side of his tray is a large slice of Wright's famous lemon bundt cake. "Don't tell my wife; she'd kill me if she saw this five-thousand-calorie bomb sitting in front of me." He pats his stomach. "She keeps telling me to eat salads, but I'm not a fucking rabbit."

"Lehayim, to life," toasts Avner, lifting his tea.

"What can I do for you, Avner? I am assuming you didn't track me down for my winning personality. By the way, you are a slippery one. My boys keep trying to follow you, but you disappear like a ghost."

Avner takes a big bite of his sandwich, ignoring the last comment. "I need some information on something called the Wealth Defense Network."

Zeke eyes Avner suspiciously. "I am assuming this has something to do with your friend Jason. Do I need to remind you that you have no jurisdiction in America?"

"Listen, Zeke, we are both professionals trying to put the bad guys away. We are on the same side. You know something stinks with Safe Harbor Bank and Jason's situation. If we work together, maybe we can help him."

Zeke leans in and says, "Tell me what you know and where Jason is. That is the best thing you can do for him. Let us handle it."

"No way, you've already proven yourself untrustworthy with the stunt at the motel."

"That was all my boss. I tried to go alone, but he insisted on the heavy stuff. Regardless, the only one who can help Jason is me," asserts Zeke confidently, as he bites into a giant pickle spear, shooting juice into the air. "I know all about your background, and if we were in Israel, you might be helpful, but not here. These are bad guys, and the longer Jason is in the wind, the more likely it is that those goons will find him."

"What can you tell me about the Wealth Defense Network?"

Zeke moves his meal off to the side and looks around. "We can't talk in here. Follow me outside."

They move to an outside table with no other customers close by. Avner removes a cigar from his jacket and clips the end. "Want one?"

"Why not? If that fucking Reuben doesn't kill me, I might as well have a smoke."

Avner hands him one and lights both with a silver lighter. Zeke takes several puffs to get it started, inhales deeply, and blows out a thin stream.

"Fuck that is good," exclaims Zeke, as a cloud of smoke obscures his face. "What is it?"

Avner blows out his own cloud. "The anniversary series of Davidoff. Outside of Cubans, they are the best."

"I will tell you about the Wealth Defense Network, and then you need to share something with me. Got it?"

Avner savors the richness and earthiness of the cigar. "Deal."

"It is known as the WDI—the Wealth Defense Industry. It is a loose group of consultants, accountants, money managers, and lawyers who get paid a shitload of money to keep the rich from paying taxes," states Zeke. He looks around to make sure no one is within earshot. "In other words, they keep the very rich even richer. They are the professional enablers. Crooks in pinstripes."

Zeke looks at Avner, noticing that the Israeli's eyes expand and then burn into him. "People don't know it, but the United States is the world's biggest tax haven. Dirty money from all over the world ends up here. Everyone thinks of Switzerland and the Bahamas, but it's all right here in our backyard."

Avner considers this as he smokes his cigar. "How do I find out more about this group?"

"This isn't an official group. It's not a fraternity where they gather once a year and talk about how to defraud tax authorities. Think of it like an industry." Zeke pauses, looks upward, and then continues. "There are perfectly legal ways to shield wealth, and there are highly illegal ways. These guys talk about tax efficiency, but there is a fine line between tax avoidance and tax evasion."

"If everyone knows about it, why doesn't the government shut it down?" asks Avner.

Zeke laughs out loud, causing a couple at the other end of the patio to look his way. "The government is part of the problem. We allow these lobbyists and professionals to create laws and the loopholes that are big enough to drive a truck through. They will always be one step ahead of the IRS." He blows a haze of smoke toward the couple, who pick up their trays and walk inside.

"If you want to know more about this, you need to speak with an expert. Lucky for you, we have one right here in Tampa. Professor

Apple Lee is ten minutes from here at The University of Tampa. She literally wrote the book on WDI. She owes me one. I helped get her kid into Tampa Prep."

Avner stands and stamps out what remains of his cigar. "Thanks, Zeke. You're not such an asshole after all."

Zeke draws some smoke into his mouth, looks up, and then lets it slowly escape. "You have no idea what an asshole I can be. Your turn. What are you going to give me in return?"

Before Zeke lowers his eyes back down, Avner is already walking away, blending into the crowd. He still doesn't trust Zeke but appreciates the professional courtesy and the tip. He also appreciates not being arrested. It is time to go to school and visit Professor Lee.

CHAPTER 40

There is a hard knock on the door, which pulls Lia from her nap. It is Saturday afternoon, and she is exhausted from the stress of the week. She comes downstairs, and Oak meets her in the entryway wearing a pair of basketball shorts and a T-shirt with a picture of Ben Franklin that reads "Ben Dranken." As with most of his shirts, the sleeves have been cut off to expose his bulbous biceps and tattoos.

Lia yanks the front door open to see Zeke with a large team of FBI agents behind him. Several black vans are parked in the driveway.

"What took you so long?" she asks.

"Lia Miles, I have a search warrant for your house and all your vehicles. Please step aside," instructs Zeke.

Lia takes the document he provides her and slowly reads it. She lets her hands tremble a little.

Let them think they are scaring me a little bit.

"Do you want me to call my lawyer?" asks Oak, as he fills the rest of the doorway.

"No, there is nothing to find here. Go ahead, Agent Michaels. Please be careful with our house."

Zeke puts paper booties on over his shoes and moves slowly around Lia and Oak. He signals to the rest of the team with his hand in the air.

Gloria Chavez approaches Lia. "We have our warrant. Now *you* can get the hell out of *my* way."

The FBI team methodically searches and examines every inch of the house. They open every cabinet and look in the closets. They move slowly and document anything of interest with a short video. When they find something meaningful, they whisper in Zeke's ear. Somewhere in the house, glass breaks.

An hour into the search, Zeke asks Lia and Oak to join him outside. They stand in a shady spot near the pool. "I know you think I am the enemy, but I'm not. We need to find Jason. He is not safe. We've researched these thugs employed by the bank, and they are serious bad guys," says Zeke.

"As I told you before, if you were to spend as much time looking for him as you are harassing us, you would have probably found him by now, and he would be home," counters Lia.

Oak steps forward. He towers a good six inches over Zeke and outweighs him by fifty-plus pounds. "You don't think Jason did these things, do you?"

Zeke considers the question. He stares down at the water as if he is in a trance. His lizard eyes slowly open and close. "No, I think he is being set up, but I can't prove anything if he stays on the run. I know he is communicating with you two and your Israeli friend. Convince him to turn himself in or to let us know where he is. I promise to bring him in gently and work with him."

Lia gazes intently at Zeke. *This man can't be trusted. He just wants the arrest.*

"Just so you know, Jason is my best friend in the world. He's also the best guy I know," states Oak. "These guys at the bank are insane."

Zeke looks up and stares at Oak for thirty seconds. "Have you had communication with anyone at the bank we need to know about?"

Oak looks away and rubs his neck. "No, I haven't."

"Think about what I've said," requests Zeke, as he hands them both a business card. "I am going to get things moving in there."

Chavez walks outside. "Zeke, we need you upstairs. We found a safe hidden in the closet."

Zeke heads to the stairs, followed closely by Lia. They walk through the bedroom to the walk-in closet. Clothes have been moved to the side, and a picture of dogs playing poker is on the ground.

"The safe was behind the picture," says one of the techs.

"Can you please enter the code?" Zeke instructs Lia.

She crosses her arms. "I don't think so. I don't believe the warrant includes our safe."

Zeke pulls the search warrant from his pocket. He points to the second page. "It clearly does. Open the safe, Mrs. Miles, or we'll have it blown open."

The agents gather around, and Lia presses in her personal code. The safe clicks, and the door unlatches. Lia opens it and walks away.

Zeke shines his flashlight into the safe. From behind, he hears Gloria say, "What's in there, boss? Tell me it is something good."

"Fucking empty and looks like it has been wiped recently."

An hour later, the FBI packs up. They bag several items and carry boxes to their vans. Men with gloves handle the electronic items from Jason's office carefully.

Good luck finding anything except family pictures and fantasy football. Lia watches them with narrowed eyes.

When they are alone, Oak asks Lia, "Do you think Jason would be safer with these guys than on his own?"

Lia shakes her head and signals him to follow her back to the pool. She turns the outside speakers on and blasts music.

She speaks into his ear. "Assume this place is bugged until I can have Avner sweep it. Be careful what you say."

"Got it."

"I don't trust them. They need to arrest someone, and the bank fabricated enough proof to pin it on Jay. He'll rot in jail, and he can't survive being locked up with animals. We need to help him figure out what is going on."

"We can talk to him when we meet. How are we going to make sure we are not being followed?" asks Oak.

"I have that covered. Just be ready when I call you—and wear something dark. We are all Jay has. We're in it together, till death do us part."

****

I look around the old tin can and realize it might be my home for a while. It is a stark contrast to my beautiful house in South Tampa, but it is time to have a better attitude until this nightmare ends. There are Clorox wipes underneath the kitchen cabinet, and I find an old broom with a broken handle and a red plastic dustpan.

Some of my best thoughts happen when I clean the house or do yard work. It is a great chance to kill two birds with one stone—clean the shitty trailer and figure out a way out of this mess.

I go to work on the fake granite countertop first. There is a layer of dust and some petrified nacho cheese that takes some work to scrub off. A few of the composite drawers are hanging off the hinges, so I use an old screwdriver to tighten them up.

I have the information on the laptop, but if I go to the FBI, they will arrest me. If I show it to Lia, Avner, or Oak and they go to Zeke, he won't believe them. I need a third party who I can trust.

The fridge is empty except for some old pickles, and there is only frostbitten ice in the freezer. I bag everything up and place it on the wood deck. I take a handful of aspirin to numb the pain in my leg.

Even if I find that person, how am I going to convince them to meet with me? Where could we meet? What would be in it for them? Is there anyone I can trust?

The linoleum floor looks like a puzzle with pieces of red, yellow, and black. I use the broom to take a layer of animal fur off the ground.

I'm not sure what type of creatures might have lived in this trailer, but a cat was definitely one of them. Luckily, there is a spray bottle of Lysol, and I use it throughout the place.

What about an attorney? Is there some kind of client privilege I could count on? Attorneys are as untrustworthy as bankers.

Once I am satisfied with the kitchen, I work on the built-in table that can be used for meals or as a workspace. I clean it thoroughly with wipes and set up the laptop in a corner. There are only two lights in the house, a dusty fan/light combo in the kitchen with three of four bulbs working and another that appears to be the same model in the living room, but it is missing the fan blades.

The rest of the living room has seen better days. It is separated from the kitchen by a brown carpet. The walls are paneled wood that is peeling off, and the windows are covered with threadbare orange drapes. An L-shaped couch is in the corner, and it is sagging on one side.

Oh my god, I have it!

I run out to the truck and grab the *St. Pete Times* newspaper that Avner tossed on the floorboard. I tear through the front page and sports until I find the financial section.

There she is—reporter Morgan Chase. Would she do it?

Morgan is a financial columnist with the paper and an acquaintance of mine. We served on the board of a local charity together and ran into each other at committee happy hours. She is somewhat of a local celebrity having worked for *The Wall Street Journal*, and she pens a popular blog about the economy and finance. She signs her work "Morgan Chase—Black, Beautiful, and Brainy." She is certainly all three.

At the bottom of an article on student debt is her e-mail.

What do I have to lose?

I grab the burner phone and take a deep breath. I type out an e-mail:

Morgan, I need to speak with you. JM.

With that done, I go back to work. There is only one bathroom, and it consists of a sink, a toilet, and a small shower. There appears to be a science experiment of some sort in the shower with many different colors of mold. There are not enough wipes in the world to clean it up.

I hear a chirp from the phone and know I have mail.

Are you crazy? What the hell is going on, Jason? The world is looking for you. They are saying terrible things.

I can explain. Just give me five minutes.

There is no response, and I realize I am rubbing my left pinky. I move on to the final room, which is the bedroom. It has one window with similar orange drapes as the living room. They are falling and not blocking much light. A mattress is pushed up against the wall and sits on the floor with no frame. The bedspread is mauve and looks like the one in the motel. I don't have the guts to check the cleanliness of the sheets.

I check the phone again, but there is still no response. I pack up the laptop as always and drive the truck to a dollar store a mile away. I pull my hood tight and keep my sunglasses on. Despite my disheveled state, at least I am not wearing pajamas like everyone else in the store.

I fill my cart with some basic supplies. I have never been to a dollar store and soon realize that not everything costs a dollar. But still, for less than forty bucks, I collect cleaning supplies, water, snacks, legal pads, and some items for my leg. I also grab several air fresheners, hoping I can get rid of the kitty smell.

Halfway back, the phone chirps again. I look down, see a phone number, and dial it immediately.

A cautious voice answers. "This is Morgan."

I pull over to the side of the road. "Morgan, this is Jason. Can we talk?" I assume she is recording the conversation, but what does it matter? I am still sure a burner cannot be tracked.

"Why are you calling me? I've been following your story. Did you really do it?"

"Of course not, Morgan. I would never do those things," I state as confidently as possible, hoping she will believe me or at least not hang up. "I need your help."

"My help?" she responds, her voice quivering a little. "What can I possibly do to help you...and why would I?"

"I am offering you the deal of a lifetime. You help me with my problem, and you get a chance to tell a story that will change your life and maybe the world."

CHAPTER 41

Avner pulls into the parking lot at The University of Tampa and steers into a spot with a large sign that reads "Visitors Only, All Others Will Be Towed." A campus security guard appears dressed in a dark uniform with a badge on his chest. He has a serious scowl that makes Avner smile.

Rent-a-cop ready to bust some balls.

"Where are you heading, sir?" he asks as he writes down the license plate number and examines the rental car. "A lot of the buildings are closed on Sunday."

Avner tried to raid Jason's closet for the mission, but all those clothes were too tight. Instead, he spent $50 at Target on a light blue golf shirt and khakis. He added his own sports jacket to finish the look. He trimmed his beard and added a pair of round glasses. Lia parted his usually messy hair on the side and used gel to make it stay in place. They filled a brown leather backpack with paper, pens, and a newspaper. They agreed that the transformation to a forty-something journalist was good enough.

"You don't look so scary," Lia giggled.

"Looks can be deceiving," replied Avner on his way out the door.

"Good morning, I have an appointment with Professor Apple Lee. I believe it is in the Entrepreneurship Center." Avner offers his friendliest smile to the guard. It feels forced and unnatural. Apex predators rarely smile.

The security officer looks him up and down and then points to a multistory building across campus. "Professor Lee is on the fifth floor. Go to the lobby and sign in."

Avner thanks him and starts his trek across the beautifully manicured campus. Palm trees, rose bushes, and azaleas landscape the property. A breeze blows a pleasant scent through the air.

From his research, Avner knows The University of Tampa is a private college with ten thousand students. Most of the kids are staring at their phones or talking to friends as they walk. Most ignore him, probably taking him for an academic or just another "old" person.

He stops to take a picture of Plant Hall which is UT's most recognizable and central building. Silver minarets sit atop each side of the building. The main entrance features cannons and a sculpture. As a lover of architecture, Avner appreciates the beauty of the building.

He notices several tours taking place for prospective students and their deep-pocketed parents. They are led by what look like current students. Avner leans into one group and hears a young man say, "UT's campus features seventy buildings on one hundred and ten landscaped acres. In the last sixteen years, UT has invested approximately $575 million in new residence halls, classrooms, labs, and other facilities."

You are not on vacation looking for somewhere to study. You have a job to do. Focus on the task at hand and get the hell out of here.

He walks several blocks on a sidewalk toward the Entrepreneurship Center. The entire time, he cannot help but think he is being watched. He moves in circles and doubles back several times. There are no obvious signs, but a trained agent knows when something is not right. He makes it to the building with palm trees in front. A student sits in the lobby behind a counter.

The young woman looks up. "Can I help you?"

"Hello, I am here to see Professor Lee," answers Avner. "My name is Yosef Mizrahi."

Avner has been using the Yosef Mizrahi alias in Israel for ages. Anytime he needs to tweak the character, Shin Bet builds a backstory including date of birth, employment, and internet searches. He'd called in a favor and asked them to hastily put together a background for a finance journalist. He hopes no one will dig too deep.

She checks her appointment book and prints off a name badge. "Please wait over there," she says pointing to a pair of green couches.

Several minutes later, another fresh-faced student introduces herself and leads Avner to the elevators. Once they are alone, she says, "I hear you are a journalist. That's what I am studying. Who do you work for?"

"You can probably tell by my accent that I am Israeli. I am a freelance journalist focused on international finance."

"That is so awesome. I bet it is so exciting," she exclaims, leaning in.

The elevator opens to an entire floor that looks more like the Google campus than a college. There are very high ceilings with all kinds of seating areas and multilayered light wood circular walls. An entire wall reads "Adapt, Inspire, Question" with faces of famous leaders from history.

"This is our Entrepreneurial Center," she says. "It's pretty cool, isn't it?"

"Very cool."

"We have students taking classes, business owners who need mentoring, and wannabe entrepreneurs. The whole thing is about collaboration. There are also lofts for reflection and a community incubator for early-stage businesses. Maybe you can mention this in your article."

Avner can't help but smile at her enthusiasm and the fact that there will never be an article. "Maybe I will."

"Here comes Professor Lee. It was nice to meet you, Yosef."

"Nice to meet you also. Good luck with your career."

Professor Apple Lee is dressed in a conservative long, gray plaid skirt with flats and a sleeveless, black silk shirt. She has strong Asian features and shoulder-length black hair.

Dressed professionally and not the old lady I expected. In pretty good shape too.

She offers her hand. "You must be Yosef Mizrahi. Please follow me."

She leads him to an outdoor terrace with views of the campus and the river. He can see the skyline of downtown Tampa in the distance. He walks to the edge to see if he can spot anyone who looks out of place.

Beats where I work. Maybe I picked the wrong profession.

"Thank you for taking the time to meet with me, Professor Lee."

"Call me Apple. And while you're at it, why don't you tell me who you really are."

CHAPTER 42

On the inside, Avner's blood pressure spikes, but on the outside, he is as cool as they come. "I'm sorry, Apple, but whatever do you mean?"

"This isn't my first rodeo, Yosef—or whoever you are. I googled you, and I am an investigative writer in my spare time. I reached out to some of my contacts, and no one has ever heard of you." She pulls her phone out of her purse and searches the internet.

"There are some articles by you, but they feel forced. Not much depth. That getup isn't fooling me either. Your eyes give you away," she states. "Soldiers and government types always have the same hard eyes. My dad was Chinese intelligence before we escaped the country. He never lost those eyes."

"I can certainly provide references if it makes you feel better. As a financial journalist, I've made some enemies and need to write under an assumed name."

"You have the only reference I need. Agent Michaels asked me to talk to you, and I owe him a favor. So let's talk, but I am only saying so much until you tell me who you are," she insists, taking a seat at a patio table.

Stay in character and work through this. We need to know about this financial network.

"Do you mind if I record this?" asks Avner. He likes this lady. She is tough, smart, and intense. He checks for a ring and sees none. She would make a good spy.

"Knock yourself out."

Avner removes his cell phone and presses record on an app purchased that morning. "It is Sunday morning at ten AM. I am with Apple Lee, a professor at The University of Tampa." He pauses and checks his notes before continuing. "What made you write your book, *Wealth Defense: The Shadowy World of Wealth Inequality*?"

"China is a Communist country that allows capitalism, except when they decide not to. Different rules apply depending on your relationship with the government. My family wanted something different, so we immigrated to the United States to live in a place where everyone has a chance to be successful," she responds, slipping into teacher mode. "Don't get me wrong, it is much better here, but there is a widening gap between the rich and the poor. And there is an entire industry that is working to make that gap even wider."

"Who are these wealth defenders, and how do I find them?" presses Avner.

"They are everywhere. As the saying goes, follow the money. If you want to find them, you need to be around the super-rich," she answers, looking over his attire. "First, you need to fit in. Have your girlfriend take you shopping for some nice clothes. You will need to educate yourself on terms like family office, shell corporations, and tax havens. The wealth defenders use all of these and are paid billions to help the rich hide trillions."

"What does it matter, Apple? The rich have always had different rules."

"Let's go for a walk, and I'll try to explain it all."

They leave the patio and take the elevator to another floor, where they order matcha teas from a coffee shop. They walk to the Hillsborough River, where some students are studying and others are lying on blankets napping off a rowdy Saturday night. The water flows slowly and peacefully. A rowing crew works in unison to move their lightweight boat through the water.

Avner and Apple sit on a park bench underneath a tree. Students jog by, and a group starts up a volleyball game at a nearby sand court. They have a great view of downtown Tampa. The light shines off the glass buildings. A brief break before the nasty weather moves in.

"This place is really beautiful," observes Avner, looking around.

"Yes, these kids have no idea how lucky they are. The ironic thing is that many of their parents are the ones we are talking about."

Apple turns and looks Avner in the eye. "Before we go on, I need to know why we are having this conversation. Otherwise, I'm done."

"I have a friend who came across a situation. There appears to be a scam at a local bank where they are aiding in tax evasion."

Apple considers the comment and takes a sip of her tea. "That would not be surprising. Wealth defense is meaningless if the rich do not have somewhere to stash their money." She smiles and waves at a couple of students walking by.

"Is this something banks do in this country? Aren't there rules in place?"

"Of course. Banks have compliance departments and *Know Your Customer rules*, but it still happens. Research HSBC, Credit Suisse, and even JPMorgan Chase. They have all been fined for allowing this to go on," she says, pulling out her phone. She completes a quick search and hands it to Avner.

Lots of corruption around money. This might not be just a Safe Harbor problem. The biggest banks in the world have been caught breaking the rules.

"These are rich people running the banks, and they want their rich friends to bank with them, so they turn a blind eye. The Swiss were the worst, but the world cracked down on them, which allowed other countries to take a bite of the apple," she informs him.

"Again, what does it matter?" asks Avner. He realizes what a complex mess they have stepped into.

Apple points to the water. "Why don't you let me take you on a trip down the money river. Kurt Vonnegut wrote in *God Bless You, Mr. Rosewater*: 'The Money River, where the wealth of the nation flows. We were born on the banks of it—and so were most of the mediocre people we grew up with, went to private schools with, sailed and played tennis with. We can slurp from that mighty river to our hearts' content. And we can even take slurping lessons, so we can slurp more efficiently'." Apple spreads her hands toward the flowing current. "Kids like the students you see want access to the money river. They want what society tells them they need. If you work for the rich, you get access to money. Sooner or later, they want you to cross the line, and you want to stay on the banks of the river, so you do it," she says. "It is a cycle of corruption."

Avner slowly shakes his head. "That's how it ties into the Wealth Defense Industry."

"Yes, it is all interconnected. It is cancer spreading to widen the wealth gap between the rich and the poor. The rich keep getting richer, and everyone else keeps getting poorer. Do you see?"

As they talk, Avner notices two people coming down the sidewalk. Clearly, they do not belong. His hand moves toward his jacket expecting trouble.

"Hello, Avner, who is this pretty lady?" asks the approaching figure of Max. Orsu stands behind, glaring at them both.

"You two need to move on. You don't belong here," growls Avner.

Max starts to slowly tap his wrist. "Don't forget about our deal. You are running out of time."

"As I said, you need to move on," repeats Avner, patting his sports coat.

They start to walk by, but Max turns back for a moment. "Nice to meet you, Apple. Maybe we'll see each other again."

"Friends of yours?" Apple inquires. "At least I know your name now, Avner."

Son of a bitch. How did those two psychos find me? Now I've put this nice lady at risk. Need to be more diligent.

Avner stands. "Definitely not friends. Don't worry about those idiots. This is a lot of information, Apple. Can we walk? I suddenly want to get away from the river."

They walk the campus, and Apple educates Avner on the basics of hoarding wealth. They discuss the family offices that are set up to further insulate the wealthy from the rules. She explains the use of trusts and new synthetic trusts created to hide and transfer wealth to the next generation. In the simplest terms she can find, she describes tax havens and shell companies, along with the use of international wires coming from places like the Cook Islands and Monaco.

They finally make it back to Apple's office. It is small but elegantly decorated with a glass-top desk and several candles. One wall has a giant whiteboard with all sorts of notes written in beautiful cursive. Behind the desk are dozens of files piled high. On the desk is a Chinese juniper bonsai tree sitting in a square base with small rocks around the edge.

Perfectly manicured, just like Apple.

"It took a while, but I finally get it. When the rich do not pay their share of taxes, the burden shifts to everyone else," Avner concludes. "When there are not enough dollars to go around, social programs get cut. This is about the haves and the have-nots."

Apple slowly claps. "You have been listening. Now what are you going to do about it?"

"I need access to the rich to start breaking down the Wealth Defense Industry. This will help solve my friend's problem. How do I get that access?"

"Start tomorrow. There is a full-day conference for family offices and their agents of inequality at the Spencer House on Bayshore."

"Great, do I just show up and pay a fee?" asks Avner.

Apple laughs. "No chance. Something like that is invitation only. You are going to need to know someone in the one percent club, which does not include me. I am a well-known member of the Tax Equality Network. I am the enemy."

"Would a movie star with hundreds of millions do the trick?"

"That would do it, but remember you are walking into the wolves' den. You need to be prepared and play a better part than you did today. If even I realized you were not who you said you were, they will see through you in a second."

"I understand. Can I ask you something else?"

Apple nods.

"Have you ever heard of anything called *The One*?"

Apple frowns and walks around her desk to retrieve a file. "As a matter of fact, that is something I have been researching for a while."

"Everyone says it is fiction. What do you think?"

She ponders the question and lights a candle. It fills the room with the smell of jasmine.

"It might be, but I am not so sure. What if this somehow fits into the bigger picture? A jigsaw puzzle where the WDI is just one piece." She looks closely at her file and pulls a piece of paper out. "For instance, with the trillions the one percent have, is it so far-fetched that they could manipulate the stock markets? Could something more sinister exist that wants to expand the spread between the rich and poor? I am not there yet, but it is possible."

"You are a fascinating lady, Professor Lee. Maybe I could thank you with a glass of wine sometime?" Avner asks, offering his best smile. It is still not natural.

Apple looks at Avner with one eyebrow cocked and a slight smile. "Let's start with who you are—really."

He considers the request and knows it is best to stick to the script. "As those idiots said, my name is Avner. That is probably enough for now."

"Well, Avner, we'll see about the wine, but you need to realize one thing as you step into this world. It can get messy when you try and separate the super wealthy from their money. They may look like your grandfather and grandmother, but they will go to any extent to protect what they feel is theirs."

CHAPTER 43

Reluctantly, Morgan agrees to meet me. The offer of a great story is too much to resist. She is tough as nails and possibly trustworthy. I gave her some background and let her do her own due diligence. We select a public spot where I will pick her up, and I explain she must come alone. She makes no promises.

"Lia, what do you see?" I ask into the burner.

She is on the rooftop at the Element hotel on Water Street in downtown Tampa. Her disguise consists of a blonde wig, floppy hat, and baggy clothes that cover a baby bump she bought online. In her hands are tiny binoculars she uses to scan the area.

"I don't like this, Jay. We don't know this lady. If you need to talk to her, let me snatch her. You should not be taking this risk."

I am sitting in the pickup several blocks away wearing a baseball hat and dark glasses, pretending to read a magazine. People are strolling down the street on their way to enjoy coffee or brunch. Being out in public is stressful but necessary. Everyone who passes seems to look my way, but I am sure it is just my growing paranoia. "No way, Lia. This is my fight, and I am going to finish it. Do you see her? Anyone watching? I just need you to get her to me so I can tell her my story."

There is a pause. "Pretty woman on the corner in front of that restaurant Naked Farmer. Dark skin and braided hair. She has on sunglasses but is looking around and keeps glancing at her watch. No one appears to be watching her. I am going downstairs."

I start the engine and move a block closer so that I can see Morgan. I call her from the burner phone. She answers, and I tell her to follow five feet behind a pregnant lady in a floppy hat, who will lead her into a restaurant bathroom to change clothes.

Lia walks out of the hotel and past her without a word. Morgan follows into the restaurant as instructed. They both exit five minutes later. Lia now wears a baseball hat and a different dress with no bump. Morgan has on an ill-fitting sweat suit and wears a beret on her head.

They cross the street toward a new part of Water Street that is under construction and then disappear between two buildings. Seeing no one follow, I drive the truck to meet them.

Lia is frisking Morgan as I pull up, and she slips a pair of blackout goggles over her eyes. She pulls anti-noise headphones out of her backpack. She whispers something in Morgan's ear, puts the headphones on, and walks over to me.

I lower myself down from the truck and hug her, but she responds with only a quick peck on the lips.

"What's wrong?" I ask.

"I'm tired of being on the sidelines, and I think this is a bad idea," she says. "We should have waited for Avner, so we could scout the area properly. Why are you limping?"

Even pouting and mad, she is beautiful. "I will tell you the whole story tomorrow night. Thanks for doing this. Did you take her phone?"

"Yes, I searched her and took her purse. I really want to go with you."

"No, I'm not putting you at any more risk. By the way, what did you whisper in her ear?"

"I told her that you are the most important thing in the world to me, and if she hurts you in any way, I will hunt her down if it's the last thing I do."

"Well, that should certainly calm her anxiety," I respond.

Lia thaws a little, and we embrace. After I lay Morgan down in the truck, we say our goodbyes. I watch my wife walk away and feel a lump form in my throat, but I have a job to do.

After half an hour, we arrive at the trailer, and I lead Morgan into the house. I can feel her trembling and regret the drastic measures we employed, but this is life or death for me.

Once inside, I lower her into a chair and remove her headphones. I sit across from her and peel off the goggles. She takes a moment to let her eyes adjust.

"Hi, Morgan," I say. "I'm sorry about all of this."

She is having trouble breathing. "Hi, Morgan? Is that all you have to say? What the fuck, Jason? I agreed to listen to you, not all of this," she says, pointing around the trailer. "And who the hell was that terrifying lady? And where is my phone?"

I hand her a water. "I'm sorry, Morgan, but that was all necessary, and I think you will understand why. I promise you are safe now."

She takes several deep breaths and looks around before settling on my face. "Where are we, and why do you look like that?"

"Welcome to my home away from home. As I told you on the phone, I'm going to tell you everything. I am being set up by Safe Harbor Bank, and I need your help."

"Why me?" She gives me a skeptical look. "Why would you trust me? And why would I believe you?"

I rub my hands over my eyes. The exhaustion is wearing me down. "I think a Russian philosopher once said something like 'You can turn anyone into a monster in two weeks.' I've been isolated and on the run for a while. I think he is right. I need to end this soon, and my only real way out is to prove what Safe Harbor has been doing."

She sits up straighter. "I don't know what you expect me to do, but tell me what you know."

Here goes nothing. Either this is the best decision or possibly the worst, but time is running out.

I lead her over to the small table with the laptop and hand her a pen along with one of the legal pads. Her hand is still shaking, and I place mine over hers. "Morgan, you are in no danger from me. If you want to leave, I will take you home right now."

She pulls her hand away. "You have ten minutes," she says defiantly. "Let's hear what you have."

"As you know, I was a security officer at Safe Harbor. They have since fired me. Anyway, my IT specialist Scott came across some troubling information."

She starts scribbling notes. "Came across it how?"

"According to him, he accessed a system that was supposed to be hidden. He found a back door and started digging. We were both concerned with some things we were seeing in the Private Wealth Group."

"So he accessed it illegally?"

I consider the question. "If you access something that turns out to be illegal, are your actions illegal?"

"I am not the ethics police. I just want to make sure I have the story right."

For the next two hours, we walk through it all, and she makes no mention of leaving. I show her the database and the secret relationship notes. She gasps when she looks at the names from all over the world. We both pace around the trailer, and I show her the video of Sebastian Keller switching briefcases and his confession on the boat. There are times she glances at me out of the corner of her eye like I might already be the monster.

We take a break and sit on the deck to drink a couple beers. The sky is overcast, and the sun is completely hidden. The clouds look like characters from Greek mythology. Random gusts of wind shake the trailer.

"This story is unbelievable, Jason. I am going to summarize it back to you. Tell me if I have it correct."

I nod for her to go ahead and rub my throbbing leg. I hope the beer and some aspirin will help with the pain. I know I need to get the limb examined soon or some permanent damage could take place—if it hasn't already.

Morgan looks at her notepad and begins. "This appears to be a tax evasion scheme on a massive scale. Thousands of high-profile very rich people from around the world depositing billions into Safe Harbor Bank via complex wire transfers and, in some cases, cash handoffs." She stops to make sure I agree, and I nod. "The bank keeps records of the deposits in a separate system and then launders the money back in by depositing it into the accounts of fictitious companies. Thousands of small deposits to avoid reporting requirements."

She takes a drink of her beer and flashes me a smile for the first time. I can tell she is warming up and starting to believe.

"The bank takes a fee, but also takes ten percent and sends that money somewhere. That is the one hole. Where is it going?"

"That's the billion-dollar question," I respond. "Neither Scott nor I had the expertise to track it through the different offshore accounts. It is wired all over until it goes *poof*."

"Speaking of Scott, you believe that Safe Harbor hired a bunch of thugs to intimidate you, and they killed him. Then they tried to frame you for it."

I picture Scott in that pool of blood and nod. My failure to keep him safe still weighs heavy on my heart. I was not the hero he needed me to be, but I'm going to change that.

"Clients are introduced to the scheme through something called the Wealth Defense Network," she continues flipping through her notes. "Your Israeli agent friend is working that angle."

I look to the sky as the rain starts to come down in big, heavy drops. We go inside and sit on the couch.

"I think you have it all," I pronounce. "They are desperate to get the laptop back and cover up this entire fraud."

"What do you want me to do with all this?" Morgan asks. "Am I seriously supposed to tell the FBI that Terrance Browning, one of the most respected men in banking, is running one of the world's biggest tax schemes and is willing to kill to protect it?"

I turn to her. "I want you to research the companies the deposits are being laundered into and prove they are fake. Then I need you to meet with Agent Zeke Michaels and corroborate my story. Tell him you have seen all the information firsthand and that I am only turning myself in if I'm promised full immunity."

She laughs. "Is that all, Jason? Again, why would I put myself in the middle of this mess? And what if the thugs come after me?"

"Because you know what I've shown you is the truth. It will be a hell of a story for you, and I know you don't scare easy. You have seen worse than this firsthand. More importantly, I've been reading your work for years. I know you believe in doing the right thing for society, and together, we can put these liars and killers away for good."

She stands up. "It is time for me to go. I'll do some research. Call me tomorrow—assuming that lady gives me my stuff back. You know a hurricane may be headed this way. You can't stay in this tin box. Where are you going to go?"

On my list of problems, Mother Nature doesn't even make the top ten.

CHAPTER 44

Avner thinks he looks pretty good in the dark blue suit with a white shirt and red tie. He trims his beard to a five o'clock shadow and adds tortoiseshell glasses to the ensemble. Lia gels his hair back and reties his tie.

They tried to squeeze him into one of Jason's suits, but Lia said something about a "fat guy in a little coat" and laughed uncontrollably. Instead, she took him to a small studio where Jason had purchased his custom-made suits in the past. The price is exorbitant, but Lia said Avner needed at least one good suit anyway. She was paying, so he didn't care.

The tailor, who was also the owner, spent an hour looking at different fabrics and measuring him. He kept talking about the suit being made-to-measure, but Avner felt ridiculous with all the preening. His mind was on the conference he would be attending and on Apple Lee. He hoped Oak's contact was able to pull enough strings to get them in.

Lia, Oak, and he had spent the previous evening discussing the Wealth Defense Industry and how it might fit into Jason's plight. The members of this group appeared to be feeding clients to Safe Harbor Bank. They'd agreed that they needed to get into the Spencer House, and Oak had started working the phones. They confirmed the existence of the Family Office & Private Wealth Management Forum. The sponsor was something called Titan Financial Group.

Monday morning, Oak had received his invitation via e-mail and a call from someone named Sterling Kennedy. The man explained that he was CEO of Titan Financial Group, and he was excited to have Oak as part of the conference. He assured the movie star that he would not be bothered, and no one would ask for autographs. Oak let him know that his financial representative Yosef Mizrahi would be attending as well.

Avner descends the stairs in his custom-made suit and finds Oak dressed in a Pink Floyd T-shirt, jeans, and a pair of black-and-white-checked Vans.

"Why am I dressed like this, and why are you dressed like that?" asks Avner.

"One thing you need to understand, Avner, is that the rich dress however we like. Only our people dress up in suits and ties. And today, you are my people."

Avner's hands stretch in and out, and he rotates his neck to try and release the stress. Each side cracks loudly.

"I don't understand why I can't go as well," complains Lia. "I can put something nice on and be your girlfriend. Avner can be my people too," she says, as she and Oak laugh.

"Sorry, Lia, you're hot but too old to be on the arm of Oak Williams. Everyone knows how I roll. Everyone would know it is an act."

Lia raises her middle finger. "Never forget I am a trained sniper, asshole. All joking aside, I need to get out of this house. I am a sitting duck here. You know I can handle myself, but I need to be helping Jason also."

"I get it, Lia, but the FBI is all over you. Just sit tight for now. Oak, we need to get going," says Avner. "Did you go home and get the Mercedes?"

"I sure did; it is in the garage."

They walk through the house and into the garage. Sitting next to Lia's SUV is a bright yellow Lamborghini Aventador. Oak hits a button on his key fob, and the doors open like wings. It is a two-seater with black interior and yellow trim. The word Lamborghini is stitched into the dash.

"What the fuck is this? I told you to be conservative, not get a yellow rocket."

Oak wipes a smudge off the sloping front of the car. "As I said, let me handle being rich, and you handle whatever it is you do."

****

Zeke and Gloria spend the day following Lia. Zeke does not believe that she is just a concerned wife. She is either assisting Jason or maybe even in on the blackmail plot. The longer Jason stays on the run, the more the FBI agent doubts his innocence.

For the first time, Lia makes no obvious attempts to escape their tail. The day is rather uneventful, with a trip to the mall and the post office. After getting her nails done, she pulls into the parking lot of Chase Bank and spends twenty minutes inside. She nonchalantly strolls out and drives away.

"Let's go see what she was up to," proposes Zeke.

They enter the branch and ask to see the manager. A young man dressed in a Chase polo shirt warmly welcomes them. "Good afternoon. What can I help you with?"

"Is there somewhere we can talk that's a little more private?" asks Zeke.

They walk to a glassed-in office in the corner of the branch, and the manager offers them a seat. The man's computer is turned away from them to stop prying eyes. The room smells like curry, and he throws the rest of his lunch into the trash.

"Thank you for visiting our branch today. My name is Brian. What can we do for you today? We have some great specials on twelve-month CDs, Mr. and Mrs....?" The man looks to them expectantly.

Zeke laughs out loud, and Gloria scowls at him. They both produce their badges and Zeke states, "We are certainly not a couple. My name is Agent Michaels, and this is Agent Chavez. We are with the FBI."

Brian's eyes widen, and he sits up straighter. A light glaze covers his forehead. "The FBI? Is there something wrong?"

"We just need a little information on a customer who just walked out."

"I am sorry, Agent Michaels. You know I can't provide information on a customer. You would need a subpoena for that. We have very strict rules regarding customer privacy."

Zeke stares at the nervous young man. "I understand the law, but I am sure you want to help us, since this could be a national security issue. Maybe we can start with something basic. The customer who just walked out is named Lia Miles. Can you confirm she has an account here?"

Brian rubs his chin while he considers the options. "I'll look it up, but I can't give balances or information on loans or anything like that." He types on his computer and looks confused. "You must be mistaken; we don't have a customer named Lia Miles."

"Could she have just cashed a check or received cash?" asks Gloria.

"Not if she doesn't bank with us."

"This is important. Can you just ask whoever helped this lady what her name is?" Zeke pulls out a picture of Lia.

The young man smiles, and his cheeks turn red. "I wouldn't forget her, if you know what I mean. I helped her myself."

"I know what you mean. Her name would really help."

Brian looks around and says quietly, "That is Mary Smith. She needed a bunch of cash."

Zeke and Gloria thank him and exit the branch quickly. "I want you to retrace all her steps from today and show her picture around. Jason and Lia are getting ready to run."

CHAPTER 45

After an exhilarating high-speed drive to the club that has Avner gripping anything he can to hold on to, Oak pulls up the long driveway a little too fast. A young man wearing a black uniform jumps to attention. Oak releases the doors of the Lambo, and they step out.

The man's eyes widen. "Holy shit, you're Oak Williams," he stammers.

Oak hands him a $100 bill and tells him not to scratch the car.

The Spencer House is a private social club located on Bayshore Boulevard across the street from the water. If a person isn't looking for it, they would drive right by, which is exactly what the members want. It is set back from the road and blocked by tall hedges. The main house has been restored into a beautiful white colonial.

The property has multiple buildings and a gorgeous water feature running down the middle with shooting fountains and manicured hedges. It is made to feel like a trip to Europe without having to board a plane.

Avner lets out a low whistle. "Look at this place. An escape for the one percent of society from real life. This is our chance to find out how the wealthy live and their strategies to avoid paying their fair share."

A beautiful long-haired blonde greets Avner and Oak at the

entrance of the main house. She has her hair pulled back into a ponytail and wears librarian frames. Her skirt is short, but not too short. She is attractive enough to make the old men sneak a peek, but conservative enough not to have the ladies hate her.

"Mr. Williams and Mr. Mizrahi, please follow me and I will get you over to the meeting room."

They follow her under an arched walkway made of gleaming white stone. Every few feet, there are large pots that hold perfectly shaped round plants. Expensive black lights hang from the ceiling. Up ahead, they can see a fountain shooting water into the sky.

The blonde leads them to a main building and past a sign that reads "Wealth Management Event, Sponsored by Titan Financial." They receive name tags and a swag bag full of high-end items including a watch, a money clip, and some information about the sponsor. A waiter in formalwear hands them each a mimosa. Oak tosses his back and then grabs Avner's drink as well.

The room is large with a stage in front. A lectern sits between two tall plants. Padded chairs have been set up in rows, and a Muzak version of the Foo Fighters' *"Everlong"* plays softly. The room smells like magnolias and old lady perfume. The audience is a mix of casually dressed older men and women joined by serious-looking folks wearing expensive dark suits. A buffet that offers fruit, muffins, and coffee has been set up against the wall

The blonde says, "I'd like to introduce you to Sterling Kennedy, Titan's CEO, if you have a minute."

"Sure," responds Avner, as Oak piles a small plate high with strawberries, blueberries, and mango.

Avner leans into Oak and whispers, "This is the guy we want to meet. If Apple is right, he can give us access to the Wealth Defenders."

In less than ten seconds, the blonde woman leads a man their way. He is tall and thin and bears a striking resemblance to John F. Kennedy. He wears a dark blue suit, and in his jacket is a simple white pocket square. A small platinum T is pinned to his jacket. It matches a pair of platinum cuff links. His thick salt-and-pepper hair is parted on the left.

"Mr. Williams and Mr. Mizrahi, thank you for joining us. My name is Sterling Kennedy, but I am not one of *those* Kennedys." His stiff laugh shows off large white teeth. "We are thrilled to have such a distinguished actor on hand today."

"Nice to meet you, Sterling," replies Oak in a somewhat bored tone. "This is my guy, Yosef."

"Nice to meet you, Yosef. I am looking forward to spending some time with you both today. If you will excuse me, I am up first on the stage. If you need anything, one of the team will take care of it."

"Sounds good." Avner makes a show of thanks.

Avner spends the next twenty minutes roaming the room and talking to the other attendees, while Oak eats at the buffet. Many of the attendees are in their sixties or seventies and either have, or are interested in creating, a family office. Most have financial people with them who either manage their money or run their office. Avner thinks other attendees seem more interested in the free muffins and coffee.

Only Avner's closest friends ever knew he'd grown up with people just like this. His father had come from wealth and was an arrogant bully who used his money to demean others, including his family. After years of butting heads with his father and being kicked out of several boarding schools, Avner was ultimately disowned and never spoke to his parents again.

Finally, the lights are lowered, and the music becomes louder. A voice emits through speakers on each side of the stage. "Please welcome our host and CEO of Titan Financial Group, Sterling Kennedy."

The man they met earlier takes the stage and is greeted with a polite round of applause.

"Thank you so much, ladies and gentlemen. My name is Sterling Kennedy, but not one of *those* Kennedys," he says, and the crowd responds with some muffled laughter. "It is an honor to be with you today to talk about that thing that makes the world go round—money. And if you are in this audience, you already have plenty of it."

Same dumb joke and staged smile. This guy is fake as they come. My parents would have loved him. Avner crosses his arms as the man continues his presentation.

Sterling Kennedy takes the microphone from the lectern and begins moving around the stage. He is clearly comfortable as the center of attention. "The question is, how do you keep what's yours?" he asks, pausing for effect. "We're going to talk about dynastic wealth. We are going to talk about wealth preservation. We are going to talk about tax avoidance. But before we do that, I want you to join me in a little mantra."

He moves down the steps and closer to the crowd. "When you have your financial house in order, you can live off the interest. Your heirs can live off the interest, and their heirs can live off the interest." Several in the crowd clap. "The thing you cannot do is touch the principal. I want to hear from you: 'Don't touch the principal, don't touch the principal.'"

Before Avner knows it, all one hundred people in attendance are chanting together. Even Oak has joined them in the mantra and winks at Avner, who feels like he has entered a bizarre universe. He hears an elderly woman next to them tell what looks like her twin sister "He is very handsome!"

"That was amazing. If you don't learn anything else today, make sure you remember to never touch the principal The question is, how do you accomplish that goal?" Sterling probes.

He walks back to the lectern and reconnects the microphone. He lets the question settle in for thirty seconds. "It starts with a family office, an organization dedicated to your family's wealth preservation and management. At Titan, we specialize in forming your family office, or admitting you to our multi-family office."

He holds up a pamphlet in his right hand. "The criteria are simple. If you have $150 million or more in assets, a family office makes financial sense. If you have as little as $25 million or greater, you can be part of our multi-family office."

Avner leans over to Oak. "Good to know the poor people with only $25 million have somewhere to go."

"Here is the plan for today," Sterling resumes. "We are going to have experts on subjects such as trusts, why you always want to incorporate your limited liability company in Delaware, how to avoid that nasty estate tax, and in general, how to defend your hard-earned income from the government."

He waves the brochure again. "We'll make sure you have one of these. We are also going to talk about setting up your families for the next hundred years and beyond. And we are going to feed you a world-class lunch and finish the day in the bar for some cocktails. There will be representatives from Titan available to answer any questions. Now who is ready to get started?"

After slightly louder applause from the crowd, the first speaker takes the stage. He goes on and on about the evils of the estate tax, sometimes called the "death tax," and ways to avoid it. He finishes by saying that no one in the room should ever pay the estate tax, and Titan will show you how to circumvent it.

Avner leans over to Oak again and whispers in his ear, "How much money do you have?"

"On me?" Oak pats his pockets.

"No, you idiot. Do you have enough for your own family office? I need to know how to play this out."

"Yes, Avner, I have enough for several family offices."

The next speaker is an attorney who discusses using art and wine as a place to store wealth. He moves on to trusts and shell companies used to shield an individual's identity from the public. And finally, he talks about something called a synthetic trust that can help people avoid many forms of taxation.

The conference adjourns for lunch at noon, and the elite are moved to the onsite restaurant for a five-course meal that includes lobster salad and key lime pie. Avner and Oak make small talk at their table before slipping outside.

"What so you think so far?" Avner asks.

"I think I need to sign up with these people and protect my principal. What do you think? Does this have anything to do with Jason and Safe Harbor?"

"I think groups like Titan are involved, but this feels like something bigger. This feels like the separation of the wealthy from everyone else, and it could all play into things somehow."

He looks around and nods at Sterling strolling toward them. "We need to get this guy alone."

"Let me handle that," proposes Oak with a wink.

"Yosef and Oak. Do you have a minute?" asks Sterling. "How are you enjoying yourselves so far?"

"Great information," remarks Avner.

Oak steps closer to Sterling. "Listen, I have Yosef and a team of accountants and lawyers who know about all these things. What I am interested in is a more aggressive strategy. Do you have somewhere private we can talk?"

CHAPTER 46

Sterling leads them through a courtyard to an entrance for the men's card room. The walls are painted dark green with black-and-white framed photos hung throughout. A fully stocked bar sits underneath a television, and a Brunswick pool table with a dark blue surface is in the corner with the balls racked. It smells strongly of tobacco, despite a sign asking members not to smoke.

Avner checks the room for exits and weapons. He does not like being unarmed, and this guy has his fur up.

Two exits, and pool cues within reach. Could easily beat this skinny guy with a stick if need be. Could also throw the pool balls into someone's face.

Sterling points to one of the tables and offers them a drink. Avner passes but Oak asks for a beer.

"When you say aggressive, what do you mean?" inquires Sterling as they all sit. He unbuttons his jacket and interlaces his fingers on his lap.

"Sterling, I make $20 million every time I do a movie, and sometimes, I can crank out two in a year. I am tired of giving it all away to Uncle Sam and every damn state and country I work in."

He takes a long pull from his beer. "Let me give you an example. I have a condo here, but my home is Los Angeles. The state of California has a twelve-and-a-half percent state tax for rich people, and now they have passed a four percent tax on home sales over $5 million and five percent for over $10 million. You know what you can buy for under $5 million in La La Land?"

"No, what?" responds Sterling with a smirk and his hands up.

"Not a damn thing. They call it the LA Mansion Tax. I was selling one of my homes that was worth $6 million and going to get hit by this bullshit tax. What I mean by aggressive is what my Realtor told me to do."

He takes another drink and starts talking louder and faster. He leans in and says, "He said to sell the house for $4.9 million and the furniture for another $1 million. Tax avoided."

"Sounds like a smart guy," asserts Sterling.

"He is. Dude is part of something he called the Wealth Defense Network. Helps the rich navigate the available loopholes to keep their money in their own pockets. That is aggressive, and that is what I am looking for."

You are doing a great job, Oak. Keep sinking the hook in even further.

"Got it," replies Sterling. "What role do you play in this, Yosef? You look like you could be security."

Avner looks to Oak, who nods his approval to answer. "As Oak told you earlier, I handle his affairs. He makes the money, and I work with my team to grow it, along with organizing his hectic life. If I must handle security, I can do that also."

Avner moves closer to Sterling and drops his voice lower. "Quite honestly, it is obscene what he pays to others. We have a team, but they only talk about tax efficiency. We want to talk about tax strategies for avoidance. As you can probably tell, I am Israeli, so we have been investigating some international investing as well."

Sterling gets up and walks to the bar. He makes a show of reviewing several bottles before pouring himself a scotch. He pulls out his cell phone and sends a text. After a sip, he loosens his tie and rejoins them.

Two large security types enter the room. Avner stands defensively and notices a bulge under each of their jackets. "What is this about?"

"Relax, Yosef. You want to talk real business, we need to check you both out. A quick look for wires, or you can simply leave the conference."

Avner signals for Oak to stand, and they are both thoroughly searched. One of the men says, "Clean," and they leave the room.

"Was that really necessary?" asks Avner.

Sterling puts his hands behind his head and spreads his elbows wide. "Better safe than sorry. Okay, fellas. Let's talk business. What you are hearing today is the cookie-cutter stuff, but Titan works with the elite to defend their money from taxation. We know the line and walk very close to it."

Avner barely restrains a grunt. *Same arrogance as my dad. Condescending and obnoxious, but smart and careful. Let's hear it, slimeball.*

"We have people in the IRS who feed us information daily on their priorities and tools. We are always one step ahead. We make the richest people in the world look like they own very little."

Oak lifts his beer and clinks Sterling's glass. "I like what I am hearing, but what about the banks? They are so regulated that they need to report everything to the government. They report everything—the size of the deposits, where they come from, who owns each account. What do they call that, Yosef?"

"Beneficial ownership."

"Yep, that's it. Every account you open, they are so far up your ass that they can see out your mouth."

Sterling smiles widely. "Don't worry about the banks. We know who's on the team and who is not. You even have some right here on the West Coast of Florida who play ball."

"Such as?" Avner raises one eyebrow.

Sterling shakes his head. "You don't get it all on the first date. We also work with the international banks. Think about the Cayman

Islands, Monaco, Luxemburg, and even Canada."

For the next forty-five minutes, Sterling takes them on a tour of dark money throughout the world. The use of shell companies, offshore accounts, and Delaware LLCs. Setting up trusts in South Dakota and using straw men in luxury real estate purchases. He is smart enough to speak in generalities and examples in case he needs to deny the conversation. As he drinks, his hands become more active, and he touches Oak and Avner on their arms.

Sterling stands and concludes by saying, "Gentlemen, the government can't tax what it can't find. Think of Titan *AS* the Wealth Defense Network. We have connections you can't even imagine. We pool millions with billions and turn it all into trillions. We not only move markets, we own the markets."

"I like what I hear, Sterling. I want to build a dynasty that carries on forever. Get with Yosef and figure it out."

They all shake hands, and Avner accepts Sterling's business card. In return, he gives him one that simply reads "Yosef" and a cell number.

Sterling finishes his drink and pops a breath mint into his mouth. He buttons his top button, reties his tie, and struts out the door.

Avner stares after him. *The master of the universe makes his grand exit. He has no idea the first domino just fell.*

Avner and Oak walk to the valet stand. They have learned all they need to know for the moment. The Wealth Defense Industry is real.

As they slide into the Lamborghini, Avner says to Oak, "You were pretty damn good back there."

Oak puts on a pair of Cartier sunglasses and turns to face Avner. "Well, I *am* an actor."

****

Terrance feels the buzzing in his jacket. He excuses himself from the board meeting and walks out onto the balcony. Looking over Tampa Bay and the approaching storm, he answers the burner phone. "Go ahead."

A female voice says, "They are getting closer to you. Jason's friends are asking about Wealth Defense. This is just a warning. They are putting more of the puzzle pieces together."

Before Terrance can say anything, the woman hangs up.

He curses under his breath and moves inside to his egg.

CHAPTER 47

Avner is the first to arrive at nine PM. He is driving an older model tan Ford Explorer, which he parks behind the trailer next to my truck. I go out to meet him and help him carry in several bags of groceries and three large pizzas. The smell of meat and melted cheese makes my mouth start to water.

"Look at you," I say. "New hairdo and shaved-down beard. You almost look handsome. What's up?"

"Don't get used to it. I look ridiculous, but it was worth it. You'll hear all about it tonight."

This is the chance for all of us to finally get together and compare notes. A lot has taken place, and we need to formalize a plan to end this drama.

He tosses me a small bottle of pills from the pharmacy. "Some antibiotics to help with your leg."

The constant waves of rain have cooled the air and allowed me to keep some windows open. I spent most of the day making notes on the data from Scott and talking to Morgan. When my eyes started burning from staring at the computer screen, I took a break to finish cleaning. The trailer almost looks presentable and smells better than it did.

"I like what you have done with the place," comments Avner sarcastically.

"I figured I might be here a while, so I did my best."

Avner removes his sports jacket to reveal his shoulder holster and Glock. He usually removes his weapon when we are together, but not tonight. He paces in the kitchen, pumping his powerful forearms up and down. He goes to the fridge and grabs us both a beer.

"Are you okay?" I ask.

I'm not used to Avner being so antsy. Maybe the stress is getting to all of us.

"Of course. I am just worried about Lia and Oak getting over here clean. You are a popular guy. Lots of folks out there looking for you. Your picture is everywhere."

He takes a long drink of his beer and pulls the drapes back to look out the window. His eyes dart back and forth over the property.

"Lia is a pro. She's probably better than you at losing a tail."

"She was a pro. It has been a long time, Jason. You've turned my diamond into a yuppie housewife."

I smile at the thought of Lia as a housewife. That is not how I would describe her. She still has a tough edge. It is just hidden behind makeup and pretty clothes.

"Here come headlights. If it is not them, let's be ready for anything."

A black Ford F-150 Raptor cautiously approaches. I have seen Oak drive it a few times over the years, but it looks to be jacked up even higher on large knobby wheels. It is entirely blacked out, including the grill and rims. Oak calls it his "everyman" truck. I remind him that not every man drives a $125,000 truck.

I feel nervous to see Lia—like it is our first date. I have butterflies in my stomach and can feel my pulse race.

I run the best I can on my bad leg down the steps and around the trailer to meet them. Oak is out first, and I give him a big hug. He laughs loudly looking at my appearance. I cleaned up the best I could. I wear black jeans and a gray T-shirt with my Glock pressed close. I shaved my beard back to a goatee and kept the dark-framed glasses.

"Who the fuck are you?" he asks, stepping back to look me over. "Dude, where is your hair?"

"When in Rome…" I give him another hug. "Welcome to my new casa. Go on in. Avner has some beers in the fridge."

He leans in close enough that I can smell his cologne and maybe a hint of weed. He barely moves his lips when he says, "Hey, Jay-Bird, remember, I need to talk to you alone."

"I know. But right now, I need to see my wife."

Oak nods and walks away, eyeing the trailer suspiciously.

I turn my attention to Lia. She opens the truck door and steps down on the platform to bridge the three-foot gap to the ground. She is stunning, and my heart skips a beat, even though her hair is pulled back and she is wearing almost no makeup.

"Don't just stand there. Help me down from this ridiculous monster truck."

I offer her my hand and feel a jolt of electricity as we touch. Once she is on the ground, I enfold her in a long, deep embrace. She steps back and looks me over.

"You really were listening all those years ago. You look like another person."

My cheeks blush a little. Appearing like this in front of Lia is embarrassing, but I appreciate that she approves of my transformation. I want her to know that I can handle this.

"I know I look ridiculous."

She tilts her head. "I don't know, I think you look kind of sexy, Jay. Kind of dangerous."

I pull her in tight and breathe in her scent. I am relieved when she hugs me back just as tightly. I take her hand. "Come on around the front. Avner is already here."

We join the others inside. They have already opened the pizza boxes and put out paper plates. I pick up my untouched beer, and Lia walks around inspecting the trailer.

"This is a total shithole, Jay-Bird," declares Oak as he shoves a piece of veggie pizza into his mouth. "When I was a kid, we lived in places like this. You remember?"

"Yeah, not exactly the Ritz Carlton," I agree.

"It's perfect," argues Avner. "No one would ever think to search out here in the middle of nowhere. It's not that bad. Lia and I worked out of worse."

Lia grabs water from the fridge. I cannot not stop staring at her, and I wish we were alone. It has been a while since we were intimate, and I've been dreaming about it in those few hours I have slept.

"That is true. This is fine, but we need to figure out a solution to this situation and get Jay back home," insists Lia.

"Did you two get here clean?" asks Avner. "That truck is not exactly inconspicuous."

"We're good. We found a transmitter on both the vehicles that the FBI left behind when they raided the house. We dropped one off at a convenience store to give those guys something to do," Lia responds as she takes a bite of pizza. She pulls the slice away, and the cheese stretches for several inches before breaking. "We drove around for an hour looking for a tail. Finally, we switched vehicles and drove that beast over here. Trust me, we're clean, and it was either the truck or that yellow Lamborghini."

"You know this is my everyman truck," states Oak proudly.

"Did you say the FBI raided our house?" I can feel my jaw clenching.

"They had a warrant and searched the house yesterday. They towed away your Tesla just to be assholes." Lia looks directly at me. "Thought they'd hit pay dirt when they found the safe upstairs. I had Avner debug the house after they left, and we threw all the transmitters into the bay. We assume they are listening anyway."

I feel my temperature rise despite the coolness in the trailer. The thought of Zeke and his team harassing Lia and going through our things makes me crazy. I crack my knuckles and take a deep breath before realizing that I am rubbing my pinky.

Lia notices and reaches for my hand. "It is okay, Jay. They are just doing their job. I knew they would come sooner or later. I was prepared."

We sit around the table and eat while catching up. It feels normal for a while, as Oak talks about what a great movie this would make. He would play the main role but could never look as silly as I do. He wants his own gun, which we all agree is a horrible idea.

Finally, Avner says, "I know this is great to see each other, but the longer we are here, the more risk there is for Jason. We need to make a game plan to get him out of this."

"Let me start." I put my plate down. "First of all, thanks for everything you have done. I never wanted to upset our lives and put you all at risk, but I need to see this through. Not only is there something illegal going on, but they killed Scott over it. I am playing this out to the end, but I need to do it on my own after tonight. I would never forgive myself if something happened to any of you."

"That is ridiculous, Jason," objects Avner. "We are a team and here for you."

"That is right, Jay-Bird. All for one and all that shit," Oak adds, as he pulls an envelope out of his pocket. "I brought you some cash in case you are running low."

I thank him and stick the envelope in my back pocket. I have plenty of money for the moment but know it could get tight.

"Jay, what have you found out so far, and what is the end game?" Lia gazes at me curiously. "Avner and Oak have been busy and need to update you as well."

I pull out my notebook and power up the laptop. "Okay, I have been working exclusively on this for days—except for cleaning and getting pretty for you all. I know a few things. There are thousands of high-net-worth individuals involved in this scam." I start moving through the spreadsheet, pointing to certain names. Oak seems to cringe as I advance through the list.

"We're talking about businesspeople, athletes, politicians, and a lot of people you would know. Even some actors, Oak. Many seem to have been recruited by something called the Wealth Defense Network. We need to find out more about this group."

"We've been on that over the last couple days," Avner informs me. He fills me in on Apple Lee, the conference at the Spencer House, and Sterling Kennedy. I am speechless.

The magnitude of the scheme is overwhelming. So complex with so many players involved. An onion with layer after layer of rot.

"That is going to take some time to process, but it makes sense. There is another term that keeps coming up. Something called *The One*. Has anyone ever heard of this before?"

Lia jumps in first. "I've heard of it. They are a fictional group that has supposedly been around for the last hundred years. It is an old wives' tale."

"Are you sure?" I ask. "I think that is where some of the money is going."

"Definitely not." Lia shakes her head. "This is boogeyman stuff. It's assumed to be a group of rich people attempting to take over governments throughout the world with the plan of creating one unified regime."

This doesn't sound like Lia. It is like she is trying to sell us on her way of thinking. Sounds like she is reading from a script. But why?

"They want one source of currency and leadership. Supposedly, they have people everywhere and are trying to topple weak countries, and they allegedly already have ties to Putin and other bad guys. They specialize in chaos and misinformation. But this is all bogus. It goes way back—before Hitler and Mussolini."

"I think it exists," offers Oak.

This night is getting stranger and stranger. There must be a full moon. Why does Oak know about The One?

"What makes you think so?" I inquire.

He avoids eye contact. "I could just see a bunch of wealthy, crazy people trying something like that. That's all."

"I am not sure I've ever said this, but I agree with Oak," concurs Avner. "I talked to Apple Lee about it, and she wasn't so sure it was fantasy. And she is one smart lady, and pretty good-looking."

We all turn to look at Avner. He blushes for just a moment and looks away.

"I am glad you are working on your social life while the world hunts for me," I reply with thick sarcasm. "There is something else. All those years ago in Israel, I think Dr. Levi mentioned *The One*." I shake my head to try and remember precisely. "I've buried that night so deep that I can't be sure."

Oak stands up and walks to the window. "This is all insane. Organized crime, tax fraud, and murder. What the hell are you going to do, Jay-Bird?"

I tell everyone about Morgan and the time we've spent together. "I'm going to keep researching and have Morgan talk to Zeke. They might trust a third party, and then I can make a deal with the FBI."

"Do you really think they will give you immunity?" asks Lia.

How does Lia know I am asking for immunity? The only one who knows that is Morgan.

We talk for another hour and agree it is best if everyone leaves. It is heartbreaking to watch Lia go. I reaffirm my vow to do the right thing, avenge Scott's death, and get back home to my wife. Most importantly, I will do it on my own, proving my worth and no longer putting my friends at risk. The hero's journey.

They all disagree with this part of my plan, but it isn't negotiable. I will see them on the other side of this mess, and we'll only talk on our burners from now on. Oak continues to tell me he needs to talk, and I promise to give him a call first thing in the morning. I have bigger problems to deal with.

CHAPTER 48

It feels good to have a plan, but I need to figure out how to strike a deal with Zeke without spending the rest of my life in prison. I am hopeful Morgan will be able to persuade him that the proof exists. I may need a lawyer working on my behalf as well, but I am not sure that is a smart move. I am not thinking clearly after so little sleep and so much stress. The antibiotics and beers are also leaving me a little spacey.

I clean the trailer and take out the trash. It is a cool night, so I sit on the porch smoking a cigar that Avner slipped me when Lia wasn't watching. I need to know more about the Wealth Defense Industry and how it fits in with *The One*. This feels bigger than Safe Harbor Bank. Something is going on behind the scenes. I respect Lia's opinion, but as Avner said, she has been out of the game for a long time.

Despite my fears, I try to think back to all those years ago, sitting tied up in front of Dr. Levi. Had he said something about *The One*? I'm just not sure. That time seems so fuzzy in my memory, and I rarely allow myself to think back. It is also possible I am going nuts. My world has been turned upside down. Maybe this is just a greedy bank helping rich people get richer and skimming money off the top, nothing more than that.

Would they really have killed Scott just over money?

After finishing my cigar, I try to get some sleep, but my mind is racing. I think about ways to get out of this mess, but most of the time, my thoughts just come back to Lia. I miss her so much and wonder if she feels the same. She whispered in my ear before leaving that she would still run away with me if I asked her to. Maybe she is the one who needs to run away from the life we've built.

****

Max, Orsu, and their team of eight park in a ditch one hundred yards from the trailer. They arrive in three vehicles, covering the final distance without headlights. The tip on the location came in, and they immediately mobilized. Max looks at his watch and notes that it is nearly three in the morning. Terrance gave them strict orders not to kill Jason Miles. They are simply to retrieve the laptop and bring him to the safe house.

Max has every intention of roughing him up—or watching as Orsu throws the guy around like a rag doll. The silly banker has caused a lot of trouble, and this job is getting old. There is more money to be made in other parts of the world where they don't have so many laws to navigate.

The team is heavily armed, wearing tactical gear and the newest night vision goggles. Max thinks it is overkill, but Terrance and his masters want no mistakes. He looks around and appreciates his prey going to such a remote location. It will be much easier to grab and transport their target without a chance of running into anyone else.

He signals with his hand for the group to move through the darkness. They all have military backgrounds and have worked together for a long time. No words are needed. Through a small thatch of trees, they can see the trailer. Max checks the pasted-on house numbers and confirms this is where Jason is hiding. *What a shithole*, he thinks.

The team spreads out, each carrying their weapon in position to administer deadly force if needed. Four men move to the back door and four to the front. Max gestures to Orsu to kick in the door. It crumbles as if made of cardboard. Another one of the team throws a flash-bang grenade into the trailer. They move in as one, while the other team breaches the back.

****

At two forty-five AM, I give up on sleep and decide to find somewhere open all night where I can get some coffee. As always, I pack up the laptop to take with me but hide the duffel bag under the sink. I have Oak's envelope in my pocket and will be back in a short while. As I walk out the door, I think about my other late-night trip to a convenience store and grab the Glock just in case.

I pull out the back of the property through an exit someone had made that leads to a dirt road. The opening is only big enough for my truck and is overgrown with trees, grass, and weeds, but I make it through. Avner suggested I always use this back road, just in case.

I drive a couple miles before I find an all-night convenience store. It is simply called La Bodega. I park on the side of the building and walk in carrying my backpack. It is completely empty except for a half-asleep teenager behind the counter.

"Coffee?" I ask.

He points to the back, where there is a pot of old brown liquid on a burner. It is not exactly Starbucks, but beggars can't be choosers. I pour a large cup and pay with cash.

I retrace my way back to the trailer and extinguish the lights as I turn onto the dirt road. As I approach, the hairs on my arms stand up, and I stop the truck. There are lights on inside the trailer and shapes moving throughout.

****

Within seconds, they clear the small trailer, but it is empty. It smells like cigar smoke and pizza. They just missed him. Max curses and punches his hand through the bathroom door.

"Rip this place apart and bag up everything," he yells.

It takes them only a few minutes to find a duffel bag and a few other items, but no Jason and no laptop. The night is a failure, and Terrance will not be happy.

Max says, "Go get the vehicles, and burn this place to the ground."

****

As quietly as I can, I exit the truck and watch through the forest as several bodies move around in my temporary home. I can hear things being smashed and someone yelling at the others. After several minutes, eight large men walk out led by Max. He directs three men back away from the property, and they return with their vehicles.

One massive man opens the trunk to his vehicle and lifts out a can of gasoline. He starts pouring it onto the old trailer. I reach for my Glock. It makes me feel confident and in control, but I realize I am outmanned and know they are much more heavily armed than me. It strikes me that everything I own besides Oak's cash, the gun, and the laptop are inside.

When the structure and surrounding weeds are doused, Max lights a rag and throws it onto the porch. The place goes up in flames, which spread quickly. Black smoke billows up out of the old structure, and the pungent smell of burning plastic fills the air. Even from so far away, I can feel the heat. The fire is sizzling and cracking. The old trailer slowly surrenders to the fire.

Max motions the group back into their cars, and they drive out the front entrance.

I sit watching the dancing flames, knowing I need to leave before the police and firefighters are called. *This must be part of my journey*, I think, watching the old place go up in a dark cloud along with all my possessions in the world.

And then it hits me. Only three people in the world know where I am. One of the few people I trust has sold me out.

CHAPTER 49

I am overcome with sadness and despair as I drive away from the burning old trailer. I simply cannot believe Avner, Oak, or Lia has forsaken me. It is impossible. These are the three closest people in my life. There must be another explanation.

I also know I need to get far away from Thonotosassa as soon as possible and find a different vehicle. All my former friends know I have the old truck, and it could have a tracker on it.

Salty tears stream out of my eyes. I can't help it, and I don't care.

I am alone now. Maybe I should toss the laptop off a bridge and go down with it.

I drive south until I weave my way to Falkenburg Road, where I can connect to the exit for Interstate 275. I sit at a traffic light and watch an electronic billboard advertising a local Cajun restaurant. It then changes to a dentist with super-white teeth advertising Invisalign. Then, to my horror, my face pops on. At least my old face. It is under the words "Wanted for Murder."

Instinctively, I slink down in the seat. It seems impossible, but things have gotten worse. Not that long ago, I had the world by the tail, and now it is closing in. Things can change in an instant.

The light turns, and I move quickly to the exit and head southwest. If there is one place someone can get lost, it is the beach. Everyone thinks of sunburned vacationers, but there is an underbelly in many beach communities that includes drifters, fugitives, and lost souls. I check all those boxes now. There are also a bunch of used car places where I can hopefully trade the truck in for another beater.

The old truck does have a radio, so I turn it on to try and calm my brain. The only channel that comes in is country music, which seems appropriate. Tim McGraw sings something about grown men not crying, and I know that isn't true as tears continue to drip down my face. My life is basically a sad country song, except my dog hasn't run away. I am sure if I had one, it would.

I feel like I might have a panic attack, and I try some deep breathing. I drink the disgusting coffee, even though it has turned cold. My head is pounding, and my vision is blurry. I need to find a safe haven where no one can find me, and I need a new look.

An hour later, I arrive in Treasure Island. It is just another Tuesday at the beach. It is a typical beach town with some beautiful hotels but also several daily and hourly motels. Before I check in to one, I need to address the car situation and change my look, but nothing is open yet. I park at the public beach access lot and walk through the picnic tables and outdoor showers toward the water. Several people are sleeping on the sand, and I wonder if that will be me soon.

I remove my shoes and start toward the water. The sand feels cold on my feet, and there is a warm breeze in the air. The radio reported that the tropical storm turned into a hurricane as it passed over the Bahamas. It is still expected to head up the West Coast of Florida, which just adds to my problems. For now, the smell of the beach is salty and fresh. Halfway out to the water, I feel exhausted. My leg is burning, and I can't go any farther. The sun is coming up, and the sky is a combination of black, blue, and orange. Truly the calm before the storm in many ways.

I should walk into the water and just keep going. Who did it? Which one of them, and why?

About a hundred yards away, I see a man approaching. He has

ripped clothes and a tangled beard. He is skinny with a sleeve of tattoos. His long hair is tucked under a camouflage hat. His only possession appears to be a faded green backpack. I consider moving out of his path, but what does it matter at this point?

"Good morning," he says. "You okay, brother?"

I smile and respond, "Yeah, tough night. How about you?"

"Every night is tough on the street, but if you have to be on your own, this is a pretty good place."

I nod.

"Mind if I pop a squat for a few minutes?"

"Sure, it is a public beach," I reply, even though I just want to be left alone in my despair.

He looks me over. "I've got a spare protein bar and water if you want it. You look like you could use it."

I realize he thinks I'm homeless like him, and he is partially right. "No, that is kind of you, but you better keep it."

He rubs his beard and turns his baseball cap backward. He reaches out his filthy hand. "My name is Gabriel, but everyone calls me Goat."

I shake it. "Nice to meet you, Goat." I don't offer my name, and he doesn't ask.

We spend the next twenty minutes chatting. He was an Army Ranger who earned the nickname of Goat climbing mountains overseas. While he made it back physically from Afghanistan, he never made it back mentally. Between drinking and drugs, he'd lost his job and his family. Lots of bad decisions. After a while, he just gave up. He is only a little older than me but looks sixty.

"How about you, stranger? What's your story?"

"I'm trying to do the right thing, Goat. Be a hero. But it has been hard. I don't know who to trust anymore. I feel like giving up."

He smiles at me with brown, jagged teeth. "You don't need to listen to me, but when I was in Afghanistan, we would be trying to get somewhere, and we always came across mountain ranges. Once we made it past one, we would find another. After a while, instead of crying about it and giving up, we learned how to climb them better." He looks out to the water and seems to say more to himself than me, "Life is hard, and there is always another mountain, but you learn how to deal with them better." He shakes his head. "I just gave up. The mountains were too high. Don't be like me, friend. Climb your mountain and then climb the next one. You'll be that hero."

He stands up. "I can tell you are a good man. If you are doing the right thing, don't give up. Just trust yourself and don't worry about others. You can do whatever you put your mind to."

Goat is right. I can do this on my own, and I'm not going to give up. His words are exactly what I need, and I vow to return the favor one day.

"You want to go have some breakfast? St. Edwin's down the way feeds guys like us. I stay there sometimes when the weather is bad. We need to stick together. It is tough out here. Even in paradise."

I shake my head. "No, I have a mountain to deal with, but I enjoyed meeting you, Goat. Maybe we'll see each other again."

"Give them hell, friend," he says as he walks away.

I sit there until several early-morning walkers make their way down the beach. If I am recognized, it will be over for me, so I make my way back to the truck. To my dismay, a Pinellas County police officer is in the lot. He is walking toward the beach when he spots me.

"Hey, you," he calls.

"Yes, officer?"

"This is a closed lot. Is that your truck?"

"Yes, sir. I didn't realize the beach wasn't open. I'll move right now."

He continues walking toward me. I do my best to avoid eye contact without being obvious. My choices are simple—be arrested or make a run for it.

He looks me over for a minute. "Let me see some ID. We've been having trouble with vagrants bothering the vacationers."

I look around for an escape route. I don't have any ID, and I am wanted by the police and FBI. Pulling my hat lower, I prepare to run.

As he moves closer with his hand on his weapon, we both hear a shout from the beach and then a scream.

He points at me and instructs, "Stay right here until I get back."

"Yes, sir," I respond, and as soon he is out of sight, I jump into the old truck. I drive quickly out of the lot. My heart is beating so fast I think it might give out. It is stupid to be out in public. Another mistake like this, and I will find myself behind bars or dead.

CHAPTER 50

I drive a few miles to a rougher area with a bunch of used car lots. Several are still closed, but I locate one offering cars in every price range. It has a couple of nicer German cars out front used as bait, but most are older models.

I exit the truck and am greeted by a salesman with a man bun and a black windbreaker. I must replace the truck, or I am a sitting duck.

"What can I do for you, my friend? That truck looks like it is on its last legs."

I smile, hoping the man will find me friendly and agree to help me out. I say politely, "I'd like to trade this in for something more reliable. Do you have anything on sale?"

"Everything is on sale. What's your name?"

I think about it for a moment. "You can call me Jim."

He offers his hand. "Nice to meet you. What's your budget? That old junker is not going to be much of a trade."

"Here is the situation. I don't have the title to the truck, and all I have is two grand in cash. Can we work something out?"

He fakes surprise. "Jim, it is illegal to take a trade without a title, and I need ID to sell you a car."

I could just pull my gun and take a car. Add grand theft auto to my list.

I suppress the desire to steal a car and consider my cash position.

"How about this. I give you the truck, two grand in cash, and an extra five hundred bucks, and you give me something reliable to drive."

He removes a small Motorola walkie-talkie from his pocket. I can't make out what he says, but moments later, a man opens the door of the building and exits with a huge unleashed German shepherd by his side. As they approach, I can hear the beast grumbling under its breath.

"Is there a problem out here?" the man asks as he instructs the dog to sit.

Oh shit, all I need now is a dog bite.

"No problem here. I just need a car. I didn't mean to offend anyone." I try to calm my wavering voice. It is hard to take my eyes off the dog, who is showing a bit of teeth.

"The guy doesn't have any ID or a title," states the salesman. "Looking for a cash deal."

The man with the dog looks at me suspiciously. "Are you a cop?"

"Do I look like a cop?" I point to my clothes and face.

"All right, drive the truck around back."

They open a gate leading to the back of the property, and I park the truck next to the building. The salesman signals me to follow him to a white, older model Kia. It has a dent on the passenger side and is missing a couple of hubcaps.

"It isn't pretty, but you can have it. No questions asked. We sold it and repossessed it a year later when the guy stopped paying. It doesn't have a title, so the risk is yours. Give me the cash and the keys to the truck—otherwise, hit the road."

"Start it up," I request. The dog growls from somewhere deep in its body.

The vehicle fires right up and seems to run okay. I go back to the truck, grab my bag, and count out twenty-five hundred bucks. I toss the sales guy the truck keys and jump into my new ride. The German shepherd does not move, but its eyes follow me everywhere.

"Nice doing business with you, Jim," the salesman says with a wave. Then he adds, "And we never met."

My next stop is a beauty supply shop on the way back to the waterfront. The place is filled with aisles and aisles of beauty supplies and, most importantly, a wall of wigs.

A shapely lady with long red hair approaches me. "Can I help you find something, sugar?"

"Yes, I am going to a costume party and need a blond wig. Do you have anything that might fit?"

She walks over to the wall of hair. Her hips sway side to side like she is listening to music in her head. "Did you have a certain style in mind, honey?"

I look over the options, not having any notion of the differences. "I am going to be a surfer with long blond hair. Any ideas?"

She looks diligently over the selection. She finds several options and asks me to sit down. We spend ten minutes trying the wigs on until we find one that fits well. She asks me if I want her to trim it and secure it. She is not buying the costume party story.

When she is done, I look ridiculous. I have shoulder-length dirty blond locks and a very dark goatee. She leads me to one of the other aisles and hands me a box of beard dye.

"Use this, and it will look more natural. You need to bleach the hair first."

I pay her and thank her for the help. She smiles knowingly, and I worry she is on to me, but she just tells me to have fun.

On the way back to the shore, I stop at an off-brand beach shop a couple blocks from the water. It advertises three T-shirts for $10, which is exactly what I can afford. I purchase two trucker hats, a straw lifeguard hat, two pairs of board shorts, and three of the advertised cheesy beach T-shirts. As I prepare to check out, I notice a long-sleeved fishing shirt and buy it as well.

The cashier agrees to let me change into my recent purchases before leaving. I exit the store a new man, but a new man in need of a shower. The blond hair hangs down from my new hat, and I fit in well with the other beach bums waking up and moving toward a day by the water. There are rumors of big waves due to the hurricane, which has the wannabe surfers excited.

After driving up and down Gulf Boulevard several times, I find a place that will work. The Grand Pelican Resort Motel has a total of ten units, all in a straight line facing the street. Each unit has a parking spot, and out front, there is a large neon sign advertising available, clean rooms.

I park and walk into the office. The attendant looks like she is ninety-five and has spent many of those years lying in direct sunlight. She smokes a menthol cigarette and welcomes me warmly. "Welcome to the Grand Pelican. You are in luck; we have one room available."

I assume the forecasted hurricane has something to do with the empty parking lot. Using my best Georgia drawl, I say, "That is lucky. I'll take it."

"Wonderful," she mumbles with the cigarette dangling from the corner of her mouth. "ID and credit card."

"Sorry, but my wallet was stolen on the way down from Atlanta. Some asshole took it directly out of my car. Can you believe that? Luckily, I have a pocket full of cash. I can pay for a week in advance." I pull several $100 notes out of my pocket and let them spill onto the counter.

She looks at me and then looks at the cash. "You seem nice enough." She shrugs, sticking the bills in her bra and handing me a key ring with two keys.

As I am reaching for the keys, I notice several flyers sitting in a messy pile. I almost choke when I look down at my face, along with several others, and capital letters that warn "WANTED FOR MURDER." Placing my backpack on top of the stack, I calmly slide them into my free hand to throw them away when I get to my room.

The noose is tightening. My face is everywhere.

"Just don't cook anything in the room, okay? Guests don't like when their room smells like fish."

"Of course not. You won't hear a peep out of me, and no cooking. I just need a few days at the beach to figure some things out."

CHAPTER 51

By now, I am sure everyone is aware that the trailer has burned down. As hurt and frustrated as I am about one of my team members double-crossing me, I can't let the other two think I'm dead.

I call Lia and let her know that I barely escaped. I promise to call again as soon as I relocate. She agrees to tell Avner and Oak what's happened and presses me for my location. I change the subject and get off the phone.

Someone will be disappointed that I escaped.

I am in the final chapter of my story. I am running low on money, have no ID, am basically driving a stolen car, and no longer know who to trust. The world is closing in on me, and my picture is everywhere. There are a couple of things I need to do before the end.

Zeke answers on the first ring. "This is Agent Michaels."

"Zeke, this is Jason. Sorry about the little trick at the motel, but I needed to see if I could trust you, and clearly I can't."

"Jason, I have always been straight with you. Job first, our relationship second. That is just how it has to be."

I walk around the small pink room studying the framed pictures of pelicans throughout. Compared to my previous home, it is nice and clean. Luckily, it does not smell like fish.

"I know who you are, Zeke. I will come in with the laptop, but we need to cut a deal. I cannot be prosecuted based on any of the bullshit from Safe Harbor. I need full immunity," I demand, just like I practiced it.

"That is a big ask, Jason. What if you are a thief and a killer?"

"You are going to be contacted by someone on my behalf. I have shared all the information with her, and she is doing her own research. She is reliable and has no reason to lie."

I lie down on the bed and continue. "You already know I'm not a killer. I am sure they figured out that Scott died before I was at his house. As far as the data on the laptop, how the hell could one person mastermind such a big scam? This thing is huge, and I have seen it all."

There is silence, and I can imagine his eyes opening and shutting. "I'm not making a deal until you come in. I don't care if you send the pope on your behalf. I give you my word that if you are not guilty, we'll take care of you."

I get up and walk into the bathroom. There is a window large enough for me to fit through. "Not good enough, Zeke. But I'll give you another tidbit. I was staying in a trailer in Thonotosassa, and Max Braun and his gang showed up late last night. I assume they were there to kill me. They trashed the place and set it on fire. Check with the police and you'll find the spot. These guys are bad news, and you should be chasing them, not me."

"Let me talk to my people, and I'll question them about the fire. How do I get hold of you?"

"You don't. I'll call you tomorrow. I'm already out of state, and I have options. The bank data includes high-profile people from around the world. If you don't deal, I call your counterparts in France or Greece and I get the guarantee they will offer me immunity. The world is a big place."

There you go, Zeke. The money shot. Make the deal.

I hang up the phone feeling good about the call. As instructed by the lady at the beauty shop, I use bleach first and then the dye to change the color of my goatee to dirty blond. It is a closer match to my ridiculous wig. I dress in my jeans and the long-sleeved fishing shirt and put on the straw lifeguard hat. Looking at my transformation, I think this might just work.

Before bed, I leave the beach for a trip to Home Depot. Slipping in just before the store closes, I purchase a shovel, a yellow work vest, plastic wrap, rope, and a gaiter face mask. My cash is getting low, but I have enough for a bag of tacos for dinner.

I need my rest. Tomorrow morning, it is time to see the one person who I know can connect the dots. It might take violence, but at this point, that is fine with me.

****

Terrance Browning lives in an affluent neighborhood in North Tampa known as Avila. The gated community has been home to athletes, socialites, and professionals since the early eighties. It is surrounded by eight-foot walls and got its name from a Spanish city. The neighborhood only has two entrances, and armed security patrols twenty-four hours a day.

Terrance's house is a sixty-five-hundred-square-foot beauty located deep in the neighborhood. A long, stone U-shaped driveway leads to his front door before snaking back to the street. The house is two stories with many sharp angles. The lawn is immaculate and lush with beautiful bushes, palms, and flowers.

I've played a lot of golf at their private club over the years. It is a gorgeous Jack Nicklaus-designed course that travels throughout the neighborhood. Terrance is an avid golfer who plays with the same group every Wednesday. Despite his persistence, he rarely breaks 100 and even more rarely reports the correct score.

My playing partner on several occasions was an ex-NFL player who we met through Lia's jewelry business. His wife loves her designs, and we became friends. The only drawback to playing golf with him was that he always insisted on the first tee time. I would give in and arrive at the neighborhood gates at daybreak. I lined up with the ground crew and neighborhood landscapers, who were allowed to enter as a group.

At six AM, I line up with the other workers. I am dressed in jeans, my straw hat, and a neon yellow vest. My long blond hair is pulled back into a ponytail. I have the shovel in the back seat, along with a bag holding the tarp, the rope, and my handgun. The laptop is stored in my trunk for safekeeping.

There are three or four other workers in every car, and a few have been dropped off at the gate to walk the rest of the way. I signal one guy over and ask if he needs a ride to the maintenance shed, and he gladly accepts. The security guard barely looks at my dented Kia and my new friend as we roll through.

I drop the worker off at the shed and drive to the maintenance parking lot. It is farther back than the member lot, but it has a view of most of the cars. There are plenty of Mercedes and BMWs along with some high-end electric cars. I scan the lot until I find what I am looking for—a black Porsche Panamera with tinted windows. Terrance loves his cars, and the Panamera is his favorite.

I have about four hours to kill until Terrance finishes his round. The lack of sleep is starting to affect my thinking, so I tilt the seat back and close my eyes. When I wake an hour later, the Porsche is gone, and it is raining. They must have called everyone in off the course due to the hurricane heading our way.

I curse myself for being dumb enough to fall asleep, and drive through the neighborhood. I park a block from Terrance's house. After putting on the gaiter mask, I grab the shovel and bag and walk to his house. Strong gusts of wind almost knock me down a couple of times, and I wonder how they played any holes earlier.

Terrance does not have a family, so I assume he will be alone before heading off to work. I walk up to his door and ring the bell. A minute later, he answers, dressed in tan slacks and a pink shirt.

"Who are you, and where is my usual landscape guy?" he grumbles with a scowl.

"I am sorry to bother you, but he wasn't available, so it looks like you are stuck with me." I shove the Glock in his face and push him inside hard. "Time for you and me to have a little talk."

CHAPTER 52

"You have no idea who you are messing with. I'm going to give you ten seconds to get the hell out of my house." Terrance's face turns a dark shade of red.

I punch him hard in the stomach and land a knee to his chin. He falls into a fetal position and curses to himself. "If you want money, I'll give you what I have. Just don't hurt me."

This is the man who has caused all this pain. He ruined my career, destroyed my friendships, and killed my friend. I want revenge. I want to hurt him.

I remove my hat and the gaiter.

"What I want is my life back, Terrance."

He looks up with wide eyes and an arched eyebrow. In the two weeks since this started, I have lost weight and developed dark bags under my eyes. Terrance looks like he has just been at the spa.

"How do you know my name? Do I know you?" He gapes at me for a moment. "Holy shit...is that you, Jason?"

"The one and only. Do you like my new look?"

"Let's take a breath and slow everything down. Don't do anything you are going to regret," he says, staring at my face and outfit.

I point the gun at his head. "You and I are going to have a long talk, and you are going to tell me everything you know about this mess. Get up and keep your hands where I can see them. You so much as breathe funny and you're dead."

We walk through the entryway under separate stairways that curve to the right and the left. The layout looks like a butterfly. Opera music is playing throughout the house. I keep the gun close to his head in case he tries to run. I am ready to shoot him if necessary.

"Where do you want to go?" he asks.

"The theater," I respond.

Before coming, I looked up the house online and found a listing on Zillow from before he purchased it. I know it has a theater room with no windows, perfect for an interrogation.

"Bring a chair in from the kitchen," I instruct.

He does as I ask, and I tell him to sit cross-legged while I spread out the painting tarp on the ground. It smells like buttered popcorn in the theater. I place the chair in the middle of the tarp, pull him up, and shove him into it. I use the rope to tie him firmly to the seatback. It is not lost on me that a decade prior, I had been the one in the chair with Dr. Levi asking the questions.

This is disgusting. Have I become the monster? Can I ever be the same person after this?

Terrance gains his composure quickly. "Jason, let's handle this like gentlemen. We've known each other for a long time. Let me out of this chair, and we'll work something out." He eyes the tarp and tries to wiggle free.

I make a show of straightening it so it covers as much of the floor as possible. "If you don't answer my questions, I am going to shoot you and then wrap you up in the tarp. Got it?"

He nods. I see sweat breaking out on his forehead. "Not exactly gentlemanly, but that's fine. What do you want to know? You can't use any of what I tell you against me. I will say I lied under duress."

I press the gun hard against his temple. All the pain and agony of the past weeks surge up in me, and I consider pulling the trigger.

Just give me a reason, Terrance. You have put me through hell, and for what?

"Jason, calm down. You have no idea what you are in the middle of. Killing me is pointless. I am one small piece of this whole thing."

"Let's start at the beginning. Did you hire Eric to run this scam?"

He contemplates the question carefully. "No, he was placed at Safe Harbor by mutual acquaintances who knew his skillset from previous banks."

"What acquaintances?"

"Before we do this, why don't we talk about making a deal? I'll match what we are giving your Israeli friend to turn you over. One million cash or bitcoin or whatever you want. All we want is the laptop."

The words hit me like a tidal wave. "What the fuck did you just say?"

Terrance smirks. "We'll match what we are giving your friend, Mr. Cohen."

I want to rub my pinky finger, but I am still holding the gun. "You're a liar."

"Oh wait, you didn't know? Your Israeli watchdog rolled over on the first offer. He agreed to sell you out to fix his money problems. He's also got some daddy issues, you know."

I knew one of my friends had turned on me, but the thought of Avner being the one makes me sick. I trusted him with my life, and he sold me out.

"What do you say? Let's make a deal. We'll give you two million, you run away with your pretty wife, and all you need to do is give us the laptop. We can fix everything else."

I am having trouble thinking, and my eyesight is blurry. My head pounds, and my legs have trouble holding me up. I need to pull it together. I block out the thought of Avner turning on me. "I want some answers. I don't want your blood money."

Terrance simply shrugs before tilting his head. "Have it your way."

"Why did you kill Scott?"

"He knew too much and was just in the way. Max and Orsu got a little too aggressive. Sorry about that."

I know at this moment I could shoot Terrance and hunt down Max. My hatred feels like it is being released through my pores. I take a quick walk around the theater room to calm down.

"Don't be so dramatic, Jason. Life is short, and we all die sooner or later. Take the money and have some fun."

"Who placed Eric at the Bank? Was it *The One*?"

"Jason, let me give you some advice. You need to stop. Perhaps you want to be a hero and do the right thing, but you are meaningless in the grand scheme of it all," he says, trying to move his arms.

"Is *The One* a real thing?"

"You are talking about a movement. *The One* has been around forever, and sooner or later, it will accomplish its goal. One little man in Tampa can't change anything. It is so big and widespread that stopping one trickle of money won't delay a thing."

"Who is behind it?"

Terrance laughs. "Who isn't behind it? The strings are being pulled all over the world. This is inevitable. You think you are doing the honorable thing, but I'm the hero in this room." His voice grows louder. "I am a believer in change, and it is happening as we speak. You and Scott are pieces of sand blowing away in the wind. You stepped into something you can't understand, so you either make a deal with me or die. Not a tough choice."

The anger has been building like pressure in a pipe, and it is suddenly released. I punch him hard in the face.

Terrance spits out blood and laughs even louder. "You don't have anyone. Your friend is dead! Your Israeli sold you out! We own your movie star friend! And your wife is working with the FBI! You are fighting a war by yourself in a ridiculous blond wig."

"What do you mean you own Oak? What does he have to do with this?"

"You really don't know anything, you moron. Check your precious laptop. Oak Williams is not only a client of our Executive Banking Group, but he has been washing cash in the fraud for years."

CHAPTER 53

"You are a liar!" I yell.

Terrance laughs louder and longer. "Check the list. You'll see. Oak is part of what you are trying to stop. You bring us down, and he tumbles with us."

I've heard enough. I leave the room and walk to the kitchen, where I find a towel used to dry dishes. I shove it into his mouth and grab my things as he attempts to shout.

"You are lucky I don't burn this place down like your assholes did to my hideout. But I don't need to. You all will burn in Hell soon enough. Tell them all I am coming for them—Max and his bear, the scoundrels at the bank, and whoever or whatever *The One* is," I scream, spit spraying from my mouth and landing on his face.

The germaphobe struggles to do anything he can to clear my saliva off his face, but there is little he can do as it drips down his cheeks. I gather as much spittle as possible in my mouth and shoot it at him like a missile.

I leave Terrance tied up, gagged, and in his germ-infested hell. I'm not a killer, but at that moment, I came close. The news about Avner and Oak is debilitating. I can't believe it, but I must check the laptop for Oak's name.

Lia would never work with the FBI. She would never forsake me. Would she?

Heading to the door, I pick up a vase and smash it on the ground. I hope it was expensive. It feels so good that I smash several more sculptures and rip paintings off the wall. A china cabinet is easy to tip over, and I throw an espresso machine into Terrance's flat-screen television.

The drive to the beach is exhausting. I am physically and mentally done. I want to pull the laptop out, but the most wanted man in Florida can't exactly go to Dunkin' Donuts for the Wi-Fi. Driving the speed limit is testing my patience, but I know if I am pulled over, it will be the end. The weather has also turned dangerous. Sheets of rain fall from the sky, and the wind blows my Kia all over the road.

Did Avner sell me out to fix his financial issues? Is Oak involved in the fraud? Does he know anything about The One? Is it possible that Lia is working with Zeke? Am I really on my own?

I arrive back at the Pelican and run inside, leaving everything in the Kia except the laptop. I power it on and whisper to the machine to hurry up. Finally it is ready, and I pull up the Project Cardinal database. I type in "Oak Williams" and then pause. No going back once I press enter, but I must know.

I press the button, and it immediately pulls up Oak's information. He has a balance of $3 million and is banked by Eric Gruber himself. I feel like I am going to throw up. Oak is part of the scam. I read through the notes, which detail how a courier brings the cash once a quarter to Eric's house.

Is this what Oak wanted to talk about? Was he going to come clean or just tell another lie? Maybe he decided it was easier to give me up.

I pull out one of the burners and dial Lia's number.

"Jay, is that you?"

"Hey, baby, it is."

"Are you okay?"

That is a loaded question. I wonder if everything I say will be communicated to the Feds. It doesn't matter. This is almost over anyway. "Have you seen Avner or Oak?"

"No, I haven't. Avner's been gone, and Oak said he was going back to his condo to pick up some clothes. But that was a while ago. He also said to tell you he needs to talk to you."

Too late, Oak.

"Lia, can I trust you?"

She pauses before answering. Her voice is soft and caring. I wonder if she is playing a character. "Of course, Jay, tell me what is going on."

"I talked to Terrance."

"Oh my god, what did he say?"

I tell her the whole story. Everything except Avner's and Oak's betrayals. She is quiet and doesn't interrupt.

"That is unbelievable, Jay. Do you think it is all true? You know Terrance is a liar."

"There's more. According to Terrance, he paid Avner a million dollars to turn me over to the bank people, and Oak is part of the Project Cardinal fraud. One of them handed me over."

"I don't believe it. Avner is your friend, and he doesn't care about money. I have known him most of my life. He is like our family."

"Maybe," I acknowledge. "But the part about Oak is true. His name is in the database, and he has a secret account with Safe Harbor."

She is quiet again. I can almost hear her mind racing and calculating.

"What are you going to do, Jay? Can I come to you, and we'll figure it out together?"

"No, I am not putting you in any more danger. This is my mess. I am going to turn myself in to Zeke and work through everything. I'm innocent, and I'm going to put these assholes in prison."

I tell her I love her and ask if we can see each other one more time.

My next call is to Zeke. As usual, he answers on the first ring.

"Are you ready to deal yet, Zeke?"

"Are you okay?"

"Zeke, this is out of control and much bigger than simple IRS fraud."

"Tell me what you know, and I'll talk to my supervisor about a deal."

I am getting frustrated and try to calm my tone. "I am ready to come in, but I want a deal upfront," I say firmly. "Talk to Morgan Bennett Chase. You have twenty-four hours. If I don't have a deal protecting me and Lia, I disappear. As I said, the world is a big place, Zeke. Not that hard to go poof in the wind."

He tells me to hold on and puts the phone on mute. After several minutes, he returns.

"We already spoke with Morgan. Assuming your story and everything she told us checks out, we'll deal."

"Full immunity in writing. I want to see it before I come in," I demand.

"That's fine. Give me the rest of the day. By the way, we are hearing a lot of chatter, and we've lost Max and his big friend. If they find out we are making a deal, they are going to strike even harder, so get hidden and stay alive."

I hope I can.

CHAPTER 54

Terrance has seen my disguise, so I bag up the blond wig and the clothes from earlier and throw them in the motel trash. I plan to stay put until I review Zeke's deal. I get some food and a single beer in a brown paper sack from the convenience store and settle in. No one knows where I am, so I feel safe. But I am nearly out of money and running out of options.

I shave my face and even out the mohawk before taking a long, hot shower. The leg wound is still bright red and tender. I dress in a T-shirt and shorts and look almost human again. It is good to see my face without a beard.

I pack up the laptop and my few belongings before sitting on the bed with my notebook and the beer. Turning to a blank page, I begin writing everything down from the beginning. I want to have a detailed history of the saga when I sit down with Zeke. I describe how Scott found the back door into the data and our code name Project Cardinal. I am as comprehensive as I can be and only leave Lia out of the story.

When I am done, I take a long drink and read it once more. It reads like a Greek tragedy. So many people and relationships are damaged for no reason. But I am still hoping for a happy ending. If Terrance and Max and all the bad guys go to prison, I will feel somewhat redeemed, but that will never bring Scott back. I listen to the wind outside and the rain pelting the windows. From time to time, a gust blows so hard that I think the glass may break.

Even if this turns out okay, there is a lot of collateral damage. Scott has lost his life, Oak will have to deal with the backlash of being on the list, and Avner will probably escape to Israel. I won't see him again, which is fine.

My main concern is Lia. Can we have a normal life? Will we need to go into hiding? Will she want to stay with me?

The adrenaline from the morning is gone, and I am exhausted. I drain the beer, put down the notebook, and close my eyes. Sleep comes quickly.

****

I am awakened by the turning of the lock on the motel door. I sit up quickly and reach for the Glock, but it is packed away with the laptop.

A giant man moves swiftly across the room and picks me up like a child. This must be the man named Orsu I've heard about. He slams me into the wall, and I hit my head hard. I see stars, but my Krav Maga training clicks in. I step on his foot as violently as I can and land an elbow to his giant head. Neither seems to faze him. He just gives a deep throaty laugh.

Max stands at the door smiling. "I told you, Jason. Big beats little every time. And Orsu is very big." He pulls out his gun and aims it at me. "As much as I would like to let him pound you to death, we don't have time. I want the laptop and everything else. Terrance wants you for himself. You should not have attacked him."

The cavalry is not coming. Muttering "bluebird" will do me no good. It is over, and I have lost. I hold up my hands in defeat. But before they are fully extended, the door explodes open. Wood splinters throughout the room. Max is knocked to the ground, causing his gun to fly out of his hands.

Avner enters the gaping doorway and shoots Orsu in the leg. Max reacts quickly, pulling out a knife and slashing Avner's arm.

"Jason, get the hell out of here. I'll take care of these two," he screams.

I stand shocked, unable to move. Am I really seeing Avner?

Why is he here if he is a traitor?

"Jason, now!" he yells as he squares up with Max. Orsu is steadying himself, but blood pours out of a hole in his leg.

I grab the backpack and notebook and run for the bathroom. I lock the door and open the window. Standing on the toilet, I ease my way out and drop to the ground. I am immediately soaked by the rain. The last thing I hear is a gunshot.

CHAPTER 55

I am frozen, thinking that Avner might be dead and that I left him behind. He told me that a hero needs to have strength for two. I am no longer a victim; I am a protector. It doesn't matter whether he set me up or not. He came back for me when it mattered.

I double back as fast as I can to the motel and scale the window, despite the intense pain in my leg as it scrapes against the wall. Dropping to the floor, I remove the Glock from the backpack and place my other hand on the doorknob. I turn it as quietly as possible and move the gun to a two-handed position, with my right hand on the grip and my index finger on the trigger. My left hand rests underneath, near the magazine as a support. Holding it just below my sight line, I kick the bathroom door open with my foot.

The scene is chaotic. Rain pours in from the shattered front door, and there is blood everywhere. I scan the room from left to right and find Orsu slumped against the wall, staring at me with eyes wide open. I instinctively fire a shot at him, but he is already dead. The rest of the room is empty. The wail of police sirens is getting louder and louder. I've got to move quickly or I will be caught. I store the Glock in my backpack and run back to the bathroom. I leap through the window again and land hard on my bad leg.

I am in agony, but I run as fast as I can. There is no way to get the car, so I will be on foot the rest of the night. It's dark, and a steady rain is falling. The wind is so strong I feel like I am barely moving forward. I am disoriented, but I need to get off the main street and go somewhere safe.

I cross the street to the beach side, where I know that a concrete path runs parallel to the sand. Because of the storm, there is no one out to see a crazy man sprinting at full speed. After a mile or two, I am winded, and I notice a half-built condo complex up ahead.

I scale an eight-foot chain-link fence and run through what looks like it might be the parking area. My leg feels like it is on fire, and my wet pants are irritating the wound. Only a few floors have been built, but it is dry and will keep me hidden. My heart is beating so fast I think it might give out. I take as many deep breaths as I can but struggle to calm down. My clothes are soaked, and the air is cold. I find a corner that protects me from the wind and drop to the ground.

What the hell just happened? How did they find me again? And why would Avner save me if he was the one who turned me in? Is he okay?

The only items in the backpack are the laptop, the notebook, and one burner. Everything else is in the motel room. I have no money and no car.

I call Lia and talk in manic, breathless sentences. "Lia, they came to get me."

"Jay, calm yourself. Who came to get you?" she asks.

"Terrance's men. Avner was there and saved me."

"Where did Avner come from? Is he with you? I thought he turned you in."

"No, there was a gunshot, and I went back for him, but he and Max were gone. Orsu is dead. I don't have anything, and I don't know what to do."

"There are FBI agents everywhere around the house, and the hurricane is bearing down on us. It is going to take me a little while to get to you. Can you stay safe until the morning?"

I consider the question. "I will do my best. I need to get out of here in case there are more of them. The police are also everywhere. I will call you in the morning to meet up."

"Jay, you can do this. You need to stay hidden and dry for the next twelve hours. I believe in you!"

"I can do it, Lia. If not, I want you to know how much I love you."

Life can change in an instant.

CHAPTER 56

I move slowly through the dark shadows of the beach and the numerous hotels until I reach The Shipwreck. It is a beach bar that Lia and I went to after a wedding many years ago. We drank margaritas and did shots until they called an Uber for us.

I'm not being nostalgic. I have a plan to get away from the beach.

Due to the bad weather, the bar is closing. I sway as I walk in and take a seat at the counter. A bartender with bright pink hair and a nose ring says, "Dude, we are closing. You can have one drink. What do you want?"

I slur my words and mumble, "Whiskey."

She looks me over. "Are you okay? You are all wet and sound like you have had plenty to drink already. Might be time to go home. Plus, a hurricane is coming."

Holding my head low, I reply, "Girlfriend kicked me out, and I lost my wallet and phone."

She smiles kindly. "Is there someone you can call if I let you use my phone?"

I shake my head. "I don't know any phone numbers. They are all programmed into my cell. You know how it is. I can go to a friend's place, but I don't have any way to get there."

She pours me a cup of coffee and goes to talk to her manager. He looks me over and nods to the bartender.

"We are going to call you an Uber on us. I am not sure they will drive in this weather, but let's see."

"Thank you so much. I appreciate it. I'll tell everyone what a great bar this is."

Twenty minutes later, a jacked-up Jeep arrives. I thank the bartender with the bright pink hair and jump in the back.

"Take me to the Gandy Storage in Tampa."

****

In the pouring rain, I key my code to enter the storage facility and walk to my unit. I no longer care about security cameras and look directly into one. The sky is dark and unleashing its fury on Tampa. The wind howls like a wolf; the storage units are shaking. It is difficult to see three feet in front of me.

I roll up the door to our unit. A lightbulb hangs in the middle of the room, and I pull a cord to turn it on. I am amazed as I look around the room. In addition to some boxes, it looks like an armory. There are guns, bullets, and several bulletproof vests. Off to the side is Lia's sniper rifle. Someone is ready for war, and I know who.

I search several boxes and find some old clothes. I change into some dark jeans and a fraternity sweatshirt. They are old and musty but dry. I lay the rest of the clothes down on the ground and make a little bed. The light flickers and then goes out. For the first time in hours, I relax, knowing this is the final night of this nightmare.

CHAPTER 57

I sleep soundly even with the warm temperature in the storage unit. Mother Nature continues to attack outside, but the darkness and solitude of the storage unit is comforting. My body hurts from lying on the ground, and my leg is tender. After seeing Lia, I will turn myself over to Zeke and begin the challenge of unraveling this mystery.

The storage facility is just ten minutes from my house, but it feels like another world. Every time I think about Avner, I am confused. It makes no sense. Why take Terrance's money and then save me? Whatever the story is, I hope he is okay. And where the hell is Oak? If Avner saved me, does that mean Oak is the traitor?

It can't be. Oak is like a brother.

I peek my head out of the storage unit to find several inches of standing water. The rain is coming down sideways, and some trees next door have been knocked over. There are no cars on the street, and the electricity appears to be out everywhere.

Going back inside, I call Lia.

"Jay, is that you? I have been so worried. Are you okay?"

"I am fine, but it was a wild night. I am not far from home. Can you lose the FBI?"

"They had to leave due to the weather. I can meet you. Where are you?"

I can sense the concern in her voice, and it increases my anxiety. Lia is always so calm and cool.

"I am at the mini-storage place over on Gandy where you stockpiled a bunch of weapons," I say looking around the small space.

"I'll be there in half an hour. Love you, Jay."

****

Lia passes through the gate and parks next to our unit. She is driving a black Wagoneer with tinted windows. I run out to greet her and give her a big hug. She is dressed in cargo pants and a hoodie with her hair pulled back into a ponytail. Her jaw is set, and her eyes are focused. We walk inside, and she begins inspecting the weapons cache.

"What's with the car?" I ask.

"I rented it with my fake ID. Everyone knows my SUV." She stops checking the weapons and looks at me. "Jay, I received a call from Terrance. They have Avner and Oak. He left his number for you to call."

This is my worst nightmare. The bad guys have my two friends. Even if they are traitors, we must do something. Lia hands me the number and her phone. I dial and put it on speaker.

"Well, hello, Jason. Nice to hear from you. I know you were concerned about my well-being since you left me tied up with a rag in my mouth, but we'll talk about that in person. I must admit, you are more resilient than I gave you credit for. I thought we finally had you until your dipshit friend ruined the party, but here we are."

"I hear you have my friends. But what makes you think I care? They both turned on me."

"Did they? Maybe not. Either way, you have two hours to return the laptop. You come alone and I won't allow Max to execute these two. You bring the FBI or your agent wifey, everyone dies and then I send the team after her. Am I clear?"

I look at Lia, and she mouths for me to say yes.

"I guess I am out of time. I'll do it, but you must promise me they will be safe."

He repeats the timeline and hangs up the phone without another word.

I am rubbing my pinky, and Lia grabs my hand. There is a sparkle in her eye that I have not seen for a long time. "We have two options, Jay. One we run, or two we save Oak and Avner and kill those motherfuckers."

I think about it for a moment and smile. I slowly raise two fingers, and she kisses me hard.

CHAPTER 58

I pull up to the address that was texted to Lia's phone. It is an old warehouse near the port of Tampa. The perfect place to kill someone and drop the body in the water.

It looks like a million other dilapidated warehouses in town. It is large, maybe fifteen thousand square feet, with a flat roof and twenty-foot ceilings. It is surrounded by a concrete parking lot in need of attention. There is a chain-link fence surrounding the property that is rusted and sagging. The properties on each side look like they have been abandoned for years. A company name is painted on the front of the warehouse, but it has faded from time and the water.

This would be a terrible place to take my last breath.

I drive the Wagoneer through the front gate, which has been left open and park near a broken-down boat. It has a hole in the bottom and is tipped on its side. I grab the new Glock that Lia gave me, even though I know it will be taken away before I enter the building. I also have a knife strapped to my leg, but I assume I will be relieved of that as well. I am still wearing the jeans and fraternity sweatshirt, but now I have body armor underneath.

I take a deep breath and exit the car, carrying the backpack with the laptop. My hands are shaking, and my eyes are darting around the property. Terrance has the upper hand, but we'll go out fighting. It is hard to believe that a couple of weeks ago I was a simple banker.

Now I am a hero ready to fight for others. Even if this is it, I've wiped away the shame of Israel. I've been brave and done the right thing no matter the cost. We will try to avenge Scott's death, but a lot needs to go the right way.

Several armed men are patrolling the perimeter in rain gear, and they descend on me as I walk slowly through the parking lot. Max exits the building. I stop and he signals me forward. He points a gun at me and screams, "Get your hands in the air and walk over here slowly."

I do as he commands, and as I approach, he punches me hard in the jaw. I wobble and drop to the ground, nearly unconscious.

When I stand up, my legs are shaking, and my wound is throbbing. "Big isn't that impressive," I taunt. He slaps me hard and pushes me violently into the wall, where he frisks me. He finds the gun and knife quickly and proceeds to grab every part of my body before punching me in the kidney. I fall to the ground again.

"That vest isn't going to do you much good when I shoot you and your friends in the head."

He opens a side door and picks me up. Out of the corner of my eye, I see one of the men on patrol drop to the ground like a ragdoll. A sniper shot from one hundred yards will do that. I move quickly through the door to keep Max's attention.

The warehouse looks like it has not been used for years. It has flickering fluorescent lights that are covered with cobwebs. The floor is cracked concrete. There is shelving on the walls and crappy wooden stairs that lead to a loft of some sort. It smells of ammonia and bleach.

Down the stairs comes Terrance in his blue blazer and pink shirt with the trademark khakis. They look freshly dry-cleaned. "The guest of honor has arrived," he says with a wide smile. His face is bruised and swollen due to my house call. He looks like a different man than the one I have known and respected for many years.

"I didn't think you would be here for the rough stuff. I figured you would leave that up to the hired help."

He laughs like a hyena. "Are you kidding? I would not miss this for the world. You have made my life very difficult, and I must be here to declare victory and watch you get what you deserve."

He moves to within inches of my face and starts poking my chest. "Plus, Avner killed Orsu before Max was able to stab him in the stomach. Surprisingly, he lived. He and the movie star turned out to be the perfect bait. I thought about grabbing your little wife, but I needed someone to get you here. I will deal with her separately."

I reach back to punch him, and he pulls a taser from his jacket. "No, no, no, not unless you want fifty thousand volts."

I release my fists and step back. A quick scan of the warehouse reveals a hopeless situation. In the center of the room, Oak and Avner are on their knees, arms tied behind their backs. Max moves behind them and holds his gun near their heads. Avner is bloody and beaten, but Oak looks undamaged—at least physically.

"I thought you said Avner took the money and you owned Oak? If so, what are they doing tied up on the ground?"

Terrance smiles. "I might have stretched the truth a little. The Israeli was too stupid to take the money, and to quote the movie star, 'No one owns Oak Williams.'"

Terrance moves next to Max. "None of that matters now. Hand me the laptop, along with the password."

"I want everyone released and then I will give it to you," I insist.

"You are not in a position to make demands. We haven't hurt your friends—well, not really," Terrance states, as he zaps Avner with the taser. The electrodes enter his back, and he twitches and spasms uncontrollably. His eyes roll back as he hits the ground.

"Stop, you psychopath!" I roar.

"The longer you wait, the less I can guarantee their safety. Your Israeli friend gets a bullet instead of electricity if I don't have that laptop in the next ten seconds."

Oak fixes Terrance with a hard look. "Don't give it to them," he yells. "They are going to kill us anyway."

Max slaps him hard across the back of the head.

I hand Terrance the backpack, and he removes the laptop. "So much hassle for one little machine. Now I need the password."

"You said you would let them go."

"We'll see. The password, Mr. Miles," he says louder.

I smile at Terrance and simply state, "Bluebird."

From a darkened corner of the warehouse comes Lia with her Glock outstretched. A perfectly aimed bullet finds Max's forehead and he drops. Terrance attempts to say something before two bullets enter his brain and his life is over.

I turn to greet Lia. Then my wife, the love of my life, shoots me in the heart. The world goes dark.

CHAPTER 59

It is like watching a scene in a movie where I am the star, but I am also an audience member viewing my own death. Lia is pressing down hard on my bare chest repeatedly. Then she tilts my head back, pinches my nose, and gives me two breaths. I can hear her say, "Come on, Jay, breathe on your own."

Avner and Oak are screaming something, but all I can hear is Lia's voice. "Come on, Jay, breathe on your own."

Paramedics rush into the building. I am aware of the commotion as all kinds of gear is dropped near me. They look around, seeing the dead bodies and Oak and Avner tied up. The body armor I was wearing has been tossed over to the side. One of them says, "What the fuck happened here?"

Lia answers calmly, "He needs help. I gave him CPR, but I don't know what happened. His heart just seemed to stop."

"What is his name?" asks one paramedic, bringing out a small bright yellow machine.

"Jay Miles."

"And who are you?" The woman turns to her, but Lia is gone.

The paramedic grabs my hand and says, "Jay, if you can hear me, squeeze my hand." She shakes her head. "He is unresponsive. We need to get his heart started. Hand me the AED."

She turns on the machine and applies some electrodes to my skin.

"Get ready." I feel a bolt of electricity hurtle through me. The show from above is over as I reenter my body.

****

I am on a gurney and placed in the back of an ambulance. Police are rushing into the building, but I am fading in and out of consciousness. It is a terrifying feeling. One minute I am conscious, and then I wake up somewhere else. Each time I rouse, I need to figure out where I am and who I am with.

I hear Oak yelling to let him into the ambulance, but the police are refusing. The ambulance takes off, and I hear a loud siren. The ride is rough and fast as they continue to work on me. I keep asking for Lia, but they shove an oxygen mask over my mouth.

My next memory is entering the emergency room at Tampa General on the gurney. I hear the paramedic say, "Male victim of cardiac arrest. We got the heart started again, but it is weak."

A crew of nurses and a doctor sweep in. I pass out again.

CHAPTER 60

When I wake up, I scream, "Lia!"

"You need to calm down, Mr. Miles," a nurse says to me.

I struggle against the wires hooked throughout my body. There is beeping, and people are rushing into the room. I hear muffled voices, but none of them make sense. I fall back into a deep, dark sleep, dreaming of my wife and her betrayal.

****

It feels like I have been at the hospital forever. I am in a private room with an armed guard outside. I am not sure if that is to keep me in or to keep others out. I spend my days reading and watching mindless television while still hooked up to several machines that make beeping sounds and hum all night. For a while, I have tubes in my nose providing me with oxygen.

After being revived, I stay in the hospital for what they are calling a "comprehensive medical evaluation." There has been ongoing cardiac, neurological, and vascular testing for weeks. Nurses come in from time to time to check on me and give me medicine. The vest saved my life, but the bullet hit me directly in the heart, causing cardiac arrest. Lia had called the paramedics and applied CPR. Then she'd taken the laptop and walked out the door. She had not only stopped my heart but also broke it. Had she not made the call and worked to revive me, I would have died.

In the two weeks that I've spent at the hospital, my beard has grown dark, and my hair is growing in. My skin is very pale, and I have lost weight. I avoid looking in the mirror whenever possible. I look worse than when I was on the run.

In addition to my heart issue, the doctors work on my wounded leg. I have a bacterial infection, and they use aggressive ointments and medicine along with something called a wound vacuum to get more oxygen to the tissues. They say my leg will be fine, but it still hurts like hell.

I just want to go home. I can't believe that Lia was the traitor, and I need to talk to her. There must be another explanation.

There has been a constant stream of visitors. Oak and Avner take shifts, and other friends stop by occasionally. Even Morgan spent an afternoon keeping me company. I tell everyone it is not necessary, but their visits help me make it through some long, depressing days. I plead with them to stop looking at me with pity and assure them that I will be okay. But I'm not sure I believe that myself.

Zeke is also a frequent visitor, once he has worn down the medical staff. At first, he shows genuine concern, but as time wears on, he wants answers. There is still a pending arrest warrant, and he claims he wants to get me cleared. I wonder if he's still looking to arrest me.

We spend hours going over the events that led us to the hospital. The FBI director has been removed from leadership due to his relationship with Terrance Browning, and both Zeke and Gloria are up for promotions.

The FBI raided Safe Harbor Bank, and although Terrance and his team had wiped names and balances from the servers, there is still enough proof to arrest Eric Gruber and many others. They all claim ignorance, blame Terrance, and lawyer up. A week later, Eric disappears. It is unclear whether he ran or was found. I assume he is no longer among the living. The board cannot explain the lack of compliance, and there is talk about selling the bank.

Zeke promises to keep digging. The complexity of the money laundering is staggering. He thinks it might take years to unravel and will require the cooperation of many other countries.

One of Max's men admits that Max and Orsu killed Scott that first night. Unfortunately, there is no one to charge, as everyone is dead. I am heartbroken and have Oak get the motorcycle out of Scott's garage. I vow to take that cross-country trip for him when I am healthy.

I ask Zeke about Lia, and he says that it is not his department. The FBI will work with several other intelligence agencies to track her down. He is sure they will find her. I am sure they will not.

Morgan writes her story about the fall of Safe Harbor Bank, with me as the hero. It is picked up across the world, and she becomes the face of the growing conflict between the rich and the not-so-rich.

****

Even though my body hurts and I am fuzzy about the events that brought me here, the doctors say I will fully recover. There is no permanent damage to my heart, and despite being unconscious for a period, my brain appears to be working fine. I am allowed to go home if I agree to an in-home nurse for a couple of weeks and a police cruiser in my driveway twenty-four hours a day. Even though everyone denies the existence of *The One*, they still think I need protection.

Avner insists on staying in the extra bedroom, and I appreciate the company. He cooks us breakfast and then we go for walks when I feel up to it. He is recuperating as well from the vicious knife wound he received while saving me from Max and Orsu.

Terrance had lied about Avner taking money from him. Avner had agreed to the deal just to survive but never spoke with Terrance again until he was captured. He was watching me from afar since the night the trailer burned down, just in case the bad guys found me. When they broke into the Grand Pelican, he rushed in and saved my life.

My strength is coming back quickly, and I am going stir-crazy. The house that I once loved is now a source of pain. I see Lia everywhere and even sleep on the couch to avoid our bedroom.

****

A couple of nights after I come home, Oak arrives with a bottle of Johnnie Walker Blue. I am in my office mindlessly staring into space. There is a candle burning, and I have Olivia Rodrigo playing on a loop. I can relate to her relationship anger, even though her boyfriend only broke up with her and my wife shot me. I start writing in a notebook to try and make sense of everything that has happened but spend most of my time doodling.

"We figure if you have the strength to talk about being shot, you have the strength to take a shot," says Oak, carrying three glasses in one of his huge hands and the bottle in the other.

I join them in the living room, and Avner fills the glasses with two fingers of booze. He raises his glass. "Lehayim."

We all drink, and they take a seat on the leather couch across from me.

"Jay-Bird, how are you feeling?" Oak asks.

"Never been better. I want to know exactly what happened. It is time."

They exchange looks and Avner begins. "Lia was playing both sides, and when she had the chance, she shot you and took the laptop. What she didn't count on was you going into cardiac arrest. She called the paramedics, applied CPR, and then left."

"Where is she now?"

"They have no idea. There is an international hunt, but I know she has gone deep. No one will ever find her," states Avner.

I finish my drink and signal Avner for another. "I can't believe she was the traitor. I lived with her for ten years. We were married. I loved her with my whole heart."

Avner finishes his drink as well and sighs. "You remember what I told you when you and Lia were leaving Israel?"

I nod. "Of course. You said that I need to understand that Lia is complicated. She had been through a lot. But this?"

"Jason, there is a fine line between a good agent and those we hunt. You must have a dark side, or you can't do the job. Sometimes that dark side swallows up everything else. The battle never goes away. No one wants to be the sheepdog protecting everyone against the wolf all the time."

"On the positive side," says Oak, "I talked to Zeke, and they finally dropped the arrest warrant. You are now free to come and go as you like. So what do you say we leave for La La Land in the morning, and you can recuperate with the stars?"

"What is going to happen with you, Oak?" I ask. "IRS fraud is a big deal."

"Jay-Bird, nothing is a big deal for the rich and famous. Haven't you learned anything? If the names ever become public, my attorneys will handle it. I'll pay a fine, and it will be over. I had no idea I was involved in tax fraud. This was all between Eric and my money people. I had no clue. I fired everyone and will get new people. Maybe Titan Financial Group," he suggests with a smile.

"Ignorance is your defense?"

"Works for everyone else," he responds.

"I've been meaning to ask you something, Oak." I put my drink down and face him. "You kept telling me you needed to talk to me, but it never happened. What did you want to tell me?"

He stands up and walks around the room, fidgeting with his

hands. "I am not sure how to say this."

"We've been friends most of our lives. Spit it out."

"You know I love Lia—or loved Lia before all of this," he mentions, sitting back down and taking a drink. "But I heard her talking on the phone to someone. I couldn't make out everything, but I think she was spying on you. She mentioned Project Cardinal. I guess I wanted to warn you, but I didn't know what to say."

I lean back and blow out some air, looking at the ceiling. "Well, isn't that a kick in the balls."

He smiles. "Doesn't matter now, but I'm serious about making this into a movie. Although I am not sure I could find someone ugly enough to play Avner."

Avner gives him the finger, and we all have another drink.

"What would you call your movie?" inquires Avner.

Oak inclines his head in my direction. "What did you say before Lia came out of nowhere and blasted those fools?"

"Bluebird," I reply sadly.

"That's it. I would call it *Bluebird*."

Wanting to change the subject, I ask, "How about you, Avner? Are you ready to go home?"

He ponders the question. "Not yet. I owe someone a glass of wine, then I need to find the mole in Israel who sold me out. I have one more bullet saved for him or her."

"Listen, I love you guys, but I need some time to sort this all out. Oak, you need to go back to LA with the beautiful people, and Avner, you need to go have your wine and maybe save the bullet. I'll be okay."

We fill our glasses for one more drink. "Remember, fellas, enjoy today, because life can change in an instant," I say.

CHAPTER 61

I stand on my deck at the Treasure Island Beach Resort breathing the salty air and drinking a cup of strong coffee. A month ago, I had been down the street at the Grand Pelican hiding as a fugitive of the law during a hurricane.

The dirty clothes have been replaced by an unbuttoned Tommy Bahama bright-blue silk camp shirt and a pair of tan board shorts. I haven't worn anything on my feet except flip-flops since arriving at the beach.

My black aviators, along with my grown-out beard, give me the sense of anonymity that I need. I spend my days working on my tan and reading Jimmy Buffet's *Tales from Margaritaville* or a thriller by one of my favorite authors. At night, I walk to a small beach bar that has great seafood and cold beer. I sit at the bar and chat with the bartender or a tourist from Nebraska or Iowa or some other cold-weather state. They always remind me I live in a place where everyone else comes to vacation.

I have been working through the five stages to deal with my grief. First came whiskey and then tequila. That was followed by vodka, red wine, and finally cold beer. At some point, I figure I will need to dry out, but that is a problem for another day.

Once Avner and Oak leave town, I start therapy. My therapist told me that sunshine every day would be good for me, so I relocated to the beach for a while. I'm not sure how long I will stay, but I am not in a hurry to leave.

My attorney filed a lawsuit against Safe Harbor Bank. The board quickly settled as they attempted to distance themselves from Terrance and the scandal. The settlement is seven figures, and there is no need for me to go back to work anytime soon.

****

I am joined by Zeke and Agent Chavez on a sunny Friday morning. It has been two months since I was shot. There is no mention of Project Cardinal or Safe Harbor Bank. We have a cup of coffee and a bagel before walking down the beach to St. Edwin's Catholic Church.

It looks like it was built in the 1980s, and little has been done since that time. There are high ceilings and a heavy wooden door. The beautiful stained-glass window shows a lion and a lamb, which I take as a good omen. On the roof is a fifteen-foot gold cross. A sign in front reads "Breakfast Out Back, All Saints and Sinners Welcome."

In the corner of the parking lot, there is a tent with volunteers handing out hot meals to those in need. The air smells like bacon and pancakes. A priest greets new visitors and talks with the regulars. He is a young man with long hair and a brown goatee. He wears a priest's collar with a black shirt, cargo shorts, and sandals.

"Good morning. Judging by your clothes, you don't look like you are here for a free meal or a ticket to paradise. What can I do for you?" he asks.

"Good morning, Father. My name is Jason Miles, and these are my friends Zeke and Gloria. I might take that ticket to paradise later, but right now I am looking for a homeless man named Gabriel. He also goes by Goat. He mentioned that he comes here for breakfast and stays from time to time."

He looks suspiciously at all of us. "Did Gabriel do something? You look like police."

Zeke smiles and says, "Guilty as charged, but we're just here to try and help him."

"Follow me," the clergyman instructs, as he leads us to a structure connected to the church.

Inside is a large room filled with cots. It is the church's gathering room as well as a sanctuary for those in need of a clean bed. It smells like sweat and Lysol. All the beds are made except for a few with men still sleeping in them. Back in the corner, Goat sits in his little space sorting through his backpack.

We walk through the room, careful not to disturb anyone.

"Gabriel, these people asked to see you," says the priest.

He avoids eye contact like a dog used to being hit. "Whatever it is, I didn't do it. Father knows I am clean and sober. I don't cause any trouble."

I step forward. "Do you remember me, Goat? We met a while ago on the beach."

He looks me over closely. "I don't think so. Wait a minute, did I sit with you on the day before the hurricane came in? You wouldn't give your name."

"That's right. I am glad you remember."

"Dude, what happened? You looked like me and now you look… normal."

"I want to let you know that you inspired me when I needed it. I was in a low place, and your kindness helped me through. I want to return the favor."

He shakes his head. "It was just a conversation, brother. You don't owe me anything."

"These are my friends Zeke and Gloria. I told them about you, and they thought they might be able to help. Gloria was in the army as well."

"I was stationed at Fort Benning and did some time overseas. Mostly in communications," she says.

"I was part of the 75th Ranger Regiment. Spent a lot of time in the sandbox," responds Goat with pride in his voice.

"Thank you for your service," replies Gloria.

Gabriel is sitting up straighter and removes his hat. His long greasy hair flows down past his shoulders.

"Goat, when Zeke gives me a day off from the FBI, I volunteer at the Veterans Resource Center in Tampa. Jason told me a little bit about you, and I think we could help you get back on your feet. If you are game for it."

There are tears in his eyes. "I gave up a long time ago. I am not sure I have it in me."

"After you've had some time to get things back in order, give me a call. I am thinking about starting up my own security company. I'm going to call it Bluebird Security Consultants. I have some unfinished business, and I could use someone like you," I say.

"Why do you all want to help me? Why do you even care?" he asks.

"I once heard that we should enjoy life because things can change in an instant. I always thought that meant change for the worse, but maybe not. Maybe things can change in an instant for the better, and the world would be a nicer place if we all tried to pass along our blessings to others."

I reach out my hand, but instead, Goat grabs me in a tight bear hug. I leave him in the capable arms of Zeke and Gloria.

CHAPTER 62

A couple of days later, I am back on the deck enjoying my morning routine. I roll out of bed whenever I wake up and turn on Jimmy Buffet or Bob Marley. After setting the right vibe, I make coffee and eggs before relocating outside. I breathe in the smells of the beach and listen to kids playing in the sand. I keep trying to journal, but words will not come. The wounds are still open, but I am hopeful they will close one day. I think about the hero's journey and realize it starts every day, so I need to stop being a victim and create the life I want.

The only clean shirt I find this morning is the same Tommy Bahama one. I am thinking of an ocean swim, so I start the day in swim trunks and bare feet.

My new cell phone rings, and I check the number. The caller ID reads "Unidentified Number," so I figure it is a spam call and ignore it.

Moments later, it rings again. It is the same number.

"This is Jason."

"Hello, Jay." The voice freezes me in my tracks.

The phone slips a few inches in my grip before I catch it. "Is that you, Lia?"

"Of course, baby."

"Where are you?" I jump up and look in all directions.

"Far, far, away, my love."

"Are you okay?"

"Yes, but I miss you."

The words are painful and beautiful. I miss her so much, but I need answers only she can give. "I need to hear it from you, Lia. Why did you do it?"

"Jay, you know I couldn't play American housewife forever. I really did try, but it was never a fit. You must have known. I wanted a normal life so badly...until you gave me one, and then it became a prison."

I know what she is saying is true, but it still stings.

"Why didn't you tell me you were unhappy? We could have done something else. I would have done anything for you."

There is a long pause. "I know you would have, but I was fooling myself. You knew who I was and where I came from. You don't just have that dry-cleaned out of you and become a new person."

"Okay, Lia, I understand it wasn't a perfect fit, but you stole the laptop and shot me. What the hell?"

"I am sorry about all of that, but it was time for me to be my real self. Even though we were the good guys in Israel, we always walked that fine line between gray and black. Ask Avner; he's the same as me. It is easy to go the other way. To be honest, I've played so many characters, I am not sure if I have a real self."

"But you shot me!" My voice raises in pitch.

"I knew you had on your vest, and it was just bad luck that your heart reacted. If I hadn't shot you, the FBI would never have left you alone. They would have figured we were in it together."

I consider her rationale, and it almost makes sense. I want to believe everything she says. "I think you are taking the fact you shot me a little lightly. I almost died."

"Think about it, Jay. I'm a trained sniper, if I'd wanted to kill you, you would be dead. I'm the one who saved you by calling the ambulance and performing CPR."

"So now, am I supposed to thank you?" I ask.

"Jay, we can still be together. When you are off the hook with Zeke, we can run away to South America or Israel. Maybe even Australia. That would be nice. I have all the money, and we can run forever."

I can't believe what I am hearing. Even worse, I want to go, despite everything that has happened. Lia makes me feel something in my heart that no one else ever has. Something I can't explain. I just want to be with her desperately. "Lia, there are a lot of people after you. You killed some bad men in that warehouse."

"I will be fine. Those men were disposable, and they became a liability."

"A liability to who?"

"There is a lot more going on than you realize. Something very big and powerful is behind this. They wanted those fools dead and paid me for the data. If you are not coming with me, you need to stay out of it and go back to your normal life."

"I don't know what you are talking about. I can't go on the run with you. You know who I am. I've got to do the right thing. It is in my DNA now. That is what this whole mess was about. Trying to do right. Be a hero—not just for me, but for us."

"That is what I love about you. I better go."

I love her madly despite all the mixed emotions, but this is the end. "Be careful out there, Lia. Maybe we'll see each other again someday."

"Maybe we will," she says sounding hopeful. There is a pause on the other end of the line. "Jay, one more thing. You sure look great in blue."

END

ABOUT THE AUTHOR

Chris Kneer has spent thirty years as a senior-level banker. When he's not in the office, he draws on his professional expertise to write page-turning financial thrillers. His debut novel, *Bluebird*, is the first in a series featuring Jason Miles. Chris lives in Tampa Bay, Florida, with his family.

For more information, visit *ChrisKneerAuthor.com* and follow him on Facebook, Instagram, LinkedIn, and X.

ACKNOWLEDGMENTS

Writing *Bluebird* has fulfilled a lifelong dream, and the experience has been amazing. I'm so thankful to have been inspired by great writers like Brad Thor, Harlan Coben, Daniel Silva, among many others who fill my shelves.

Reading and writing have always been important to me. My parents, Warren and Connie, passed along a love of reading to my sisters and me. Still, to this day, I finish a book every couple of weeks and rush to the bookstore when a favorite author releases something new.

Writing a book is a journey; every author's path is different. There are ups and downs, highs and lows, and nagging self-doubt. Some days, words flow effortlessly; others, stringing a few sentences together is hard. On those tough days, you need a support system, and for me, it started at home with my family.

My wife, Jodi, has always encouraged me to chase my dreams. While writing *Bluebird*, she was always supportive and my number one fan. I would have never finished the book without her.

In addition to tapping into my creative side, writing also helps me teach my son, Andrew, that you can accomplish anything you put your mind to. We should all spend our precious time chasing passions and trying new things. Every minute of writing is a minute less with your family, so I appreciate the understanding, and I can't wait to see what passions he uncovers.

Thirty years ago, I was barely surviving Nebraska's cold and snowy winter when I read Jimmy Buffet's *Tales from Margaritaville*. I was inspired by Tully Mars and his Horse, Mr. Twain, and their quest from Wyoming to the Caribbean. When I finished, I told my parents and best friend Morty I was moving south. While I didn't have a horse, I had a bright red Eagle Talon and a fold-out map for my journey to Florida.

I moved with a pillow, a spaghetti pot, and a thousand dollars and somehow built a fantastic life in the sunshine. I will forever be thankful to the Zaritsky family for allowing me to stay with them and treating me like family in a strange new town.

I never had a doubt that Florida was where I was destined to be. Over the years, I met my wife, raised a son, made many friends, and was blessed to have a wonderful career in banking. Tampa Bay is the perfect setting for my series, *Cigar City Thrillers*. It is a fantastic destination with sandy beaches, eclectic towns, and a history that the wildest imagination could not make up. Over the years, I've met some interesting characters that remind me that Florida can be "A Sunny Place for Shady People."

There were so many who offered me a hand while climbing this mountain. When I had given up on writing, our friend Melissa Hefty convinced me to keep going. That afternoon, I took out a pad of paper and started working on *Bluebird*. Melissa always speaks positively, reminding me to encourage others because you never know if a few kind words can change someone's trajectory.

Without my sister-in-law, Breanna Murrie, I would never have finished or released *Bluebird*. She has been my non-profit IT expert, social media facilitator, website creator, and general expert in anything else I need to know. I owe her several cases of red wine.

Through pure fate, I was introduced to Ali Bumbarger, a story coach and editor. At that time, I knew little about writing or how to structure a story. As they say, "I didn't know what I didn't know." Ali patiently worked with me and, to this day, will respond to any questions I have. She is amazing at her profession and a wonderful person.

Aryn Van Dyke with Van Dyke Marketing is the Book Rockstar.

She taught me marketing strategies and created excellent content. Her expertise in all things book marketing is invaluable, and she helped me find an audience for *Bluebird*. I am excited to work with her on future books.

Nadia Geagea Pupa with Pique Publishing agreed to take on this project and was irreplaceable. Taking a book from draft to a finished product is a Herculean task. Nadia and her team provided great advice and took *Bluebird* from a dream to reality.

I also want to thank my beta readers, who took time out of their busy lives to read *Bluebird*. Not only did they give me constructive feedback, but they also convinced me that others would enjoy it as much as they did. Thank you to Cecilia Shinn, Beth Desjardins, Ruth Banowetz, Karen Bricken, Breanna Murrie, and Barbara Schiebrock.

Finally, thank you to the readers. In today's world, there are many options for your free time. It means a lot to me that you would spend some time with Jason, Lia, Avner, and Oak. Hopefully, you are excited to welcome them back on their next adventure in Cigar City.

STAY UP TO DATE

To learn more about upcoming books in the *Cigar City Thriller* series, visit *ChrisKneerAuthor.com*.

- Chris Kneer, Author
- @ChrisKneer
- @chriskneerauthor
- @Chris-Kneer

Milton Keynes UK
Ingram Content Group UK Ltd.
UKHW021223201024
449794UK00015BB/76/J